To Gordon

A FINE HOUSE
IN
TRINITY

Lesley Kelly

SANDSTONEPRESS
HIGHLAND | SCOTLAND

First published in Great Britain
Sandstone Press Ltd
Dochcarty Road
Dingwall
Ross-shire
IV15 9UG
Scotland.

www.sandstonepress.com

The publisher acknowledges support from
Creative Scotland towards publication of this volume.

ISBN: 978-1-910124-95-6
ISBNe: 978-1-910124-96-3

Cover design by Blacksheep, London
Typeset by Iolaire Typesetting, Newtonmore.
Printed and bound by CPI Group (UK) Ltd, Croydon CR0 4YY.

Sunday

They tell you that Edinburgh is the most beautiful city in the world, the Athens-of-the-Whatsit and all that shite, but see when you're stuck on an East Coast train staring at Marionville industrial depot, you could be looking at the arse-end of anywhere.

I drain my lager and have another half-hearted flick through the *Daily Record*. For the first time in weeks there's nothing about the Stoddarts in it. I try reading the sport to take my mind off things but can't focus. Six weeks I've been thinking about nothing but coming home, thinking moving South was a huge mistake. But now I'm here I'm not so sure. It's probably the booze talking, and the thought squatting in my brain that tells me I'm not going to be too popular when folks find out I'm back.

There's an announcement and the train lurches forward the last couple of miles, past Calton Hill Observatory and into the station. I heave my rucksack off the shelf and let myself be swept along by the tourists and the locals squeezing out of the sliding doors. I have a nervous shufty up and down the platform. I'm not quite sure what I'm expecting to see: a welcoming committee of Isa Stoddart's laddies with pit bulls, perhaps, or the ghost of Lachlan Stoddart shaking its flabby fist at me. But there's nothing out of the ordinary, just the usual commuters, tourists and Big Issue sellers. I buy a copy of the magazine off a laddie who looks like he's been round the block a few times. He winks at me and I sense a kindred spirit.

The possibilities. A drink at Shugs. Straight to the lawyers. Find myself somewhere to stay. But before any of that there is one visit I've got to make.

Marianne opens the door, sees me and screams. She does her best to slam it in my face but I manage to get my size 9s in the frame before she gets it fully shut. This doesn't stop her battering the door off my foot.

'Marianne.' (batter)

'I'm not here to cause any trouble.' (batter)

'It's just that...'

This time she slams the door so hard I have to move. Jeez, I'm hurting. For a wee lassie she's pretty damn strong.

One of her neighbours sticks her head out her door to see what all the racket is about. She takes a good long look at me, obviously trying to memorise my appearance for a statement to the Polis if anything happens to Marianne. *Well, officer, he was average height you know, 40s, I'd say, with dark hair that's going grey and he was very, very, thin. He looked in a bit of a state, to be honest, like he'd been sleeping rough for weeks.*

I turn and stare at her. 'You seen enough, missus?'

She tuts in disgust and goes back into her flat.

I drop to one knee and shout through the letterbox. 'It's just that with Lachie dying, you know, everything's changed now, hasn't it?'

'No, it hasn't,' she shouts back and throws something at the door.

I sit on my heels for a minute, then poke the letterbox

back open. 'Is your Uncle Mick around?'

'Just get lost, Stainsie.'

I know when I'm beaten and hobble off down the corridor. I'm half a dozen steps away when I hear the door open.

I turn back in anticipation and get a face full of dirty water. Never piss a woman off mid-mop unless you want to end up wearing the moppings.

'I'm glad that bastard Stoddart is dead.' With that thought she flicks her blonde curls over her shoulder, and slams the door again.

It's nice to be back.

The lawyer's office is near Princes Street, in one of the Georgian townhouses that make up the centre of town. Edinburgh New Town was built in the 1800s to tempt decent and respectable citizens out of the overcrowded tenements of the High Street. It worked at the time. Pity it's full of lawyers now.

The inside of the building is ultra-modern. The whole place has been painted white, and all the way up the staircase there is contemporary art with wee spotlights shining on it. The receptionist is encased by a huge semi-circular Perspex desk and is eyeing me suspiciously. I'm letting the place down with my three-day-old stubble and my rucksack. While attempting a discreet sniff of my oxters I catch the receptionist's eye; she doesn't look impressed. I swing my bag to the floor and nearly knock over a row of pot plants.

Murmuring an apology, I tell her about my meeting with Miss Spencely. The receptionist silently points a bright red fingernail in the direction of a waiting room.

She can't get me out of reception fast enough. She doesn't even offer me a cup of tea; I've had better treatment in the cells at Leith Polis Station.

I could tell the jumped up wee besom that I'm not just some dosser, that I've travelled the world, had lassies far better looking than her in more countries than I can remember, but what's the point? In reality my glory days are past. The time when my hair was black, my muscles were firm, and lassies lost their knickers after one wink of my eye is long gone. What am I now? Absentee father, false friend, liar?

She's got a point. If I was her I wouldn't want me hanging round either.

'Mr Staines?'

Miss Spencely is not what I was expecting. When I got the call on my mobile from Miss Spencely of Bell Muldoon Solicitors I assumed she'd be some middle-aged spinster. Instead she's a twenty-something looker with a figure that I wouldn't dare describe aloud, and long dark hair that falls poker-straight to her shoulders. Why do all young lassies these days have hair that looks like it's been ironed?

'Mr Staines,' she says again, offering me a perfectly manicured hand. I do a sly wipe of my paw on my jeans then give what I hope is a firm handshake. 'So glad you could take the time to see us.'

'No problem. I'm led to believe by your message it's in my own interest.' I lower myself into a not particularly comfortable seat.

She gives me a sad smile and a slight shake of her head. 'I wish I had only good news for you Mr Staines, but

I'm afraid it's a little complicated. You are aware of the recent death of Mr Lachlan Stoddart?'

'Oh yes. Unfortunate business.'

'Were you aware that you are the sole beneficiary of Mr Stoddart's will?'

I stare at Miss Spencely's unnaturally shiny hair while I try to take this in. I'm surprised enough that Lachie even had a will, never mind that I'm in it. After all, I wasn't top of his Christmas card list when he died.

Miss Spencely is staring at me, awaiting a response.

'He may have mentioned something about it.'

She smiles politely and continues. 'Mr Stoddart had very little money in his own name, but as you are probably aware, the death of his mother, Mrs Isabella Stoddart, settled a considerable amount of money on him.'

A lot of good it did the poor bastard. Still, it's an ill wind and all that.

'Did you know Mrs Stoddart well?' Miss Spencely asks.

I start to cough and she offers me a drink of her water. I nearly choke on it. *Know Mrs Stoddart well?* Well enough to have had nightmares about her since I was five years old. Well enough to know what she did to people that didn't pay their debts. Well enough to want to keep out of her road, even after she's dead. Miss Spencely is still waiting for an answer so I keep it factual, 'I worked for her up until her death, actually.'

'Really?' She looks surprised. 'In what capacity?'

I shrug. 'Doing this and that.' *Babysitting her Number One Son.*

She pauses for a second, then, sensing she's not going to get any more out of me, continues. 'Unfortunately,

5

there are a number of issues relating to the settlement of Mrs Stoddart's will.'

This makes me sit up straight. I knew it was too good to be true. 'What kind of issues?'

The solicitor stops to pour herself a glass of water. *Jesus, woman, cut to the chase.*

'At the time of her death Mrs Stoddart had sunk most of her money into the conversion of a large Victorian house into a block of flats. However, subsequent to her passing we have been contacted by a number of her creditors who would appear to have some claim over her estate.'

'Meaning?'

'Meaning that we are unable to wind up either of the estates until these claims have been examined more closely. Consequently we will not be in a position to pay you any sum from Mr Stoddart's estate for quite some time.' She drains the glass of water. 'If ever.'

My head falls, involuntarily, into my hands. After a second a thought hits me and I sit back up. 'So, this house she was converting – where is it exactly? And what happens to it now?'

'It's on York Road. The Trinity area of Edinburgh – are you familiar with Edinburgh?'

I nod.

'Here are the plans.' She slides a set of architect's drawings across the table and starts to flick through them. 'This is the original house, Mavisview, which is being converted into three flats.'

I pick up the picture. It shows a three storey, stone-built house set in its own grounds. The building is not quite symmetrical.

'It's got a tower.'

'Yes, Mr Staines, I believe a lot of houses in that area have. Anyway, work on Mavisview is at a very early stage. The other part of the development is much more advanced.' She flicks to a drawing of a more modern block of flats. 'This is being built in the grounds of Mavisview, and I'm informed, is more or less completed. There are six one-bedroom flats in the block.'

'Nine flats on one site? This development must be worth a fortune.'

She shakes her head. 'I wish that were true, Mr Staines, but this kind of development is always a speculation.'

Her eyes flick away from me as she says it, and I wonder if she's being straight with me. I open my mouth to speak but she continues on.

'However, in discussion with the late Mrs Stoddart's business partners, we have decided that it makes sense to continue with the development for the moment.'

We look at the pictures in silence for a minute, until I have an idea. 'As an interested party I hope you have good security on the site.'

She blinks. 'Good security?'

'You know – a night watchman or something to keep the neds off the foundations and that.'

'Well... we don't have anyone there at the moment but I suppose I could look into that.'

'No rush, Miss Spencely, I'm sure you know what you're doing.'

A house conversion with no security.

I think I've just found my accommodation for the next few weeks.

I spend the last of my money on a carryout, then take

7

a leisurely walk down Dundas Street in the direction of Trinity. I'm in no rush. I want to wait until it's dark before I break in, in case any of the neighbours see me and do their duty as a citizen. Trinity's that kind of place; if you farted round there they'd be on the phone to the Council worrying about the impact on the ozone layer.

I don't really know the area that well. *The posh bit of town.* As a kid I'd no friends there, no business being there. Maybe that's not changed. Now that I'm taking a proper interest in it I can see that, posh as it is, there are layers of affluence. The first layer is solid family housing, one-up-one-downs, usually with a bit of garden to the front. I'm not knocking them – I'd be working a hundred years before I could afford anything like that.

Push through that layer, and you come to the houses round Lomond Park. Huge, stone built properties with driveways and gardens hemmed in by iron railings. Not as posh as they seem at first glance: if you look closely you can see a second door or a side path that hints at furtive subdivision.

But for real old-money luxury, the streets round Russell Place and York Road take some beating. The oldest of the houses round here, they are by far the quirkiest. It's as if creating the new area of Trinity gave them confidence to build whatever they liked. Want some Greek columns either side of your door? No problem – this is Trinity. Mock Tudor frontage? On you go – this is Trinity. Pointy Gothic turrets on each corner? Get building – you know where you live. And of course, make sure that every second house has its own tower.

I stop outside Mavisview. She must have been a beauty in her day, but the old girl is showing her age. A couple of the windows on the upper floor are broken, and there are a handful of tiles missing off the roof. The garden is completely overgrown, with only the different shades of green to identify which was once a lawn and which a weed-covered flower bed. The general look isn't improved by all the building crap that's been left lying. There are planks of wood and bits of pipe all over the place.

The new development looks more or less complete. It's your typical modern complex: no character and rooms the size of rabbit hutches. Nonetheless I opt for this for the night, mainly because some daft prick's left a ground floor window open round the back of the block. When I'm officially in charge of all this, some heads are going to roll. Though judging from the way the lawyer wifey was speaking, that's not going to be any time soon.

I unroll my sleeping bag on the bare floorboards. It's not going to be comfortable, but it will be wind- and watertight, which is an improvement on where I've spent my last few nights. I get into the bag and crack open one of my cans. I light up a fag and I'm finally ready to go over what's happened today.

In my head I replay the conversation with the lawyer, because there's a lot of things I'm still not sure about. This site not being valuable? I don't buy that. Way I see it, if this place is finished and sold on, there must be enough to pay Mrs Stoddart's debts, and be something left over.

The beer and fags are working their magic and I can feel myself starting to relax. The last thought that goes through my mind before I fall asleep is that so long as I'm awake and out by 7 am nobody's going to be any the wiser that I've been here.

Under normal circumstances I pride myself on knowing

how to deal with Her Majesty's Constabulary. If, for example, two representatives of the Queen's law enforcement agency were to come across me sound asleep in a place I had no business to be, I know that the correct response is to sing them profuse apologies, with a chorus of 'it'll not happen again, Constable,' while hinting at the amount of paperwork involved if they do bother to book a lowlife such as myself.

Unfortunately, when I am kicked awake by the Plod after oversleeping by some four hours, with the mother of all hangovers, the first thing that comes out of my mouth is, 'You can't touch me – I own this building.'

This causes much mirth. The bigger of the two Polismen, who I recognise from my last visit to the station, says, 'My apologies, Mr Trump. I didn't recognise you lying there. Maybe I was a wee bit put off by the sleeping bag and empty *Special* cans, or maybe it was the resemblance you bear to this wee runt called Staines that's wanted to help with our enquiries into the death of a Mrs Stoddart?'

I stare at them in disbelief. They're not pinning that one on me. 'I had nothing to do with that. And how did you know where to find me?'

'Don't flatter yourself - we didn't expect to see you here.' He stamps on one of my empty cans in a manner I find quite unnerving in my present state. 'Not that we're not delighted to stumble across you.'

I sit up and pull my sleeping bag round me. I wish I was wearing more clothes. 'What are you doing here then?'

'The builders knocked through a wall in the big house and found a body.'

'Shit.' Just my luck.

'Shit indeed. Would he have been a tenant of yours,

Mr Rachman?' He gives me another prod with his foot. 'Anyhow, get your clothes on because the Super wants a word with you.'

'Which Super?'

Please not Jamieson, please not Jamieson.

'DS Jamieson of course.'

As I sit in the Interview Room waiting for Danny Jamieson to turn up, I make a neat list in my head of all the possible reasons he could want to see me. It's not beyond the realms of possibility that he just wants a chat for old times' sake. After all, he *was* at school with Lachie and me, even if the toffee-nosed bastard never said two words to us. Best case scenario – a couple of old acquaintances catching up.

The worst case scenario is that he's found out about me pumping his wife on her Hen Night and has been waiting to frame me for the first suitable murder. On the other hand, maybe he also pumped some lassie on his Stag Night and is not too bothered about Babs and me. After all it was eight years ago, and you know, what happens on tour, stays on tour.

Who am I trying to kid? He's going to kill me.

'Staines.'

'Hiya Danny, I mean DS Jamieson. How's it hanging?'

Danny looks like he's not slept for a week. His ginger hair is receding fast, apart from an optimistic tuft that's clinging tight to the middle of his forehead. His face is the colour of wet suet, and I'm sure I can see white hairs sprouting in his moustache. He ignores the pleasantries and waves a folder in my face. 'The late Mrs Isabella

11

Stoddart. Anything you'd care to tell me about her death?'

'I am as baffled as you are, I swear to God.' Aye, well, maybe not quite as baffled. A picture of a heavily-indebted blonde goes through my mind. If Danny was a half-decent cop at all he'd know the answer to Mrs Stoddart's death lies in her tallybook; even Lachie knew that much. If he was any kind of plod at all, he'd at least wonder where the tallybook was.

'Really? 'Cause here's the funny thing – all over the scheme people can't wait to grass you up to me as Mrs Stoddart's killer.'

'What?' I can't believe what I'm hearing. 'People think I killed Mrs Stoddart?'

He nods. 'That's what I'm hearing. You,' he points at me, in case I've not got the message, 'killed Isa Stoddart.'

We look at each other over the interview table. I don't understand what's going on, and I'm starting to panic.

He drops the files onto the desk. 'Care to tell me why everyone is grassing you up?'

This is no good. No good at all. 'There are some right backstabbing bastards out there that would tell all sorts of lies about a person.'

'You're not wrong. And I think to myself, I've known Stainsie a long, long, time. Can I really picture him as a murderer? Can I really picture him repeatedly battering a woman over the head? So, I pull out your records and what do I find but Mr J Staines with a cast-iron alibi.' He waves Isa's file at me again. 'Isabella Stoddart – Pathologist's Report - estimated time of death, early hours of February 4th.'. He picks up another folder. 'Joseph Staines – early hours of February 4th – sleeping it off in a police cell in Gayfield Square.'

12

He flings both the folders onto the table. 'Why is half of the scheme trying to finger you for a murder you couldn't have committed?'

'Jealousy of my good looks and high-flying lifestyle?' I don't know exactly what the bastards are up to but I'm going to find out.

Danny doesn't laugh.

I'm getting so desperate to move the conversation away from me being an alleged murderer I try a high-risk tactic. 'How's Babs?'

He throws me a sharp look but he answers. 'She's fine.'

'And the bairns – is that three you've got now?'

'Number four arrived two weeks ago.'

'Jesus! You've been blessed and no mistake. Is the wee one keeping you up?'

Danny shakes his head, but, try as he might, he can't quite stifle a yawn.

Danny knows that I'm not being straight with him, but he's got nothing of substance on me, so two hours later I find myself free to go. I'm not quite sure what to do with my freedom due to my current cashflow problem, but I scrape together enough loose change for a couple of cans of *Special* and head for my favourite bench at the Foot o' the Walk.

It's a great spot for people watching, and I'm on the lookout for a certain someone, possibly the only person who can shed some light on my reincarnation as an assassin of elderly crime bosses. Michael Murphy, known to most people as Wheezy, and to Marianne as 'Uncle Mick.' I've known him a long time, although I wouldn't exactly call him a friend. But, then, these days I'm not sure I'd use that term about anyone. Anyway, if old times' sake isn't enough to persuade him to help, I'm pretty sure he'll know it's in his own best interest to get me back out of town as soon as possible.

Mr Murphy shouldn't be hard to track down, but I'm reluctant to show my face in the pub or the bookies until I've worked out what's going on. However, if my instincts are correct, sometime this afternoon he'll scurry out of Shugs and along to his favourite book-maker, so if I sit tight and keep my eyes open, like a small, scruffy comet he will pass through my orbit.

After about ten minutes my patience is rewarded when I see a donkey-jacketed figure hurrying along the other side of Great Junction Street.

'Wheeze,' I shout and wave him over. God, it's good to see a friendly face.

He turns and stares at me, open-mouthed. Rumour has it that in his day, Wheezy was quite the Dapper Dan. One of the old guys from Shugs told me that way back when, all the lassies were after young Michael. Which just goes to show what a lifetime of alcohol, gambling and dental neglect does to you, because the kisser on him now would frighten a ghost.

He hobbles across the road as fast as his legs will carry him, all the time hurling a string of obscenities in my direction, which leads me to believe that he's not quite as pleased to see me, as I am to see him.

'What are you doing back? Does Marianne know you're here?'

'Aye, I went round to see her.' And I've still got the bruises on my foot to show for it.

'Did she take it all right?' His face is scrunched with worry. One of Wheeze's very few redeeming qualities is

14

that he's genuinely fond of Marianne. Possibly because she's the only family member he has that still speaks to him.

'Oh aye – she invited me in for a cup of tea and a range of sexual favours.'

Wheezy smacks me so hard I drop my can. 'That's my niece you're talking about.'

Shit. I'm not being overly tactful here. 'Sorry, pal – shouldn't have said that.'

Wheezy grabs my shoulder and leans in toward me, until his face is an inch away from mine. His breath smells like a pub toilet. 'Ach, save the apologies – you're coming with me.'

I stare past him at my can, which has rolled as far as the man selling hot chestnuts from the fake Victorian oven. He's not noticed yet that he's standing in a wee pool of *Special*, and I suspect he's not going to be happy when he realises.

'Aye, Wheeze, whatever.'

'I have to say I'm very disappointed, Staines, very disappointed indeed.' Father Paul shakes his head to emphasise his unhappiness. I feel like I'm fifteen again and in confession admitting to lustful thoughts. I stare at Wheezy. For a man who hasn't set foot in a church since his bairns were christened, he's suddenly very pally with the priesthood. Needs must, I suppose. He glares back at me over the top of the sports page of the paper, and jerks his head in the direction of the priest, indicating I should pay attention. Father Paul continues with the lecture.

'We gave you that money in good faith, in return for

15

you leaving town with...' he lowers his voice, 'a certain *item*. We certainly didn't expect to see you back here a mere six weeks later.'

'Amen to that,' says a voice from behind the paper.

Father Paul looks mildly irritated at the interruption, then returns to his interrogation. 'Are you looking for more money, is that it?'

'God no, I just...' And I'm not entirely sure how to answer that question. I don't feel inclined to share the real reason for my return.

'Are you thinking blackmail, perhaps?'

'That'll be it, Father,' the sports pages pipe up.

'No!' I grab the newspaper out of Wheezy's hand. He smirks at me, and I realise I can't think of a convincing explanation for my reappearance. 'I'm just...' I tail off.

Father Paul sighs. 'Right. We can't have you wandering round the scheme shouting your mouth off the first time you get drunk. You can stay here where I can keep an eye on you.'

'In the Priest's House?'

He nods. I can't say I'm too struck on this idea. The Priest's House consists of three floors of Gothic misery, and the general gloom isn't helped by Father Paul having taken out every second bulb in an effort to save money. I play for some time.

'Will your housekeeper not mind?'

'While you are living here, Staines, you *are* my housekeeper.'

Wheezy snorts.

'And perhaps your first task could be to see Mr Murphy to the door?'

A couple of hours later I've had time to reflect, and

16

on balance, things could be worse. I've got free digs and all that's required in return is that I stay put and see that Father Paul gets fed of an evening. I live up to my end of the bargain by giving him a hearty meal of sausage and mash, and he departs to continue ministering to his undeserving flock. I've not had a chance to talk to Wheeze about Danny's comments, but then he wasn't in what I'd call a cooperative mood. I'll seek him out again tomorrow, if he's not round here at the crack of dawn, threatening me with further violence for upsetting his niece.

Father Paul has given me a bedroom on the first floor. From the smell of damp, it's not been used for a year or two. I wrestle with the window for a good ten minutes before I can persuade it to open, then prop it up with a copy of *Lives of the Saints*. There's not much in the room, just a bed, bedside table and a wardrobe full of old clothes. I go through all the pockets methodically and I'm rewarded with a bundle of fifty notes that has worked its way into a coat's lining.

I reap even more rewards in the little sitting room next door. There's a drinks cabinet that doesn't seem to have been opened since Noah was a lad. I'm just in the process of opening a dusty bottle of *Macallan* when I think I hear a noise. Not anything loud, more like a chair or something being knocked over. I wonder if Father Paul has a cat, though to be honest he doesn't strike me as the Saint Francis of Assisi type.

I'm a bit jumpy so blame my paranoia and continue hunting around for a tumbler. I've just laid my hand on a wee crystal number that will really do justice to the *Macallan*, when I hear what I could swear is the sound

17

of glass breaking. Perhaps the cat that Father Paul never mentioned has upset something in the kitchen. I pour myself a healthy measure and settle down in an armchair. There's a television in the corner with a layer of dust over it. Nothing happens when the on switch is pressed. It's disconnected so I get down on all fours to look for the socket.

I plug it in, press the button and the ten o'clock news appears. I've just settled back on my heels to admire it when the picture disappears and the lights go out.

At first I assume that I've fused the lights; maybe sticking an old TV set on was not such a good idea. Then I hear the distinct sound of someone moving about downstairs. There's nothing to hand to use as a weapon except the whisky bottle and I'm damned if I'll risk wasting a twenty-one-year-old malt. On all fours I shuffle over to the curtains and pull them open. They shed some light into the room, but it's fairly dark outside now as well. I carefully open the door and feel my way to the top of the stairs.

My best bet is to head for the front door then leg it, so I edge down the stairs keeping my back to the wall. I make it down one and a half flights before smacking into someone large and unmoveable, and bounce arse-over-tit down the last half-flight. My trip leaves me face down on the hall carpet, which immediately sets me off coughing. It's not seen a Hoover for quite some time.

I push myself up onto all fours as quietly as possible. It's dark as the Devil's heart down here and I'm trying desperately to get my bearings. I try shuffling gently forward but the movement of my hands unleashes another set of dust bunnies, which makes me start coughing again.

Next thing I know I've got a boot resting on my neck.

18

It pushes me gently back down until I'm eating carpet again. I hear a match being struck and the room lights up briefly. The intruder takes a draw on his cigarette and speaks.

'So, Stainsie, you're back then?'

1939–1949

See, if I had to blame somebody for the state of my life, if I had to root around in the dark recesses of my past and choose the one person that I could legitimately point a finger at and say, 'It was you. You started all this. You started me on the drinking, the sleeping around, the not holding down a job. Everything. It was you.' See, if I had to do that, I know exactly who I'd name as the culprit, and I know exactly the date of his crime. The date? 24ᵗʰ July 1948. The person? Josef Wiśniewski. My grandfather.

If you'd met him though, God rest his soul, you'd have thought him the sweetest old fellow going. And to give him his due, my grievances aside, he was a good man. He steered clear of most of the vices of men of his generation. His wages never went to line a bookie's pocket. He never had his fill in the pub then gave his wife the benefit of the back of his hand. I never even heard him curse, although maybe he confined his bad language to his mother tongue. And he was always, always good to Granny Florrie (who wasn't really our granny but, well, we'll get to that one later).

In fact, to my eyes the man only had one fault – an overwhelming love for Her Royal Highness Queen Elizabeth II. I know not everybody would see that as a flaw, but when you grew up in the Workers' Republic of Leith like I did, it seemed a wee bit odd at least. But, Christ, the man was mad for royalty. His front room had so many pictures of Elizabeth II it would have put your average RUC canteen to shame.

But to understand why he did what he did (and by-the-by ruined my life) you have to understand where he was coming from. Grandad Joe was born in 1924 in a wee village just outside Lvov in Poland. To hear him talk, it was a bloody countryside paradise. A rural idyll. Birds singing in the trees, sheep in the fields, yadda yadda. The only fly in the ointment was that he was Polish, and most of his neighbours were Ukrainian, but for the most part they all rubbed along together.

There were five of them – Dad Filip, Mum Ewa, and his two younger sisters, Alicja and Anna, and Filip had high hopes for a couple more junior farmhands in the next few years.

By 1939 Joe was fifteen. He was at the local school with ideas in his head about going on to university (first one in his family to go, if he made it, and everybody was rooting for him). He wasn't really keeping an eye on world events, to be honest none of them were; politics was an urban thing - what did the government of Germany have to do with getting the harvest in? What did they care who was in charge of the Soviet Union? Stalin knew squat about keeping your chickens happy. No, Joe was not worried. He was spending the best part of his time mooning over the lassies in his class, with big plans for getting into their knickers. After all, they were not short of hay to roll around in.

But that's the thing about politics – just 'cause you

21

choose to ignore it, doesn't mean that it'll choose to ignore you. On the 1st September 1939 German forces invaded Poland from the north, south, and west. A couple of weeks later, the Soviet Red Army invaded the eastern regions of Poland with the full support and cooperation of the *Führer*.

Filip was worried, but as he kept telling Joe, Poland wasn't on her own. The British and the French would be sending in troops any minute, there would be a bit of bloodshed, he couldn't deny it, but Poland would be liberated.

He was still holding to this line when the Red Army arrived at their house to tell them they didn't live there anymore. Eastern Poland was now officially part of the Ukraine, and therefore the Soviet Union. Poles were no longer welcome to stay. Within days, Joe and his family were booted out of their house, and were on a train bound for the Soviet Union, and a life of communal paradise on a labour farm.

Siberia was cold. Brutally, mortifyingly, cold. Before he left Poland, the coldest Joe had ever been was on the ritual 3 am trip to the outside lavvy in the middle of winter, standing there with his hands shaking and hoping his wee man didn't get frostbite, and by the time he got back to bed he was always so damn cold he needed to go again. That kind of cold? Siberia on a good day. In summer.

Wee Anna was the first to go. It started with a cough, then she lost her appetite for the meagre rations that were on offer, then she couldn't get out of bed. Two months after moving to the camp, Ewa woke to find Anna dead beside her. She didn't have long to grieve though, because within six months, both Ewa and Alicja had also passed away.

So, Joe and Filip were left on their own to try to make the best of life on the farm. They were used to life being hard back in the Ukraine but it didn't compare to this. No equipment, no horses – they were trying to farm the soil with their bare hands. Just when they thought they couldn't stand it any longer, politics found them once again. By 1941 Stalin and Hitler were no longer bosom buddies, the Poles were no longer the enemy, and they were pretty much free to go, if they could find their way back to Lvov.

Joe and Filip got themselves on the first transportation they could find back to Poland. Joe would have been on top of the world, if it wasn't for the fact that he'd noticed that Filip had started with that oh-so-familiar cough. Sure enough, Joe waved goodbye to his last remaining family member somewhere in Azerbaijan, as the train door was opened and Filip's corpse was dumped by the side of the track.

At the age of ieghteen, Joe was orphaned and alone in the world. He joined the Polish Army, and saw out the rest of the conflict in Italy. Come the end of the war, the Polish situation had become a bit of an embarrassment to Churchill. Stalin was keen to hang on to control over Poland, and Churchill was not going to rock the boat, so it was the bum's rush for Poland and the Polish Army.

Joe was flown to England, and demobbed. He was then given the choice – get flown back to Poland and take his chances with Stalin, or stay in England and take his chances here. He talked it over with his pals and they all came to the same conclusion. God Save the Queen.

One of his pals had a brother living in Edinburgh, so the pair of them took the next train North. Old Joe'd got a few bob in his pocket from the demob, so when he got to Edinburgh he decided he was going to get a room to himself. *Lebensraum.* He'd never had a room all to himself before, between his sisters, the labour farm, then five years sharing with other squaddies, but Joe decided – the good life started here.

He waved goodbye to his friend then wandered down the cobbled streets of Edinburgh until he saw a 'Room to Let' sign and chapped the door. An old wife answered.

'I looking for room.'

The old wife looked him up, and down.

Joe, sensing reluctance on her part, tried to reassure her. 'I have money. Can pay good.'

'Oh, aye. And what's your name, son?'

'Josef Wiśniewski,' he said proudly.

To his surprise the woman started shaking her head. Through the rapidly closing door she said, 'Oh no, son, I'm not having any of you Poles staying here. You lot should be long gone by now.'

And with this welcome to Scotland, Joe realised that not everyone was all that grateful for their war effort.

Joe was sleeping on a bedroom floor with five other men and working twelve-hour shifts down Leith Docks. But he was not without ambition. He could do well in this country, he thought, if only he could be a bit more, well, British. He looked at his fellow Poles, all living on top of each other, drinking themselves insensible at weekends, and wondered if there wasn't more to life than this.

One Sunday morning he was out for a walk when he

24

saw a sign in a newsagent's window. 'English lessons. Good rates. Enquire within.' Suddenly it all became clear to Joe. He was going to improve his English, get a job in an office and go to night school. He'd get his degree, get a better job and woo some Scottish lassie. He pushed open the door to the newsagent's and nearly fell over the step in his haste to begin his self-improvement.

Miss Ailsa Morrison was a very proper-looking young woman. She explained that she was a qualified primary school teacher and was offering English lessons in the evenings. Her father did not approve of her teaching foreigners so she was holding the lessons in the back room of the newsagent's. She named her price.

In the first lesson he learned about English nouns, and noticed how beautiful Miss Ailsa Morrison's eyes [noun] were. The second lesson covered verbs and adverbs, and Joe noticed how delightful Miss Ailsa Morrison's laugh was. She laughed [verb] beautifully [adverb]. By the time they reach prepositions he realised he was completely in [preposition] love with Miss Ailsa Morrison.

Ailsa, for her part, played her cards close to her chest. It must have been obvious to any observer that she'd got a lovesick Pole on her hands, but she didn't encourage, or for that matter, discourage, him. She was, however, happy to listen to his stories at the end of each lesson. He told her about his family, his experiences in Italy, and what life was like for him in Scotland. When he suggested they meet for a walk one Sunday afternoon, she blushingly accepted.

After six months of careful tutoring, Joe felt confident

25

that his English was good enough to start implementing his plan. So he headed into town and presented himself at the first office he came to. There were three men in the office, so he addressed himself to the one who looked the most senior.

'I am looking for work.'

The man looked him up and down in a way that was becoming familiar. 'Oh aye. And who might you be?'

'My name is Josef Wiśniewski.' Joe hated himself for the small hint of defensiveness now in his tone.

The two other men sniggered.

'The boss doesn't employ papes.'

Joe thanked them for their time, and hurried back to find out what a 'pape' was.

'Oh, Joe,' said Ailsa, 'It's a rude word for a Catholic.'

Joe considered this new information. 'But I do not go to church. How do they know I am Catholic?'

'Well, your name I suppose.' Ailsa sighed. 'It's a Polish name and Polish people are Catholic.'

'I fight a war for this. I fight for Poland and now I cannot get accommodation and I cannot get job because of my Polish name.'

'Oh, Joe,' said Ailsa again. 'I'm so sorry.' And she took his hand.

They were sitting side-by-side in the room at the back of the newsagent's. The newsagent had gone home.

'Do not be sorry. It is not your fault. My name is my name and I proud of it.'

Ailsa was so moved that tears welled up in her eyes. Joe noticed her distress and wiped the tears away with his calloused hand. They were sitting very, very close together.

'Oh, Joe,' said Ailsa for the final time that evening. Joe put a finger to her lips and kissed her.

'We can't, Joe.'

They were sitting a respectable distance apart in the back room of the newsagent's.

Joe threw his hands up in a gesture of disbelief. 'I learn the words for nothing.'

'And you said it beautifully,' said Ailsa, tactfully ignoring the fact that he had just asked her to marry 'it'. 'But my father will never approve of me marrying a foreigner.'

Joe leaned forward and took Ailsa's hand again. 'Why not? I work hard, I get better job, I work harder for you and for our babies.'

'The babies are the problem.' Ailsa pulled her hands back to her lap. My father's never going to accept his grandchildren growing up called Wiśniewski.'

Joe got to his feet. In one sentence Ailsa had confirmed all his fears. He walked slowly out of the room, and was halfway through the shop before he heard Ailsa call his name. He paused, looking at the tins of peas and the posters about sugar rationing.

'I can still give you English lessons.'

He shook his head and opened the door.

Joe wandered the street for hours that night. He asked himself 'in my position, what would Queen Elizabeth II do?' (although I'm not sure she'd really have the frame of reference to imagine herself as a penniless twenty-four-year old Pole). But in a blinding flash of royal inspiration, Joe realised what Bessie would do, old Miss Saxe-Coburg-Gotha herself. What she would do is change her name to that of an inoffensive local town. So, he borrowed a map of the UK from work, closed his eyes, crossed himself for luck, rotated his arm three times above his head and came down hard.

On Staines.

Three days later he marched into the Victoria Street Registry Office and changed his name by deed poll. On 24th July 1948 Josef Alojzy Wiśniewski officially became Joseph Aloysius Staines.

Now, I'm not saying that things couldn't have been worse. A couple of inches northwest and I'd be going through life as Joseph Bishop's Itchington. At least that would have spared me a lifetime of 'stain' puns. In Joe's position I might even have done the same thing. I can relate to his motives: he was too proud of his name to change it to get better digs, or a half-decent job, but the first whiff of a bit of skirt and he'd renounced all his patriotic fervour. I've done enough daft things over lassies myself.

And, I know that there was no malice in it. Old Joe didn't realise when he went into the Registry Office, the repercussions his act would have twenty-five years later. He didn't know the impact on my first day of primary school when the teacher sat us in alphabetical order. If old Joe hadn't messed with nature I would have been nestling safely in between George Thompson, who went on to be Dux of the school, and Angela Young, who everyone agreed was the prettiest Gala Queen they'd ever clapped eyes on. I could have spent my formative years sandwiched between brains and beauty.

Instead, on my first day of school I sat down, turned my head, and stared into the fat, four-eyed face of Lachlan Stoddart.

28

Monday

The boot is removed from my neck, and I roll over and take a few choking mouthfuls of air. A hand reaches down and pulls me up.

'Thanks, pal,' I say, but I've no idea who I am talking to.

'This way,' says the voice and pushes me toward the kitchen.

I bump into the kitchen table and bounce my backside into one of the kitchen chairs. The mystery man flicks the switches back on in the fuse box and the weak light of Father Paul's economy bulbs fills the kitchen.

'Surprised to see me, Stainsie?'

Standing opposite me and looking mighty pleased with himself is, well, I don't actually know his *name*, but I know he's one of Mrs Stoddart's thugs. I'd never troubled to find out what he was called – to me he was just one of the laddies with pit bulls that followed her everywhere and I wasn't that keen to pursue a friendship with them.

'Good to see you, eh…'

'Bruce.'

We sit for a minute in silence. He pulls a bit of fluff off his leather jacket. He's a bit of a dapper dresser, is Bruce. I remember that much about him. I can't recall ever seeing him dressed in anything other than head-to-foot black, which makes a nice contrast with his heavily highlighted hair. I like that kind of attention to detail in

29

a thug; half his time spent kicking the shit out of OAPs who can't meet the 2000% APR on their debts, the other half drinking tea and leafing through *Heat* magazine in some lassies' hairdresser's or other.

'Can I get you a cup of something, Bruce?'

'No, no, don't trouble yourself. I'll just say my piece and be on my way. Now, the thing is, I believe that you've got something that belongs to me.'

This confuses me a little. As far as I was aware the sum total of my possessions is a rucksack full of dirty washing. 'I'm not quite with you, Bruce.'

He leans back in his chair, contemplating his perfectly-manicured nails, and sighs. 'Then I'd better start at the beginning. I've been Mrs Stoddart's right-hand man for some years now, as we both know.'

If you say so. I rack my brains to see if there could be any truth in the statement. Bruce looks about a year or two younger than me, and I'd first become aware of him and his highlights maybe five, six years ago. Did that make him a likely candidate for taking over the Stoddart empire? Still, this wasn't the time or place for that kind of debate. I nod furiously.

'Oh aye, Bruce, I know that.'

'And me and Mrs S had an understanding. Lachie, God rest his soul, was not what you'd call a businessman.'

Too right. The poor bastard didn't know his arse from his elbow never mind which way up a balance sheet would go.

'Mrs S was relying on me to look after the family business if anything were to happen to her. Which it has, God rest her soul. So, I start looking into her affairs and what do I find? The one-and-only copy of her tallybook is missing.'

Aw Christ.

'I respectfully ask Lachie if he's seen it recently, and the daft little prick – God rest his soul – says that he's given it to you.'

Bruce gets up and wanders over to the kitchen dresser. He pulls out a knife; using the knowledge I gained at catering college, I'd say it was a boning knife, ideal for cutting through raw meat and possibly small bones. With the knowledge I've gained in the years since I left catering college, I'd say it was very bad news indeed for me.

He sits back down at the table, and starts working the point of the knife into the wood. He's making quite a mess of the polished surface. Father Paul's not going to be too happy about that. Then I think that that's really the least of my worries, seeing as the last time I saw Ma Stoddart's tallybook it was floating down the River Tyne. Bruce continues with his theme.

'And I was a bit worried at first because I thought that Lachie's jakey pal is an even dafter wee prick than he was. But then, then, I thought even Stainsie will know what that book is worth. He'll not have done anything stupid with it.'

I wouldn't underestimate my stupidity, especially when there's a lassie involved. 'Aye, about that...'

''Cause if he was, for any reason, unable to return that book to me,' he stabs the knife head first into the table top. He stands and uses all his weight to push it in. The knife stands upright on its own. 'I'd cut the daft prick's balls off.'

'OK,' I say, getting swiftly to my feet. 'I don't actually have it to hand at the moment. Is there somewhere I could deliver it to you?'

31

Bruce laughs but doesn't move. 'You've got one week to find it. And don't worry about delivering it – I'll find you. Wherever you are staying.'

He's showing no signs of leaving so I try changing the subject.

'So, are you still partners with that other laddie with the dog?'

'Duncan? Naw. Him and me had a disagreement about who was in charge.' He smiles and tries to pull the knife out of the table. It doesn't move. He holds my gaze as he manoeuvres the blade slowly to and fro. The bloody thing still won't shift so he starts putting a bit more welly into it. This puts an unacceptable strain on the band that's holding his ponytail in place and his hair bursts free. On the plus side at least it means he's not staring me out anymore, but I can't help feeling that he's a man that doesn't like having his grooming interfered with. He lets out a couple of grunts then puts a stack heel on the table leg, and using all his weight, finally releases the knife, leaving a crater the size of a small orange in the table top.

He takes a minute to rearrange his hair and continues the conversation. 'A big disagreement.'

I watch him wielding the knife. 'How big?'

He laughs. 'Let's just say you'll not be seeing him again.'

An image of the Polis finding a body in Isa's development comes into my head.

'When you say I'll not be seeing him again…'

'Unless you end up in the same place as him,' he gestures hell-wards with the knife, 'because you don't get me that book.'

Clear enough. I start wondering how long I should give

32

it after Bruce leaves before I pack up my things and get out of town. Should I wait an hour or two, or is he likely to hang around to see if I try to run off? I decide that it makes sense to hang fire until the morning.

Bruce is just about out of the door when he stops and turns round. 'Do you know a blonde lassie that lives in the banana block? What's her name?' He makes a show of racking his brains. 'Marion, is it?'

I try to look as if I don't know who he's on about. 'Naw, don't think so.'

'Marianne!' He smiles. 'That's her name, isn't it, Stainsie? 'Cause a wee birdie tells me that you and her were pretty tight before you left town.'

I shake my head. I'm trying hard not to show that she's the last person I want dragged into this but when I speak my voice is an octave higher than usual. I sound like a chipmunk. 'No, honest pal, you've got it wrong.'

He walks back into the room and stands in front of me. I get a whiff of his aftershave as he leans forward and rests his hands on the back of my chair, one either side of my head. 'Now, I'm not sure of *all* the names in Ma Stoddart's tallybook, but I do remember that hers was in it. I just want you to know that, if for any reason, that book doesn't reappear, say 'cause you left town or something stupid like that, I just want you to know that I'll be starting my debt collecting with her.'

He steps back and gives my seat a kick. I jump about a mile.

'But I'm not an unfair man, Stainsie. If wee Marianne's a bit short of cash, I'm willing to negotiate how she pays me.' And in case I've not got the message he grabs a handful of his leather-covered groin and leers at me.

Turning on his heel he gives me a cheery wave and disappears through the door. I watch him go and wonder how much more trouble that lassie is going to get me into.

1973–1980

I enjoyed my first day at primary school. Of course, I didn't know then that this was the first day of a suffocating friendship with a psychopath, a friendship I'd still be trapped in thirty years later. My first impression of Lachie was entirely positive. His opening line to me was, 'I've got a spacehopper.' I was too young to play it cool.

'Really?' I said, eyes wide.

'Aye. And a Pong game.'

'Fantastic.'

'And,' he paused for effect, 'we've got a colour TV.'

That was the clincher. Lachie was going to be my new best friend. I was in it for what I could get out of him, and, to be honest, that didn't change much over the next three decades.

Friendship with Lachie wasn't too bad at first. He delivered on the material goods side of things, and I played my part by keeping my mouth shut and looking suitably impressed at his lifestyle. And what a lifestyle it was. On my first invitation round for tea after school I couldn't stop myself gawping.

The Stoddarts lived in a seven-bedroom villa looking out onto Leith Links. Even in 1973 there weren't that many of the big houses still intact, with most of them converted into apartments, or nursing homes. The ground floor of the house was used by Lachie's dad, Guthrie, as offices; he'd sub-divided the huge front room into an office for himself, and a reception area. The reception desk was often taken up by Mrs Ainslie, who did the books for Guthrie while chain-smoking Silk Cut. The fact that Guthrie's office didn't have any natural daylight didn't seem to bother him; perhaps he saw some advantage in the fact that, when the door was shut, nobody, not even Mrs Stoddart, could see what he was up to.

The rest of the ground floor was used as store rooms for Guthrie's import/exports, with the family kitchen, living room and bedrooms on the first storey. Lachie had more or less exclusive use of the second floor.

The house had gardens that stopped just short of being labelled 'grounds', with a swing, climbing frame and a treehouse, all for Lachie's use. To a laddie who'd spent his first five years in a ground-floor flat in Balfour Street, this was really living the good life.

And the *dolce vita* didn't stop there. Lachie had a bedroom and a playroom to himself, stocked with the finest toys that a five-year-old could aspire to: on top of the spacehopper, Pong, and the seventeen-inch colour portable, there was a wide selection of Dinky cars, vans, planes and tanks, an Action Man Soldier with moving Eagle Eyes and a talking Action Man Commander, and a jumping battery-powered Evel Knievel Stunt Cycle.

Yet there was more. No two weeks in Scarborough in July for Lachie. His family went on holiday twice a year to Benidorm! To the best of my knowledge Benidorm was in a whole other country, and getting there involved going on an aeroplane (an experience that in my opinion would have been even more exciting than the holiday itself).

But did this abundance of material goods make Lachie happy? Did it buggery. He rarely went into the garden, never mind climbed the branches to his treehouse. Even when his father nailed a ladder to the side of the oak, Lachie still couldn't be bothered dragging his tubby little arse up the steps.

New toys appeared and were discarded or broken with a callous disregard for their expense. The previous Christmas I had been given an Action Man Adventurer, one of the lesser Action Men as I was now beginning to discover. My dad had gone on at such length about how I was to treat it properly or he wasn't forking out for a toy for me ever again that my mother had found Action Man still in his box two months later never having had a single adventure. She'd enquired if I didn't like it and I'd burst into tears and said I was too scared to play with it in case I broke it. Such was life in Balfour Street.

The holidays were similarly taken for granted. I'd press Lachie for details of what it felt like to fly. He shrugged his shoulders with all the boredom of a seasoned traveller.

'You know.'

This infuriated me. 'No I don't, I've never been in a plane.'

Lachie snorted at this, as if he found this very unlikely. 'What – never? How do you go on holiday then?'

I didn't feel inclined to share details of the four of us setting off to Scarborough in an overloaded Hillman Avenger, so I tried to steer the conversation back to the wonders of flight.

'Isn't it scary?'

'Naw.' And then he gave me one clue to how the other half lived. 'You get a meal served in a wee plastic tray, and it has the meat in one section of the tray, and the potatoes in another, and your pudding in another.'

I shook my head in disbelief.

There were other less material advantages of my friendship with Lachie. Nobody bothered us in the playground because everyone had more sense, even at age five, than to mess with the son of Guthrie Stoddart. Guthrie ran a tight ship, with interests in (in no particular order): prostitution, debt collection, drugs running, smuggling, and any other opportunities that living in a port presented to him.

I suppose he was a scary man; he was followed everywhere by laddies with muscles and pit bulls, and bad things tended to happen to people that got in his way. My dad visibly paled when I told my parents about my new friend Stoddart.

'Not Guthrie Stoddart's laddie?'

I shrugged. 'I dunno. He lives down by Leith Links and he's got a spacehopper and Pong AND a colour TV.'

There was a long silence as my dad tried to process whether having your son befriend the hardest family in Leith was a good thing, or a bad thing. Eventually my mother spoke.

'Well, Alec, at least he'll not be bullied at school.'

Guthrie Stoddart didn't scare me though. With my limited frame of reference, it was inevitable that I'd compare Guthrie to my own dad. Where Guthrie was tall and muscular, my dad was short and slight. Guthrie had a mop of curly black hair and sideburns that made him look like an exotic gypsy. My dad had short brown hair and a moustache with a hint of ginger that made him look just like everyone else's dad. And, of course, Guthrie was providing a life of unimaginable excess for Lachie, whereas I had Balfour Street and Scarborough.

In later years I could rationalise that at least my dad was providing what he did by the honest means of ten-hour days working for the Council, but my five-year-old self had weighed and measured my dad with my *Fisher Price* Junior Kitchen Scales, and found him severely wanting.

And to be honest, Guthrie didn't give me any reason to fear him. I never met him without my hair being ruffled, and Lachie and me being given ten pence to go to the shop. He always went out of his way to talk to us, teaching us several rude songs that would have had my father's eyes popping out of his head in fury had he known. He provided us with sugar-heavy snacks that my mother would never have allowed at home. In short, he was a perfect gentleman in all our encounters, and as such held no terrors for me.

The Stoddarts' was always full of people, all of them more exotic than my parents and their friends. There were dark-skinned men who winked at us as they came and went, laddies with white-blonde hair who spoke in a spiky foreign language, and lassies who wore short skirts and swore a lot. Human flotsam and jetsam that floated on a high tide from Leith docks to the Stoddarts' house, and at the centre of it all, Guthrie Stoddart: ringmaster of his seaside circus, prince of the promenade.

For all that I loved the bustle of the Stoddarts', and for all that I loved being near Guthrie, there were still things I saw and heard that confused me. When Lachie and I were playing in his room we'd often hear shouting: sometimes Guthrie himself, sometimes his laddies, other times voices we didn't recognise. Lachie didn't seem frightened by this and I took my cue from him.

There were other things that I couldn't so easily shrug off. One day Lachie and I came bursting through the front door to see a man kneeling at the foot of the staircase. He was weeping and rocking back and forth, as the usual Stoddart traffic manouvered round him, ignoring his anguish. My dad was quite adamant on the issue that men didn't cry, for any reason whatsoever, so I was quite surprised to find that a grown man actually could turn on the waterworks. I turned my face away as we passed him and ran up the stairs as fast as I could.

Another time when Lachie and I were playing in his room we heard the sound of a man screaming.

'What was that?' I said, although Lachie didn't look quite as surprised as I did. We heard another scream.

'We should go and see who it is,' I said. We were deep in our hero worship of Spiderman and Batman at the time, so it seemed only natural to go and investigate. We pelted down the stairs as fast as we could; I was running toward the batcave and from the jerky movements Lachie was making I'm pretty sure he was swinging on a spider's web.

On the bottome tread we found our path blocked by the short but solid form of Mrs Stoddart.

'Away back upstairs and play, boys.'

We didn't argue with her. That day I went home early

and sat in our kitchen, watching my mother prepare mince and tatties for my dad's dinner.

Much as I loved Guthrie, I didn't get off to the best of starts with Mrs Stoddart. When I'd been palling about with Lachie for two, maybe three months, there was an incident that set the tone for our relationship. I was on my way back to Lachie's room from the bathroom when I heard a strange sound coming from the kitchen. I'd not yet developed the ability to ignore bizarre goings-on *chez* Stoddart, so I pushed open the door. There, loud and proud, standing on the kitchen table was a chicken. Now even at five years old I understood that chicken drum-sticks didn't grow on trees, ready-coated in breadcrumbs, but my first thought wasn't that this was Lachie's dinner. No, I was jealous that on top of everything else Lachie's parents had now bought him a pet.

I stepped into the kitchen to get a closer look at the squawking beast, and saw Isa Stoddart step forward, take the bird's neck in both hands, and twist it firmly. The squawking stopped abruptly. I let out a scream and burst into tears. Isa looked up in surprise, then did something that I'd never seen her do before or since.

She laughed.

For the first few years I knew Mrs Stoddart, she wasn't all that involved in the business, with most of her time spent as a full-time mammy to Lachie. The kitchen was the hub of the Stoddart empire, and Mrs Stoddart would sit in her favourite chair, watching everything that was going on but not saying much. Nobody gave her any trouble though; Lachie never answered her back, the laddies with dogs never gave her any lip, and I never heard Guthrie raise his voice in her direction. Years later, when Guthrie disappeared suddenly and Isa took over the family business, I don't think anyone was entirely surprised.

I didn't subject my Ma to the comparison with her Stoddart counterpart that I put my dad through. There was no need – Ma so obviously beat Mrs Stoddart hands down. Ma was pretty and kind, and smelt of peppermint. She was always hugging my wee brother Col and me, and saying how much she loved us, and if she occasionally sat in the kitchen crying for no reason that we could see, or took to her bed of an afternoon, or threw a couple of plates across the kitchen, well, these were just quirks.

The only other comparison I made was a further one between Guthrie and Dad. Guthrie treated Mrs Stoddart like a queen. In fact, everything I know about how to treat women I learned from watching Guthrie run around after Isa. The man never came through the door without flowers or chocolates for her, which maybe helped to explain the size that she ended up. My dad never came through the door without a list of complaints about my Ma and her housekeeping, and I bet Lachie never lay in bed listening to his dad shouting and swearing at his mother.

My Ma was right about me not being bullied, but there were downsides to palling around with Lachie. For one thing, he didn't like me having other friends. I obviously hadn't understood the terms of our friendship, that the access to the Stoddart riches was a deal for me, and me alone, in return for my exclusive loyalty. In the early days of our friendship I was keen to bring the Stoddart fun factory to a wider audience. It didn't seem fair to keep

42

the treasures all to myself, and anyhow I was keen to see the inside of the treehouse, which didn't seem imminent if left up to the host to suggest it, so I raised the issue.

'Lachie – is it all right if Jonno comes round with me to your house tonight?'

He stared blankly at Jonno as if he'd never seen him before, instead of having sat a couple of seats away from him in the classroom for the past three months.

'Naw.'

Jonno and I exchanged glances. I hadn't thought of this. I assumed that Lachie would be as happy as me to have a few more pals.

'How not?' said Jonno, with more than a hint of aggression in his voice.

Lachie pushed his glasses back to the bridge of his nose and said, ''Cause I say so.' He wandered back into the school.

'What did he say that for?' said Jonno, looking aggrieved.

I shrugged.

'Are you still going to go?' I wasn't sure what to do, but Jonno made me an offer. 'You could come to the Links with us.'

I wrestled with my conscience for a minute but to be honest, for all his worldly goods, spending every afternoon with Lachie was a bit of a bore. I had a fantastic afternoon with the lads in the Links, which was only marred by the look on Lachie's face the next morning.

'Where were you yesterday?'

'In the Links.'

'I thought you were coming round to mine?'

I didn't say anything.

'Are you coming round this afternoon?'

Again I didn't say anything. I'd enjoyed my afternoon of freedom and I didn't really want to give it up.

''Cause my dad's bought me something I want to show you.'

In spite of myself I was intrigued. 'What?'

'A rocket that you can set off in the back garden.'

Space travel! He had me back.

And we settled into our friendship, forsaking all others. Not that making friends would have been an option with Lachie around. So, why did I hang around with the useless bastard? Well, the joys of accessing Pong and colour TV gave way to the joys of accessing Transformers, video games and illicit cigarettes. Why did he hang around with a freeloading bastard like me? Simple – he needed me.

Lachie was never going to strike terror in the hearts of the primary school children of Leith, but he was enough of his father's son to feel that he should be top dog in the playground. So he cast his eye around for a sidekick, and, using the superb judgement that characterised his later life, chose the only child in school less likely to be able to land a punch than himself.

We were the crappest bullies in the world, the Keystone Cops of playground enforcement. Most of Lachie's attempts to assert his authority took the form of him deliberately bumping into someone, then trying to make something of it. Lachie had the common sense not to push it too far: he wasn't wandering around bumping into Primary Sevens or anyone like that. His usual targets were the quieter members of Primary One, with his favourite target being George Thompson.

George was a bookish laddie, no good at sport, and with a tendency to cry if he got hit. He was way brighter than the rest of us, and ended up a Professor of Surgery at some teaching hospital in England. I often wonder if it was his early experiences at Lachie's hands that gave him the will to succeed and get the hell out of Leith.

The deal was this. Lachie would seek out George at lunchtime. I'd do my best to distract him onto other pastimes, but it was a hard job, seeing as Lachie had no interest at all in football, chasing lassies, or watching the bigger laddies smoking, all of which appealed to me. Poor George would be sitting on his own, reading whatever *Ladybird* book he'd borrowed from the Library that week. The book would start shaking when he saw us appear but he never looked up.

'Oi, George.'

He always ignored Lachie, who would then up the *ante* by knocking the book from his hand.

'Leave me alone.' George, mindful, no doubt, of what his mammy and daddy had told him about the Stoddarts, would try desperately not to escalate the situation, but Lachie wouldn't have it. He'd turn to me and say, 'You get him, Stainsie,' as if I was his equivalent of Guthrie's laddies with pit bulls. I'd always refuse to fight, which would lead to him calling me all the names, allowing his quarry to make a run for it. And even George got the better of us; the teacher appointed him classroom monitor and he got to spend lunchtimes tidying up the classroom instead of mixing with the hoi polloi in the playground. Our reign of terror was over.

So, Lachie had none of the brains required of a criminal

45

mastermind and I had none of the brawn required of a henchman. In fact, the only person that thought I had something to offer to the world of crime and extortion was Guthrie Stoddart, and he was very clear about what I could do for him.

Tuesday

Next morning I'm up well before Father Paul. I've had a sleepless night going over and over what's happened but two things are pretty clear to me:

I know who killed Lachlan Stoddart.

And I know who's been spreading rumours about my homicidal tendencies.

Bruce.

He's got the motive – get Lachie out of the way so that he can take over the running of Mrs Stoddart's empire and get me fingered as the likely culprit. After all, no one was expecting me to reappear. He's got the form – he as good as said to me that he's done in the other laddie-with-the-dog, who is, no doubt, currently the body-in-residence at my new home. And he's got the brains. Well, this is maybe the weakest part of my theory but you can't spend all that time with Mrs Stoddart without picking up an idea or two about ruthless business practices.

The trouble is that I can't prove this, which leaves me open to a kicking if I stick around, or Marianne in danger of finding out if Bruce is a natural blonde or not, if I don't.

I've no idea what I'm going to do. As I go down to get my breakfast my mind changes with every tread of the stairs. *Creak.* I'm out of here. *Creak.* I'll stay and face the music. *Creak.*

Then, when I get to the landing, it hits me. I've got seven days until Bruce comes knocking on my door. Seven days to find something concrete that links Bruce to the killings. Then I point Danny Jamieson in that direction, the pony-tailed prick ends up in the slammer, and Marianne and I ride off into the sunset. Or something like that.

I clean the table up as best as I can, but there's no mistaking the fact there's been a woodwork massacre. Father Paul arrives for his breakfast at the back of eight.

'What on God's earth happened here?' He points at the mess with his spoon.

The gesturing cutlery reminds me of last night and I give an involuntary shudder. 'Sorry, Father, I was chopping some vegetables and the knife got away from me.'

He runs his finger along the battered surface. He doesn't look convinced at my explanation but reaches past me for his muesli.

'I am sorry, Father. I'll pay for the damage once I'm sorted with a job.'

'Don't bother about it,' he says with a wave of his hand. 'We've more important concerns, like minimising the fallout of you being back in town.'

'I'm not here to cause any trouble, honest. But I ran out of money and...' I'm still not sure how that sentence should end. I only came back to see Miss Spencely. My plan was to be in and out of Leith in 24 hours, right until I ran into the business end of a kitchen implement wielded by Bruce. I'm not inclined to share the news of my potential inheritance with a priest though; I don't want guilt-tripped into giving it to the widows and orphans of the parish.

Father Paul is choking on a mouthful of oats and raisins. 'You got through £1,700 in six weeks? Did you have some help?'

Aye and she wasn't worth it. A man of the Lord is not going to be impressed at me spending his parishioners' cash on loose women so I start prevaricating.

'No. But £1,700 is not a lot of money to start a new life, what with accommodation, and, eh, finding somewhere to stay, and...'

He holds up a hand. 'Save it, Staines.' He reaches into his pocket and pulls out a crumpled envelope which he puts in front of me.

I point at it. 'What's that?'

He pushes the envelope toward me. '£200. I know you're probably after more but it's all I've got.'

I stand up and try to look outraged. 'I'm not after more money!'

There's a long silence while he tries to work out if I'm serious. The thought of that money lying there is killing me; £200 would set me up nicely. I wander over to the window so I don't have to look at it.

'Take the money, Staines. You've no business here. Not anymore.'

I keep staring out the window. I hear the scrape of his chair and he appears next to me and puts the envelope into my hand.

'For the last time, take this and go.'

I shuffle from foot to foot. 'I can't.'

He looks bemused. 'Why?'

And I'm about to give him chapter and verse about Marianne, Bruce, and the real story of what happened to his kitchen table when a thought occurs to me. If I tell him the truth there's no way him and Wheezy are going to let me leave town. If I don't confess, I can do my best to save both Marianne's and my skins but if I'm not looking too successful I can still scarper when it suits me.

I hand him the envelope back. 'I don't want your money. I just need somewhere to stay for a couple of days.'

He doesn't look happy but he puts the money back in his pocket and nods. 'Just keep your head down, OK?'

Father Paul sets off to a 10 am funeral. I'm still feeling bad about the table so I decide to do a bit of tidying to try to make up for it. You can tell that there's been a man living here on his own. It's not like the place smells bad or nothing, but there's just a something in the air that I recognise from places that I've lived before. In fact, it's not a something at all, it's an absence. It's all the things that the house *doesn't* smell of: perfume, washing over radiators, dirty nappies, all the everyday smells that a proper home has. You could put me in here blindfold and I'd know that a family never lived here.

I have another look round the upper storeys of the house. On the first floor, in addition to my room and the sitting room I found last night, there are another couple of empty bedrooms and a toilet. I make a mental note to have a wee check of the coat pockets in the wardrobes on this floor as well.

I wander up and down the corridor on the second floor but I don't go into any of the rooms, 'cause one of them's got to be Father Paul's, and I wouldn't feel quite right about looking. I don't envy him his life, living all alone in this place.

50

Deciding I've had enough prying, I head back down to ground level and root around in a couple of cupboards until I find an ancient Hoover. Judging by the spiders' webs round the handle, housework hasn't been high on Father Paul's agenda. I run the vaccum over the downstairs carpets, and wipe a cloth over most of the surfaces in the kitchen until my conscience is clear.

Then I settle down with a cup of tea and yesterday's paper, which Father Paul's left lying. There's a tiny article referring to the body in the York Road development. It doesn't say much:

A BODY has been discovered by builders working on a housing development in the Trinity area of Edinburgh.

The remains were found at around 10 am on Monday, and it is not yet known if it is the body of a man or a woman.

It is believed they had been there for some time. Police are working to establish the cause of death.

The papers haven't linked this to the Stoddarts yet, but when they do they'll have a field day. The Stoddarts have barely been off the front page, between Isa's murder, and Lachie's suicide.

I drink my tea and leaf through the sport pages. I'm not quite sure of the terms of my curfew, and whether I am actually allowed to leave the house without Father P's express permission. He's not left me a key so I'm snookered for getting back in. I'm on the point of exploring the house for a spare key when the doorbell goes. Surely I'm allowed to answer the door. When I open it I wish I hadn't bothered – Danny Jamieson's standing there with a face like fizz.

51

'You've not been quite straight with me, Staines, have you?'

I give a shrug. I'm not going to open my mouth and admit anything, until I work out which *particular* thing that I've not told him he's mumping about.

'Are you coming in?' I don't open the door any further but Danny pushes past me and strides into the kitchen. I follow him in.

'How did you know I was here, by the way?'

Without turning round he says, 'I've got my sources.'

'Pretty good ones, seeing as I've only been here about, oh, 24 hours.'

Danny laughs and sits himself at the table. 'All I can say is that Father Paul is very open-minded, even for a priest.'

I don't understand what he means by that so I ignore him and stick the kettle on. 'So, what are you nipping my head about today, Danny?'

He gives me a humourless smile. 'I had a very interesting chat with Charlotte Spencely, whom I believe is known to you?'

I nod. 'Nice lassie. Great legs.'

'Aye, anyway, you omitted to mention in our recent discussion that you are the executor of Lachlan Stoddart's will, and I'm led to believe, the sole beneficiary?'

I get a couple of mugs out of the kitchen cupboard. 'I did try to tell your officers when I was experiencing Polis harassment at their hands, that I was in fact the soon-to-be owner of the premises that they were evicting me from, but for some reason they didn't believe me.'

'Strange that. You have the look of a man with money.' Danny smirks. 'And if that kettle's for me, don't bother. I'm in the mood for something stronger.'

'Give me two minutes.' I nip upstairs for the *Macallan* I unearthed last night. I'm sure Father Paul wouldn't mind, under the circumstances. I'm surprised though; Danny's not the type to have a drink while he's on duty.

I can't find any whisky glasses so I use the mugs and pour us a healthy measure each. Danny isn't saying much so I try a conversational opener.

'So, has Lachie's body turned up then?'

Danny grimaces. 'Aye. Only not where we expected to find it.'

'Where did the poor bastard wash up?'

He gurns again. 'I suppose it'll be in the papers soon enough.' He sighs. 'An old guy out walking his dog round John Muir Country Park discovered some human remains.'

My chin hits my chest. 'Lachie?'

He nods.

'But you found...'

'Yes, we found his clothes on Gullane beach.'

'Jeez-o.' I'm shocked. 'Although when you think about it, isn't that the oldest fake suicide trick in the book?'

He looks furious. 'There was more to it than that, you cheeky bastard! What do you think we are – incompetent?'

'Perish the thought.'

Danny glares at me as he reaches into his pocket for his fags and lights up. He doesn't offer me one but he doesn't object when I help myself.

He's looking a wee bit stressed. He empties his mug and gestures at the bottle. 'Going to fill this up then?'

'No bother.' I give him another generous helping.

'The thing is, Stainsie, I know Lachie was a daft bastard and all that, but, right, we knew him since he was five

53

years old.' He takes another long swig. 'You should have seen the state of him.'

We both contemplate our whiskies in silence. 'So, he'd never been in the water at all?'

'Looks like it. But somebody wanted us to think that he'd done himself in.'

We both take a long drag on our fags as we think about this.

I can't resist having a pop at him. 'So you *did* fall for the old clothes on the beach trick then?'

Danny looks embarrassed. 'Well, there was a suicide note as well. At least...' He gives me that look again, as if he's trying to decide whether to trust me. He rolls the mug around between his palms and carries on. 'The thing is, I'm not sure now that it was a suicide note. Here...' he digs into a pocket and pulls out a bit of paper. 'Tell me what you think.'

It's a photocopy of a letter, and I can see right away it's in Lachie's handwriting, and it's got his creative spelling.

To make matters worse, it's addressed to me.

'Stainsie,

I know you didn't do ma mammy in. Don't ask me how but I just do.
I'm not coping here. Its to dificult.
Go and get in touch with us cos I want to say goodby.

Lachie'

'It could be a suicide note,' I say.

Danny nods. 'Or it could be Lachie deciding it's getting

54

too hot for comfort and him thinking he's going to head out of town for a while.'

'Aye.'

He points to the photocopy. 'So, you didn't actually receive any correspondence from Lachie since you left?'

'Me? No, he wouldn't have knew where to send it.'

'See, Staines, that is what I don't understand.' He leans forward. 'You and him pal about since the age of five, but his mammy dies and you leave town? Shouldn't you have been there at his side offering him comfort in his time of need?'

I get a mental picture of Lachie alone in his mother's house, the poor daft bastard trying to cope with life on his own, with Bruce and God knows who else hovering in the background, and my stomach turns over. It's not something I want to dwell on.

'Stop guilt-tripping me, Danny.'

He's not going to let this go. 'I just think it's odd. You have business that's so urgent you have to leave town at the very time your mate needs you most, and then I start getting people telling me that you were responsible for Isa Stoddart's death, even Lachie mentions it,' he points to the letter, 'when we both know very well it wasn't you.' He downs the last of his whisky. 'Staines – what's going on?'

There's a part of me that would like to tell him the truth, just to see how he would react. Danny is staring at me, waiting for an answer to his question.

I shrug. 'I don't know, my timing's never been good.' I pick up the *Macallan*, which is now only half full. 'You want another one?'

He grabs my hand to stop me pouring any more and asks again, 'What's going on?'

I shrug again and he sits back in his chair glaring at me.

'I could haul you in, you know, just on the basis of what people have been saying about you.'

He's right, and I suddenly wonder *why* he hasn't arrested me. And if I'm a suspect, he's just shared an awful lot of information about the case with me.

He's not glaring at me any longer, and he says softly, 'Mrs Stoddart's death, Stainsie. Just give me a name.'

A certain blonde pops into my head again, but the funny thing is, I'm starting to have a rethink on that one.

Danny looks knackered, and something not that far off desperation passes over his face.

'Are you asking for my help?'

He leans back and stares up at the ceiling. 'Staines, do you know the last time I had a good night's sleep?'

I shrug. I don't think it's the kind of question he really expects me to answer.

'Seven years ago. I've had seven years of bairns waking me up two, three, four times a night. I'm so damn tired I can't think straight. I haven't solved a case in years. I need a fucking break before they move me onto permanent traffic duty.'

I pour us both another whisky and he doesn't protest this time.

He stares at me. 'Don't you think you owe me, Staines?'

I choose to believe that he's talking about the times he's turned a blind eye to me being drunk and disorderly. I'm about to move the conversation on to Lachie's death and give him Bruce's name when it occurs to me that I could milk this situation a bit further. Be nice to have *him* owing *me* a favour for a change.

I take a slow drink of my whisky. 'God's honest truth,

56

Danny, I don't know who killed either of the Stoddarts. But I'm going to do a bit of asking round the scheme and I swear I'll get back to you.'

Before he leaves, Danny insists on putting his number into my phone. I'll give it a day or so then drop Bruce's name in his shell-like. I'll maybe even have some evidence by then.

An hour after I get rid of Danny the doorbell rings again, and I open the door to see Wheezy standing on the step. He's not looking much friendlier than the last time I saw him, but he's still an improvement on my last couple of visitors.

'Wheeze.' I keep my voice as non-committal as possible. I'm pleased that he's come round but I'm not going to kiss his arse after the way he spoke to me yesterday.

He scuffs his boots around in the dirt on Father Paul's doorstep before answering. 'Staines.'

I open the door a fraction in a gesture of reconciliation. 'Are you coming in then?'

He makes a big show of thinking about it. 'Well, I really just came round to make sure you were still here... but - OK, just for five minutes.' He plonks himself in the chair recently vacated by Danny.

I stick the kettle on and we sit in silence for a few minutes.

'Marianne's beside herself with worry.'

I run my finger round the crater left by Bruce's knife. 'She's nothing to fear from me, you know that.'

He bangs the table. 'Do I, Stainsie? I don't know what to think.'

We glare at each other for a minute. Wheeze weakens first. 'So, are you planning to stay in Leith?'

It's a good question. The kettle boils and I stand up to get it. 'Maybe. I've been made to feel so welcome.'

'Aye, well. Have you been to sign on yet?'

I fling a couple of teabags into mugs with more violence than is really necessary. 'No. I haven't really thought what to say to the lassie at the counter. "Have you been looking for work Mr Staines?" "No, hen, I've been a bit busy, what with leaving town with a stolen tallybook."'

He takes his tea from me and I sit back down at the table. 'Where did you go anyway?'

'Newcastle.'

'Jesus!' He slaps his tea back down and half of it splashes over the side of the mug. 'You really know how to lay low – an hour and a half down the East Coast line? Why didn't you just pop down to Dunbar till it all blew over?'

I ignore his outburst and pass yesterday's paper to him. 'Have you seen this?'

He reads in silence then speaks. 'Another body?'

'It's Danny Jamieson that's leading the investigation.'

Wheezy laughs. 'Did he ever find out about...?'

'Christ, no. I'd not be here talking to you if he had. So...'

He looks suspicious. 'What?'

'So, Danny's sitting there thinking that he's maybe got three related murders on his hands.'

Wheezy folds his arms. 'Well, we're not going to tell him different.'

'Wheeze?'

'Aye?' He's irritated with me.

'Know what I've got my doubts about?'

'What?' His irritation is growing.

'Well, your Marianne, right, wee slip of a lassie, has a disagreement with Mrs Stoddart about her debts and manages to knock her out and...'

'For Chrissakes.' Wheezy looks round nervously as if the Priest's House is bugged.

I lower my voice. 'Manages to knock out Isa Stoddart, five foot nothing but built like a tiny brick shithouse, with such force that she kills her. Does that sound likely to you?'

Wheezy sits forward in his chair, and whispers back forcefully. 'Are you suggesting that she knocks her out, and some other bastard comes along and finishes off the job? Because that doesn't sound likely to me. Anyhow, Marianne's stronger than she looks.'

I remember my reception at her door. He's got a point.

'What I don't understand, Wheeze, is that Jamieson's had me in for questioning. There's a bunch of gabby bastards on the scheme mouthing off about *me* doing Mrs Stoddart in. Would you know anything about that?'

'Naw,' he says, unconvincingly.

I give him a look.

He doesn't hold my eye and shifts about in his chair. 'OK, OK, I'd heard that as well.'

'Thanks for warning me.' A thought occurs to me. 'Did you start the rumours to protect Marianne?'

'Naw!' He sounds more convincing this time. 'Though I have to admit I wasn't unhappy that you were getting the blame.'

'Thanks, pal,' I say, with as much emphasis on the 'pal' as I can muster.

He's still wriggling about on his seat. 'You weren't

supposed to be coming back! What difference did it make to you?'

Now I slam *my* mug down. The table's swimming in tea. 'What if they'd set Interpol or someone onto me?'

He ignores my question. 'Why did Jamieson not bang you up?'

'He's no proof that I've done anything.'

'Jeez-o. Do you think he suspects you're up to something?'

Damn right he does. 'Maybe. I don't know. But I'm only telling you this because of something he said while I was there. He said that Mrs Stoddart was killed in the early hours of February 4th.'

He shakes his head. 'Naw – she was *found* in the early hours.'

'Naw – he definitely said she was *killed* in the early hours – he had the whaddyamacallit report. Which would make Isa's time of death about eight hours later than when your Marianne clocked her after Mass.'

Wheezy's concentrating so hard he looks like he's going to burst.

'So, your Marianne hits her, she then staggers along Constitution Street for *eight hours*, without anybody spotting her, before collapsing and dying at the Foot o' the Walk in the early hours. That doesn't sound likely to me.'

Wheeze leans across the table and grabs my wrist, soaking his arm in tea. 'And you're sure – Jamieson's had a pathologist's report on this?'

'That's what I'm telling you.'

He sits back and folds his arms, ensuring that his clean sleeve is now covered in tea as well. He nods his head, and a slow smile spreads across his coupon. 'Right, Stainsie – that's you and me got some investigating to do.'

'What's *he* doing here?'

Everyone turns to look at us. All conversation stops as the barflies stand there with their pints halfway to their mouths, and their gobs wide open. If Big Malky employed a piano player, by now he would have stopped tinkling the ivories and be hiding under a bar stool waiting for the shoot-out to begin.

As a valued customer I'm not too pleased at the welcome I'm receiving. We're long term regulars at Shugs, which would be a proper spit and sawdust pub except Big Malky sees sawdust as an unnecessary expense. The pub itself has been in existence since Victorian times, and it still maintains some of the gaudiness popular in pubs found in ports. Big Malky is not really a fan of heritage; the tiled mural showing the travails of the working man is largely hidden by fading posters promoting a range of real ales, several of which are no longer in production. The floor mosaic that spelt out 'Shugs' and 'Welcome' is missing several squares, and is covered up by a mat for regulars to wipe their boots on arrival. And the stained glass windows seldom illuminate the room with colour, as most days Malky doesn't bother putting the metal shutters up.

We'd started drinking here when it was run by Malky's dad, who'd had a brief Premier League career in the 1950s. Big Malky had inherited his mother's build and her ability at football. It didn't stop him taking an interest in the game though, and Shugs sponsored a local kids' team. The less-than-charitable talk in the back room was that he sponsored the team to ensure that Young Malky got a game, as the youngster had a build more suited to rugby, or as Wheezy would have it, sumo. The juniors never won anything but that didn't bother the regulars too much. At Shugs, failure was a way of life.

'I said, what's he doing here?'

'Malky, I'm not deaf, you can talk directly to me.'

I slightly regret this line of reasoning when Malky reaches over the bar, grabs a handful of my jacket and pulls me toward him.

'I know that, but the thing is, I don't really want to talk to you at the moment. Not when the word is that you've had money off of half my regulars for doing them a wee favour involving you pissing off out of town, and now I see you reappearing here bold as a two-dicked dog. Do you think that is good for business, Stainsie? Do you think you drinking here is an advert for my premises?'

I think that Shugs' customers are probably immune to advertising and are more swayed by the twin facts of Malky's low prices and high tolerance levels. But seeing as I am apparently pushing that tolerance to its limits, I keep my mouth shut.

'Here – take this, Malky.'

While I've been otherwise engaged, Wheezy's dipped my pockets and got hold of some of the cash that I took from the Priest's House. How he even knew I had money is beyond me; the man's got a nose like a bloodhound when it comes to used notes.

'That's £20 down, the pair of us'll stay in the back room, everybody's happy, OK?'

Malky thinks for a minute, then pockets the twenty. 'Two pints of lager coming up.' He points to the two of us and then to the snug. 'I don't want either of you showing your faces out here.'

Which is going to make getting the next round in difficult, but I decide not to argue.

'So, what do we know so far?'

I finish my pint, belch, and sit back to think.

'Well, we know Isa Stoddart was murdered, but not who did it.'

Wheezy nods. 'Aye.'

'We know that Lachie was murdered, but not who did it.'

'Aye, I knew the daft bastard hadn't topped himself.'

Call it a guilty conscience but I don't like hearing Lachie slagged off like that. 'Show some respect, Wheeze, the man is dead. And his heart was in the right place.'

'No it wasn't! The laddie had no brains, no bottle, and no heart. He was the whole cast of the Wizard of Oz in one chubby wee body.' He sees me about to protest again and quickly moves on. 'Anyhow, as you said, he's also dead.'

'Now,' I lower my voice, 'Assuming that we don't already know who murdered Mrs Stoddart...'

Wheeze looks over both shoulders and nods.

'... it seems to me that the chances are they two murders are related. But now there's this other body turned up.'

'Uh-huh.'

I'm about to launch into my theory about who the latest body is, and who is behind this killing spree when Wheeze beats me to it.

'I've got a theory on who that body is. Get us another pint and I'll share it.'

I decide that I'll hear Wheezy out, mainly for the satisfaction of telling him he's wrong. I'm not convinced that it's my round but I know from long experience that a man could die of thirst waiting for Wheezy to dig deep so I saunter up to the bar, trying not to look worried that Malky might kill me. I needn't have worried; he contents himself with a snarl and some ludicrous overcharging.

I place the two pints in front of us.

'So - shoot.'

'Two words – Guthrie Stoddart.'

I snort in disbelief. 'He's not dead – he ran off with some young bird.'

Wheeze raises an eyebrow. 'Or so we were told. What if Isa had him topped?'

'Why would she do that?'

Wheezy puts his hands on his head then flings them out in a manner I find a little on the theatrical side. 'Found out about him having an affair. Fancied the business all for herself. *She* was having an affair. I don't know, but I remember Isa in those days and she was a hard ticket even then.'

'You and Mrs Stoddart must be about the same age, right?'

He slams his pint down. 'How old do you think I am?'

I'd not given that particular question much thought before. 'Sixty, sixty-five?'

'I'm fifty-two!'

'Oh. No offence, Wheeze, but you're not wearing well.' He's looking daggers at me so I move onto my theory. 'And thanks for sharing that ridiculous theory but I actually know who that body is, because I know who committed all three of they murders.'

64

He puts down his pint. 'Who?'

'Bruce.'

He looks blankly at me. 'Who?'

'Remember Mrs Stoddart's laddies-with-dogs? The one with the long hair?'

He looks at me for a minute then bursts out laughing. 'The big jessie with the dyed blonde tresses and the leather trousers? I don't think so.' He picks up his pint, then starts laughing so much he has to put it down again.

I ignore him. 'He's not that much of a ponce. He told me he'd killed the other laddie-with-a-dog.'

Wheeze thinks for a minute. 'Right enough, I've not seen him about for a while.' He's beginning to get interested. 'So, you think he's the body that's turned up in Isa's house?'

'I do.'

I'm not sure if it's the drink talking or what, but I feel the need to unburden myself.

'I've not been quite straight with you, Wheezy.'

'Aw, shit.' He drains his pint and sighs. 'What now?'

'Nothing bad. Well, I don't think it's bad.' And I fill him in on me being Lachie's rightful heir. When I'm finished he leans back in his chair and stares at me for a long time.

'You are undoubtedly the single jammiest bastard I have ever met.'

'Wheeze, we ought to tell Marianne what I found out. She might remember something that could help us.'

'It'd better be me that tells her – you're not exactly in her good books. That poor lassie. She's had it hard.'

I don't need guilt-tripped about Marianne. In light

of my current predicament *she* should be feeling guilty about *me*. 'Aye, aye.'

'Her man ran off, and her stuck there in they banana flats with her laddie. That's no place to be bringing up a bairn, no garden or nothing. You know what they call that style of architecture?'

'Naw.'

'Brutalist! And bloody brutal they are too…'

And he's off on one before I can stop him. I tune out for a bit. I've heard this rant before; the evils of social housing is one of his favourite topics.

'See social housing in this country, right, it's always been about controlling the working class. Have you ever looked at an aerial picture of a Council housing estate, Stainsie?'

'No, Wheeze, I can't say that I have.'

'They built all these new estates with big long straight streets, so that they could place a machine gun at one end of it and mow down the whole working class in one go if they ever decided to riot.'

I think for a minute. 'Well, that would certainly work with the banana flats, so named for their strong resemblance to a straight line.' I don't think he picks up on my sarcasm.

'See the working classes, right, we've been sold down the river by every government since Ramsay MacDonald.'

'Another pint?'

'Aye, well, just a quick one then I'm off to see Marianne.'

It's dark as a docker's joke when I finally leave the pub. By the time I thought about leaving, Wheezy was lying with his head on the table snoring softly to himself, so

I thought I better take it on myself to give Marianne the good news. I know Wheezy has a key for her flat, so I dip his pockets before I go. I figure she might not be too pleased to see me but when she hears what I've got to say she'll calm down.

The pubs along The Shore are half-empty. A damp Tuesday in April is never going to be a good night for business. The pubs make their money on Friday nights, when the Scottish Government workers and other office staff round here head out after work, and every night during summer when the tourists are in town. And don't get me started about what it's like during the Festival. Even Shugs gets tourists that have got lost. We generally just leave the stray travellers to it, apart from Wheezy who insists they take his picture, then charges them for the privilege.

For all that it's a tourist trap these days, there's still a hard core of old Leith round here. It's the kind of area where it's easy to end up in the wrong place at the wrong time, so I keep one eye looking over my shoulder while I hunt for Marianne's flat. I've a bit of difficulty tracking it down again because all the floors in the banana flats look the same, and to be honest, I'm not at my sharpest after a few pints. Eventually I find a door that looks familiar, and I'm reassured by a little brass plate with 'Murphy' screwed on the doorframe. I knock but don't get any answer.

'Marianne.' I try shouting through the letterbox but she still doesn't come to the door, so I use Wheeze's key. I'm no sooner through the door than she hits me with something. I fall over and she keeps hitting me.

I roll into a foetal position. 'Jesus Christ, Marianne, it's me, Staines.'

'I know that.' She takes another swipe at me and I

uncurl long enough to grab hold of her weapon.

'Do you always repel intruders with a Magic Mop?'

'It was the only thing I had to hand.' I let go for a second and she has another go at me.

I grab the implement with both hands this time. 'Will you stop that?'

She stops trying to hit me with the mop and starts trying to stab me with it instead. 'You bastard! What are you doing here? Is it sex you're after? Do you think you can blackmail me into bed?'

I let go and roll over toward the door. Marianne is still standing with the mop held aloft like the last revolutionary in that French musical thing. I check my watch and notice that Marianne is in her pyjamas. It's maybe a little bit late to be making a house call. I try for some humour.

'Can a man not turn up unexpectedly at a lassie's house at 11.00 at night for any reason other than sex? I'm a wee bit old for making booty calls.'

She's still frowning, and her mouth is pursed tighter than a cat's backside. 'I'd sooner go to prison than sleep with you.'

This doesn't surprise me. 'That's useful to know, thank you very much, but I'm actually here with some good news.'

She lowers her weapon and I take the opportunity to get to my feet.

'I think I can prove you didn't kill Isa Stoddart.'

'What are you talking about?'

'Make me a cup of tea and I'll tell you.'

I don't know what Marianne borrowed money off Mrs

Stoddart for but it certainly wasn't for fixtures and fittings. She sees me looking at it.

'The Council's supposed to be doing the kitchens up this year.' She sounds quite defensive and I decide I better not insult her interior décor on top of everything else.

'No, no it's nice. Retro.'

Her hand's shaking slightly as she puts a mug of coffee in front of me, so I try to lighten the mood a little.

'Your laddie must be a sound sleeper.'

She does a tiny shake of her head. 'He's at his dad's.'

I'm more interested in this information than I should be. I know that whoever Marianne does or doesn't keep in touch with is none of my business. 'He still sees his dad then?'

Her face twitches and I think she's going to tell me to piss off, but she keeps it civil.

'Sometimes.'

I realise I've overstepped the mark. 'I didn't mean to…'

She cuts me off. 'Can you just tell me why you're here, Stainsie?'

'OK. Right.' I'm not quite sure where to begin, and I'm a little distracted. Marianne's PJ top is on the skimpy side, and it's pretty cold in the kitchen. I make a God-Almighty effort to focus. 'I had a conversation with Danny Jamieson.'

'Who?'

'The Polisman that's leading the enquiry into Mrs Stoddart's murder. I was at school with him.'

She nods.

'Anyhow, he says that Mrs Stoddart died in the early hours of February 4th.'

She doesn't say anything.

69

'Like about eight hours later than when you hit her.'

'Oh God – was she lying there dying all that time?' Marianne looks distraught.

'Well, possibly. But it doesn't seem all that likely to me. Plus she'd have to drag herself from the Church all the way to the Foot o' the Walk, where she was found.'

There's a silence while she thinks about this, and I take the opportunity to ask something that's been on my mind. 'So, how many times did you hit Mrs Stoddart?' I can't quite imagine the scene. The way I picture it if she didn't go down on the first blow you would be in deep trouble.

She looks confused. 'Just the once.'

'But Jamieson said something about her being repeatedly battered.' I'm getting excited. 'Marianne, I think we can prove it wasn't you.'

She's not looking convinced. 'So, what do you think happened to her?'

'I'm not sure. But I do know that you were not the only one that had a grudge against her. I'm thinking someone else found her, and finished off what you started.'

She's got the same sceptical expression that her uncle had when I put the theory to him.

'So, Marianne, what we need to do is work out who did do it and tell the boys in blue.'

'Why?' She stares me out. 'I mean, why are you bothered who the Polis think did it?'

Because I want to leave town without worrying about you being sexually assaulted by a well-coiffeured thug. But she's probably got enough to fret about without adding that to her list.

I sigh. ''Cause at the moment people keep grassing me up as being responsible.' I get to my feet. 'I'm not going to get a moment's peace until someone gets arrested.'

I pick my coat up off the back of the seat and ease my arms into it. 'And with Danny Jamieson on the case I'm not convinced it'll ever get solved.'

I haven't eaten all day, so I head round to my favourite chip shop on Leith Walk. Lachie and I weren't really big on cooking so we were round there every second night. It's owned by Mac and Logie, who are brothers, and they were always pretty good to us. Half the time they never even charged us for our chips, and there's been many a night when they've seen me home when I was under the influence.

'I'm back!' I say, wandering into the neon-lit shop.

There's a brief silence, then Mac says, 'You're barred.'

'What?' This is confusing on all kinds of levels, not least because I don't know exactly what you have to do to get barred from a Leith Walk chip shop. If they banned every customer that was rude, drunk or didn't actually have the money for their purchases the whole street would be deserted after 9.30 pm. A few years ago a drunk guy cut off his knob and wandered into a chip shop round here waving it about. I bet he still gets served a fish supper when he asks for it. Though he's probably gone off the battered sausage.

'How am I barred?' Then it occurs to me – these guys probably owe Mrs Stoddart money as well. 'I'm not here to cause trouble – I've destroyed the tallybook.'

'Tallybook?' says Logie. 'Who's interested in a tallybook?'

Mac butts in. 'We're not giving you any more money, Stainsie. We're not scared of you. You're no Mrs Stoddart.'

71

Ordinarily I'd be offended at the implication that I was less frightening than a five foot nothing old lady, but in Isa Stoddart's case they're quite right. So, she's been having protection money off of them. No wonder we got good treatment here.

'You've been paying Mrs Stoddart off?'

'Aye, Stainsie, as if you didn't know that.'

'I didn't!' They're not looking convinced and frankly I don't blame them for doubting my integrity. You lie down with dogs, you get up with fleas. 'Swear to God!'

Logie places his hand on top of the counter. 'Did you never wonder where I got this?'

The skin on his hand is scarred, as if he's been badly burned. 'You had an accident with the deep fat fryer?' I say hopefully.

He smiles, grimly. 'I didn't have the money for Mrs Stoddart one week and she sent one of her thugs round. This wasn't an accident Stainsie. That bitch had her man hold my hand in the fat.'

I'm beginning to feel queasy.

Mac carries on. 'We've been having a chat with the other shopowners round here and we're quite happy to make sure you leave town again, if you get my drift.'

I always get people's drift and it's never good. 'Hold on a minute here'. I raise my hand to start pointing at the pair of them then quickly lower it when Logie makes a grab for it with his mutant melted paw. 'Before there's any vigilante justice here, can I just say I'm no longer part of the Stoddart empire. The person you need to be worried about is Bruce.'

'Who's Bruce?' says Mac.

'One of Mrs Stoddart's laddies-with-dogs,' answers Logie.

72

They both stare at me.

I'm still hungry and the smell of deep frying is driving me insane. 'Can I have my chips?'

'Naw!'

I'm beginning to think that I'm not the popular man-about-town that I thought I was. There was me thinking people laughed at my jokes 'cause I was funny, and slipped me a free fish supper now and again 'cause I was a good bloke.

I was wrong. Seems nobody in this town would have given me the time of day if it wasn't that they saw the shadow of Mrs Stoddart over my shoulder.

As I wander back up Leith Walk looking for somewhere that'll serve me, I hope Mac and Logie put the word out that I'm not looking for trouble, otherwise my head is going to end up in someone's deep fat fryer.

1980

My mammy died for the first time in 1980.

I woke one morning in late May to find the sun streaming into the room I shared with my brother Colin. This was a good sign. We were counting down the days to the school holidays and the weather was looking promising.

'Col.' I threw a sock in his direction as I groped around the bedroom floor to find the clothes that I'd dumped there the night before.

'Col!'

The Colin-shaped lump in my brother's bed grunted and pulled the covers further over his head. We went through this rigmarole every morning. Back then he wasn't what you'd call a morning person.

'Col!'

He grunted again but didn't move. I lost patience with him and pulled all his bedclothes onto the floor.

'You didn't have to do that,' he said, as he did every morning.

The first sign we got that this was not a normal day was when we walked into the kitchen to find my father sitting there, smoking a cigarette. This was unusual both because he wasn't normally there at this time, and also I didn't think I'd ever seen him sitting at the kitchen table. Usually he consumed all his meals sitting in front of the TV.

'You not at work the day, Dad?' I asked, making for the fridge.

'Your mother's not well.' He stopped for a long draw on his fag. 'She's in the hospital, so I thought I'd better stay home this morning and make sure you got your breakfast.'

Col and I exchanged a glance. My Ma not being up at this time was not out of the ordinary. We didn't usually see her before we left for school, and were quite adept at getting our own Rice Krispies without any adult help. The fact that my dad wasn't aware of this didn't strike us as odd at the time.

I was curious about this turn of events. 'What's wrong with her? She didn't seem ill yesterday.'

'Can we visit her?' Col was hopping from foot to foot, a sure sign that tears were on the way.

I looked to my dad for reassurance. 'Will she be back before the holidays?'

My father slammed his hand down on the table. 'Will you stop with all the questions?'

To the casual observer this might seem an odd way to respond to two young laddies who had just found out their mother is seriously ill. But if we noticed anything amiss, we never remarked on it at the time.

'When's she coming back?' said Col, with a quiver in his voice.

'Not for a while, son.' Dad stubbed out his fag, and stood up to empty his ashtray into the bin. With his back to us he added, 'Maybe never.'

This did strike both of us a slightly abrupt way of breaking bad news to young children, odd even to two survivors of 1970s parenting techniques such as ourselves.

We responded with the only weapon we had, and both started to cry.

'How come?'

'It's not fair.'

'I want my mammy.'

My father's face crumpled. He sat down and pulled Col onto his knee. 'I know, son, I know.'

Two days later Dad told us Ma had passed away. It was to be a small funeral; so small that neither of her sons were invited. When we asked Dad why we couldn't go, he said it would be too upsetting for us.

Col and I weren't happy about this, and plotted our campaign under the bedclothes in our room. We cornered Dad in the living room where he was having a quiet five minutes with the *Daily Record*.

'About the funeral, Dad' I began our interrogation. 'Who's going to be there?'

Dad sighed but didn't lower the paper. 'Well, me, obviously, and your grandad.'

We could have guessed that. 'Aye, and who else?'

The paper rustled slightly. 'Oh, people from your mother's family.'

We wanted specifics. 'Like Uncle John…?' I asked.

'and Tom…?' asked Col, looking to me for support.

I nodded and added, 'and Kirsten?'

The *Daily Record* was looking more uncomfortable by the minute. 'Aye. Probably all of them.'

'But Kirsten's younger than us, and if she's getting to go we should get to go.' I couldn't fault Col's logic on that one.

Dad stood up, threw the *Record* on the ground and

stamped on it. 'You're not going,' he said as he left the room, leaving both his paper and his relationship with his sons in tatters.

The day of the funeral we stayed home with Granny Florrie, who, although not our real granny gave us more comfort than flesh and blood ever could.

'It was for the best, lads. She didn't suffer.' She had an arm round each of us, holding us tight to her bosom, which wasn't all that pleasant really 'cause she was an awful skinny woman. 'She's in a better place now. Who wants ice cream?'

Col wasn't of a mood to be placated by mint chocolate chip. He had questions about all of this, and as she was the only adult present, he was determined to get answers from Florrie.

'So, what did my mammy die of?'

Florrie was looking a bit hot, although it wasn't a warm day. There was a flush to her face and she took off her cardigan and draped it over the back of her chair. 'I'm not exactly sure, son, you'd have to ask your father.'

'Was it her liver?'

Both Florrie and I looked at Colin in surprise. He had been giving this some thought. I was quite impressed; I was still struggling to come to terms with the idea that Ma wasn't here anymore and Col was already onto making medical diagnoses for her demise.

'Her liver? What makes you say that son?'

''Cause Iain Ridley in my class said that his ma said that she wasn't surprised that Ma was dead after all the strain she'd been putting on her liver.'

Florrie was looking hotter by the minute.

77

'Aye, well, maybe, son, but you'd really have to ask your father about that.'

Col contemplated this for a minute or two. 'So, where is she now?'

Florrie started fanning herself with a rolled up newspaper. 'At the cemetery, son, being buried. Where else would she be?'

Colin looked slightly bemused. 'I mean, is she in Heaven?'

Florrie looked relieved. 'Oh aye, son, definitely. That mother of yours is with God now, looking down on her two laddies and feeling very proud of you both.'

Now I'm puzzled. 'I thought Ma was being cremated?'

'Ice cream, boys?' Florrie leapt to her feet.

I could hear every window in the kitchen being opened. When she came back through with two heaped bowls, she switched the TV on and wouldn't be drawn into conversation.

Wednesday

The sound of a door slamming wakes me up. It must have been Father Paul heading out to Mass. Maybe I should make the effort of going to church while I'm staying here; it seems like the least I can do in return for the free digs.

The last time I went to Mass must have been my laddie's baptism, which would make it, Jesus, how many years ago would that make it? I decide to head to the bathroom rather than lie there thinking about my shortcomings as a parent.

The back of my hands are skinned, and the hot water stings as I wash them. I rub a few bit of dirt off and watch it spin into the plughole. My shirt is missing a couple of buttons and has a few flecks of paint attached to it. I'm momentarily confused, then remember climbing back in through one of the downstairs windows due to Father Paul not giving me a set of keys. I'm not sure if he was making a point about me being under house arrest, or if he just forgot. He's a busy man.

I eat my breakfast in front of the TV to see if there's any info about the Mavisview body, or about Lachie's death, but there's nothing on the regional news. I'd like to go out for a paper but my lack of keys puts me off. Another half-hour of channel hopping persuades me that I can't face a whole day sitting in the Priest's House. I turn out every drawer in the kitchen until I successfully locate a spare back door key.

I almost wish I hadn't bothered. The sky is metallic and the rain's coming down in lumps. It's the kind of rain that drenches you on the way down, then bounces off the ground and soaks you again on the way back up. I cast a glance over my shoulder to the Priest's House and the comfort of daytime TV, then sighing, leg it to the paper shop.

Manny, the owner, is standing behind the counter flicking through a magazine. He's halfway through his usual shopkeeper's welcoming smile when he realises it's me and the smile grinds to an abrupt halt, leaving him with his teeth bared as if he's about to lunge forward and sink them in my neck. The smile retreats completely and he speaks.

'I heard you were back.'

'Looks like it,' I mumble.

He grins and reaches across the counter to give me a hug. Manny's dad moved here from Malta in 1950. Manny's lived all his life, as far as I know, in Leith, but he still has a Mediterranean attitude to life.

I push him away. 'Aye, aye, get off me. I only came in for an *Evening News*.'

He laughs. 'They're not in yet but you'll get a *Scotsman* on the stand.'

Manny goes back to flicking through his magazine and I wander round the shop. I rifle through the papers, looking for information about the murder. The *Scotsman's* got a feature about it on page 2. There's a picture of Mavisview as it is today, and also an old photo of it from its heyday, with a bit about its history. I decide to come back to that later and go straight to the update on the Polis investigation.

It's a bit of an anticlimax, seeing as the first set of tests the Polis have had on the bones haven't managed to tell them very much, beyond the fact it's a body, and it's dead. And any facts they do know about the body they're not releasing to the likes of us just yet.

But in spite of that, the journalists have excelled themselves and managed to come up with a double-page spread of guesswork. There's a half-page discussion about whether the body's some poor chambermaid that was done wrong by her employer and ended up under the floorboards, nicely illustrated with a black and white drawing of a lassie with a drawstring cap and a mop. She reminds me of Marianne.

On the other page there's a picture of a wee laddie climbing into a fridge, accompanied by an article stuffed with frightening statistics about the number of children that die or injure themselves every year playing places they shouldn't be. They've got this down as some local kid who has being playing a game of hide-and-seek that's gone fatally wrong.

I can't wait for the morning's *Scotsman*. If they manage to get four pages' worth of news out of the story before we even know if it was a man's or a woman's body, once they find out the Stoddarts were involved they'll be able to write a bloody book.

I hear voices raised in the shop. Peering round the paper rack I see Manny getting some grief from a couple of the local neds. I recognise the pair of them from the scheme. They're a whole nightbus full of trouble.

'Gie us 20 L&B.' One of the neds is leaning across

81

Manny's counter. I'm not sure if he's doing that to intimidate Manny or because he can't stand upright.

The shopkeeper stands his ground. 'Give me some money first.'

Ned Number One leans away from the counter, staggers a wee bit and leans back in. 'Gie us the fags you Paki bastard or I'll have you.' Manny suffers a lot of misplaced racism. In the years he's had this shop I've heard him called every nationality under the sun except Maltese.

Manny's holding firm on the No Fags line, but the second ned isn't having it. He's not staggering, and peering round the paper rack I see a flash of blade as he gets a knife out of his coat. 'Gie us the fags, Paki.'

I should really do something, but I'm not keen on rugby-tackling a knife-wielding ned, so I hide back behind the paper rack and hope they don't notice me.

The door buzzer sounds.

'You can come out now, Stainsie. They've gone.'

I slink out from behind the papers, and slope up to the counter. 'You OK, Man?'

Manny reaches under the counter and pulls out a duster. He gives the front counter a wipe. 'Aye. Bit light on fags though.'

He nods at the *Scotsman* which I'm still holding in my hand. 'You taking that then?'

I've read everything of interest to me in the *Scotsman* already. 'Naw – I'll pop back for a *News* later.'

It's not really Manny's day. I give him a guilty wave and back out of the shop.

As I pull the door shut behind me, I bump into Wheezy.

He grabs my lapel. 'I've been looking for you.'

I brush his hand off my clothing. 'And now you've

found me.' Despite his attempts at manhandling me he doesn't look in a bad mood.

'Let's go and have a look at that house of yours.'

In the cold light of day, I'm beginning to regret telling Wheeze about my inheritance, but, what's done is done and I quite fancy another look at it, although I'd prefer to go on my own. 'It's not really the weather for a visit, Wheezy.'

He pulls a face. 'Och, away with you – a bit of rain never hurt anyone.'

We get the 16 bus. Wheezy is in an educational mood and insists on treating me, and the rest of the bus, to a potted history of the Trinity area.

''Course, Stainsie, son, it's all ships, ships, ships, round there. It's shipping money that got all those nice mansions built.'

'Really.' I know from bitter experience that he's going to lecture me whatever I say, so I keep my input to a minimum.

'And the street names. Half of the streets are named after ships: Stirling Road, Zetland Place.'

'Last time I looked, Wheezy, Stirling and Zetland were places, not ships.' I draw a little ship in the condensation on the window to emphasise my point.

Wheezy snorts. 'That's just the response I'd expect from a historian of your calibre.'

I ignore him, and rub my hand over the window. It destroys my drawing but at least I can see out into the world. The tide is in and the boats in the Newhaven harbour are bobbing up and down contentedly. Maybe I'll buy a yacht when I'm minted, and name it *The Isabella*. The irony of that would keep Mrs Stoddart spinning in her grave for a year or two. We hop off the bus at the Chain Pier Inn and walk up York Road. It's a steep climb and Wheeze moans all the way up.

'Jesus Christ, Stainsie son, this is some climb. I'm not sure I'll be visiting you much when you're lord of the manor.'

I stop and feign amazement. 'Really? You won't be round eating my food and drinking my booze? You're breaking my heart, Wheeze.'

We reach the wrought iron gates at the end of Mavisview's drive. I point to the house with a flourish. 'This is it.'

He sticks his face right up against the gates for a better view. 'Christ! How many of the Addams family are still living here?'

'Very funny. It looks a lot better on a sunny day.'

'And this is the new block?' He gestures to the modern development. I nod.

'Jeez-o. They look about as comfortable as a rabbit hutch. What are you planning on calling them - Jerry-Built Mansions?'

He's got a point but I'm not giving him the satisfaction. 'Shut up.'

'Sorry, sorry.' He doesn't look all that contrite. 'It's really all very nice. Super.' He clears his throat. 'Mavisview was built in the 1800s for a shipping magnate if I'm not mistaken.'

'Piss off, Wheezy.'

'No, seriously, you can tell that this house was connected to shipping by the fact it's got a tower. All the shipowners had a tower so they could keep an eye on their ships down at Leith docks.'

84

I'm not sure if he's taking the mick or not. 'Really?'

'Oh aye. I can just see us sitting in the wee tower room with a fine malt or two, watching the yachts on the Forth.'

He laughs and we walk back down in the direction of the Starbank Inn.

Halfway down Wheezy stops and gestures back up the hill. 'So, you really own all of that?'

I look up then back down the road and across the Firth of Forth to Fife. I'm not entirely sure I know the answer to Wheezy's question. 'Not yet. According to the lawyer wifey there's a load of debts attached to the project and the whole thing might have to be sold off.'

Wheezy snorts. 'Sounds like a load of bull to me.'

I agree. 'You know this, Wheeze, I had the feeling all the time I was in her office, that the lawyer wasn't being quite straight with me.'

He slaps my shoulder. 'Of course she wasn't! The more complicated they make it, the more money you have to pay them in fees to sort it all out.'

'I could do with a look at all the papers the lawyer lassie had.'

He thinks for a minute. 'I've got a plan, Stainsie.' He winks at me and gestures back over his shoulder. 'We'll have you living in Amityville there in no time.'

'This is never going to work.'

Wheezy and I are standing on Hanover Street looking at the lawyer's offices. We've raided the back bedroom of the Priest's House for a couple of suits, and I've had a shave, so I daresay we're looking presentable. Well, I am, anyway. Wheezy's beyond hope. I've never seen Wheeze in a suit before and I'm finding it quite disturbing. It just doesn't look right, like seeing a monkey in a wetsuit, or a giraffe dressed as a French maid.

'Aye, it will. Just do what we agreed.'

The receptionist clocks me, and acts much less frosty this time. She shows us into a meeting room, and fusses around getting us coffee and biscuits, flashing us a substantial amount of cleavage while she dishes out the Chocolate Bourbon. I'm not sure if this improved treatment is because this time I'm not sporting the two-day stubble and carrying all my goods and chattels in a rucksack, or because Miss Spencely's told her about my new status as the heir to a property empire. Either way I'm not that bothered now that she's tipping me the wink. Never question a lassie's motives, that's my motto.

'Miss Spencely will be through in a minute.' She gives me a big smile, which I return, while Wheezy rolls his eyes. 'Thanks, hen.'

It's half an hour before she turns up, full of apologies, and sits down, placing a couple of folders marked 'Stoddart' on the table.

'So, how can I help you, Mr Staines and er...' She looks in the direction of Wheezy.

He throws her a wide smile, revealing a frightening lack of dental hygiene. 'Mr Murphy. I'm an, eh, business associate of Mr Staines.'

I break in before Wheezy can start building his part. 'We were just wondering if you could give us an update about the will?'

She smiles politely. 'I'm not sure I've a lot to add to our last conversation.' She reaches for one of the folders and gets the plans of Mavisview out. 'As I said to you before it could take some considerable time... are you OK?'

86

Wheezy is grabbing his left arm and gulping for air.

'Oh. My God. Not his heart again.' I fall to my knees beside him. I haven't acted this hard since I was second shepherd in the school's nativity play.

Miss Spencely has half stood up in her chair. 'His heart?'

Holding Wheezy's clammy hand in mine I turn to her and ask, 'Could you get some help, Miss Spencely?'

'Of course, I'll go and phone an ambulance.' She gets to her feet, her long dark hair flapping.

As soon as she's out of the room I help Wheeze to his feet. I grab the papers out of one of her files and Wheezy gets the papers from the other. We shove them all in my bag, then head out to reception. The receptionist is on the phone ordering our ambulance, with Miss Spencely hovering over her.

I wave to them as we go past. 'I'm just going to take him out for some air.'

Miss Spencely looks confused. 'Oh – are you sure that's wise?'

I nod solemnly. 'He'll be fine.'

'Can you give us change for the machine?' Wheeze bangs a tatty fiver down on Manny's counter and gestures at the photocopier.

'Five pounds' worth? What are you photocopying – is it your first novel?' He throws his head back and laughs. 'What's it called? Jurassic Jakeys? Anyway, much as I'd love to take your money, I can't – the machine's bust.'

Wheezy and I exchange a look. 'Shit – what do we do now?'

'You could try the library?'

87

'Naw thanks,' says Wheezy with a brisk shake of his head.

Manny leans on his counter. 'What's wrong with the library?'

I look at Wheezy but he's not catching my eye. 'We're not very popular there.'

Manny's intrigued. 'In what way?'

I sigh. 'In a we're-barred-from-there kind of a way.'

Manny folds his arms and smiles smugly. 'Well, there's nowhere else round here that does photocopying.'

All the way to McDonald Road, Wheezy's ranting.

'There was a time, right, when your honest working man could spend his days sitting in the library, reading the papers, having a wee flick through the magazines...'

It's stretching the imagination a wee bit to call Wheeze an honest working man seeing as he last had a job in 1984, and the only resemblance he has to a working man these days is a donkey jacket he won in a pub bet. Added to that, your average working man doesn't tend to sit around libraries during the day, what with having to go to work, but I let him go on.

'... not getting hassled by some over-promoted wee lassie that doesn't recognise we have rights.'

'Fair do's, Wheezy, we were making a bit of a racket yon time.'

'Nonsense.'

Getting barred from places happens to Wheezy a lot, and in fairness to him it's not always his fault. He's barred from all the pubs on Leith Walk that have a trivia machine due to his extensive general knowledge, which always strikes me as a little unfair. And he's banned from being within 500 metres of his ex-wife, but who's to say who really has the moral high ground on that one? Marriage breakdowns are never easy, and having met Mo I don't think she's really living in fear of a middle-aged asthmatic with a limp.

His exclusion from the two libraries in Leith is, however, his own fault, in both cases for attempting to read the newspapers while severely under the influence of alcohol.

The library is pretty much deserted.

Wheezy points to the library reception desk. 'There she is – Little Miss Hitler.'

'Behave yourself. Remember why we are here.' I slick back my hair in an attempt to look respectable. 'And give me some money.'

He reluctantly digs the fiver out again and nods his head toward the photocopiers. 'I'll wait by the machines.'

The librarian looks up.

'I thought I banned you and your friend.'

'Aye, you did. And you were right to do so under the circumstances. My friend and I were out of order, disturbing this house of learning.'

I flash her my pearly whites. She doesn't crack a smile. This is going to be more challenging than I had anticipated.

'Thing is, we've got a bit of a photocopying emergency. All I'm looking for is to purchase two photocopying cards, do the business, then we are out of your hair so fast you'll never remember we were here.'

She stares at me, then sits back in her chair and crosses her arms.

'Really?'

'Tell you what,' I put Wheezy's fiver down on the counter, 'think of this as a good behaviour bond. Any nonsense out of us, you can put it in the charity box. '

She sighs and takes two photocopying cards out of the drawer.

'Very well. That's £2 for the cards.'

'Ah. Can you take that off the fiver?'

'Are you making any sense of these?'

I look again at the piece of paper in my hand. 'Not really, Wheeze – what about you?'

We're sitting in the Priest's House with the contents of Miss Spencely's files spread across the kitchen table; there are piles of company details, bank statements and accounts everywhere.

Wheezy sighs. 'I'm not sure, right, but looking at these I'd say Isa was up shit creek by the time she pegged it.'

I take a swig of coffee. 'How come?'

He brandishes a bunch of bank statements. 'Well, look at these: healthy - bloody healthy in fact – up until about six months before she dies. Then she's withdrawing left, right and centre. None of these accounts has got more than a few thousand in them.'

Just my luck to be bequeathed the Stoddart millions at the point where they're going bankrupt. 'There goes my inheritance.'

'But then she's got that house that she's working on – most of these payments are to builders and developers. Except for this one – look.' He fans out the statements for the last couple of years. 'There's been a regular payment of £20,000 into an account at the *Banco Popular Español* every month.'

90

It could only be one person. 'Guthrie?'

'Aye, if he's not dead and is hiding out on the *Costa Del Paedo*. But the funny thing is the payments stop completely about six months ago.'

I take a look at bank statements. 'So, what happened six months ago?'

Wheezy shrugs. 'Guthrie dies? Their divorce finally comes through?'

I snort. 'What, after a mere twenty-five years of living apart?'

'Aye, well, they probably didn't want to upset Lachie.'

We laugh, then I feel a bit guilty. *Poor Lachie.*

I go to take another swig of coffee when a thought occurs to me. 'A house that size in Trinity must have set her back a fair bit. Maybe she's economising.'

'Aye, well here's another funny thing – look at how much she paid for it.' He shoves another piece of paper under my nose.

'£250,000?' That doesn't seem right. 'I'd have said it was worth twice that!'

'Twice?' Wheezy looks outraged. 'Four time more like.'

'Who did she buy it off – was it some kind of dodgy deal?'

Wheezy shuffles the papers around until he finds the right bit of paper.

'Says here the previous owner was a Miss Agnes O'Neill. And look at this – the correspondence address for her is Marrot Muir Nursing Home.'

I don't like the sound of that. 'You don't think Mrs Stoddart and her thugs have ripped off an old lady?'

Wheezy snorts. 'I think it's exactly the kind of thing

that Isabella Stoddart would have done. You can picture it, can't you, some old dear, living on her own. No relatives, or none that take an interest anyway. Isa's round there, befriending her, just sign here on the dotted line, Miss O'Neill, before one of my thugs rips your elderly head off.'

'What are you two up to?' We're so caught up in our theories that we've not heard Father Paul come in.

'Ah nothing much, Father,' says Wheezy while I shuffle the papers together. 'What about yourself?'

Father Paul picks up the kettle and holds it under the tap. 'Just been visiting my incapacitated flock – hospitals and nursing homes, you know. The usual.'

'Have you heard of a nursing home called Marrot Muir, Father?'

He turns round, kettle in hand. 'Yes – it's one of those big old houses in Trinity. I've got a parishioner in there in fact.'

Wheezy and I exchange glances. 'Who's that then, Father?'

'Oh –from before your time, Michael. Agnes is a very elderly lady – she was housebound for over thirty years before she moved into nursing care.'

'Would that be Agnes Smith, Father?'

He shakes his head. 'Oh no. O'Neill is her name.'

Wheezy and I exchange another glance, and behind Father Paul's back he mouths the word 'coincidence' to me, and starts laughing.

I show Wheezy to the door. My coat is hanging behind the door and I pull it off the peg. 'So, what now, Wheeze – down to Shugs for a quick one?'

'No.' He goes to pull the door shut behind him but I manage to grab it before it closes.

'No?'

'Naw, you've got to get these papers back to that lawyer lassie.' He makes another attempt at closing the door. 'She'll be doing her nut.'

Right on cue my mobile rings.

'How many messages is that she's left you now?'

I scroll through Miss Spencely's irate text. I haven't told Wheeze that her first text told me that I could have seen all the papers that I wanted without stealing them, what with me being the lawful executor. 'This is the sixth.'

Wheezy puts his hand on my shoulder. 'Phone her and say it was a mistake and you picked her papers up in the heat of the moment, and that you're on the way to return them right now.' He gives me a little shake, just for emphasis.

'Why me? Aren't you coming with me?'

Wheeze steps out of the house and finally succeeds in pulling the door shut behind him. Through the wood I hear him shout. 'It's not a two-person job.'

I'm cursing Wheezy all the way back to Hanover Street, but he's got a point. I don't want to get Miss Spencely her jotters, or have her set the Polis on me, so I reckon I'll post them through the door, then text her to say that I've done it.

But when I get to the offices there's still a light on, and I didn't want to be nabbed by some lawyer-type as I put them through the letterbox, so I think I'll hang around until it's All Quiet on the Western Front. I don't want to sit around in full view in case anyone notices me taking

93

too much of an interest, so I settle myself in a doorway. I've just got my fag lit when the door of the offices opens and Miss Spencely appears.

She spends a minute or two locking up and putting the alarm on, and as she does so a sports car pulls up, and the guy inside leans over and opens the passenger door. She flashes him a big smile and climbs in, throwing her arms round his head.

Lucky bastard, I think, until the car pulls away and I get a good look at the driver.

It's Bruce.

All the regulars are propping up the bar in Shugs. Wee Craigie West is holding forth about his wife's shortcomings as usual; although if you are 5' 1" and you manage to get yourself a wife that's 5' 7" in her stocking soles you think you'd be counting your blessings, not slagging the poor woman off at every opportunity. Jimmy Gillespie is nursing a pint of *Special*, a chaser, and his usual dour expression. Tam and Ricky are nodding along to Craigie's ramblings, with Wheezy dotting about in the background. Nobody turns round when I walk in.

Craigie's being philosophical. 'What is it about women, that from the moment you marry them they get uglier and more crabbit with every passing day? Is it, like, some kind of illness that they all have?'

'Aye,' I say, 'it's called Crone's Disease.'

Nobody laughs.

Craigie shifts uncomfortably on his bar stool. 'You owe me a tenner for a service I bought that you never rendered.'

I think this a little unfair. 'No, I do not. My job was to get that book out of town, which I did.' Nobody specifically said I couldn't come back, although everyone seems to have assumed I wouldn't. Maybe they thought with £1,700 in my pocket I'd have drunk myself to death within a week.

Big Malky's drying glasses down the other end of the bar. He glares at me, obviously still worried that I'm putting his customers off their drink.

'So, where is Ma Stoddart's tallybook now?' asks Craigie. I sense there is interest from the others on this issue. You could hear a pin drop as they wait for the answer. Maybe I should ask them all how much they owed Mrs Stoddart, then I could pass the information on to Bruce and get him off my back. I might give that serious thought if they keep giving me a hard time.

'I destroyed it.'

Craigie relaxes. 'Really?'

I nod. 'Aye – you've no worries on that score.'

Craigie thinks for a minute and looks at the others for reassurance. 'Well, that's not so bad I suppose.' He's not an unreasonable man when you get him off the subject of his wife.

'So, where did you go?' asks Tam.

I debate with myself whether to tell them the truth and in the end decide it can't hurt. 'Newcastle.'

'Really? I thought you'd have gone somewhere more exotic like, you know, Bournemouth or that.' Tam isn't widely travelled.

'I've seen the world already, Tam, and most of it sucks. Anyhow, I was only bunking down there for a few weeks while I decided what to do next.'

Wheezy grabs my arm and drags me down the bar toward Jimmy Gillespie.

'Jimmy – tell Stainsie here what you were telling me earlier.'

He looks up slowly from his pint. 'About what?'

'Your cousin's laddie.'

He nods, slowly. He's not a man to do anything in a rush. 'Oh, aye. Know my cousin Margaret, Stainsie? Works in the card shop in Great Junction Street?'

I don't but I decide it is quicker to nod.

'Well, her laddie's been working on the house in Trinity that's been in the news – you know the one where they found the body?'

I look at Wheezy. I hope he hasn't been telling the whole scheme that I'm about to become a millionaire, or anything like that. 'I may have heard something about it on the news.'

Jimmy nods. 'Lewis, that's her laddie, says that the house is in an awful state, but the gaffer's been telling them that they've got to keep all the 'original features', which I don't really understand myself 'cause if you're going to spend a fortune on a house surely you want state-of-the-art fireplaces and that.' He stops for another mouthful of his beer. I take the hint and order the three of us another round. 'Ta very much, Stainsie. Anyway, Lewis and this other laddie are working on one of the bedrooms on the top floor, and it's got one of they seats built into the bay window. Lewis and the other laddie are assuming that this is one of the original features that they're not supposed to be touching so they're given it a wide berth, when the gaffer comes in and tells them off for being a pair of arseholes, and can't they recognise a botch job from the seventies when they see it?'

I laugh. 'That's harsh.'

'Not really.' Jimmy pulls a face and takes another swig. 'Lewis *is* an arsehole. I had him and his pal do some wallpapering for me and they made a right arse of it and no mistake. Anyhow, Lewis and the other laddie set to ripping out this window seat, taking care not to damage the floorboards, because, of course, the house is to have stripped pine floorboards throughout...'

'Of course.'

'... which I don't really understand 'cause who spends all that money on a house and then has to get out of bed onto freezing cold boards every morning? Any road, they get the window seat removed and they notice that a section of the floorboards has been cut up, like as if to form a trapdoor. Lewis's pal says how the gaffer's not going to like this, and Lewis says maybe they should have a wee look at what's underneath the trapdoor in case it's a false floor or something, and maybe the floor's not ruined.'

His nephew sounds quite a turn. 'That was very enterprising of him.'

'Naw the money-grabbing wee bastard thinks maybe a previous owner's got their valuables buried there, and him and his pal can pocket them.' He shakes his head. 'Tight-fisted wee toad. £40 he charged me for that wallpapering, and me family and all. Still, the wee prick gets his comeuppance when they unscrew the trapdoor and Lewis sticks his bonce down the hole. Just about brains himself on the skeleton that was buried there.'

We all laugh. I've never met Lewis but it sounds like he had it coming.

'So he starts screaming like a lassie which brings the gaffer and all the other workies up the stairs, and the gaffer has to get the Polis involved, so that's Lewis been sat on his arse for the past three days, waiting to get the all clear to start work again.'

We all contemplate our drinks for a minute.

'So, was it a body from ye olden days do you think?' I ask.

Jimmy shakes his head. 'Naw, I don't think so. The papers are talking a load of shite about this being some hiding place from the old days. I'm telling you that window seat was thirty year old, tops. And another thing: Lewis said the skeleton, well the body anyway, had had its hands tied behind its back with a length of flex, so it can't be that old.'

'So, are the Polis charging the owner of the house for murder?'

He shakes his head again. 'No – the last owner of the house was some old wife, and Lewis said that she was only living in a couple of rooms on the ground floor. He said the top floors of the house were in a terrible state, birds nesting there and that kind of shit.'

'Interesting,' I say.

Wheezy nods. 'Interesting.'

1980–1982

When he was twelve, Colin found God. I don't think that it was directly related to my mother's death. Too many things had happened in between her death and God's appearance on the scene. Not least, her resurrection.

When my father and grandparents were doing their best to erase Ma from the scene, you think it would have occurred to one of the daft well-meaning bastards, that there was just the teeniest, tiniest, possibility that one day Col and I would be walking home from school, and run slap-bang into the ghost of our dead mammy, half-cut and weeping about how much she's missing us. Do you not think?

When Ma inevitably did turn up at the school gates we had a lot of questions for her. Actually, we had one question really, along the lines of, 'How come you're not dead?' But she was too drunk to answer anything, so she just hugged us to her and kept saying, 'My babies, my babies,' which was kind of nice.

My father must have thought his worst nightmare had come true when he saw the three of us sitting in the kitchen. We had been pouring coffee into my mother all afternoon in the hope that she'd sober up enough to tell us what the hell was going on, but all we had managed to do was move her on to a tearful phase, and we both knew not to mess with her when she was like that. Tears generally turned into throwing things.

So, when poor old Dad walked in, she's sat there in floods, rocking back and forth and still chanting, 'my babies, my babies,' the novelty of which had worn off by now. He didn't say anything.

'Ma's not dead,' said Colin helpfully.

'So it would appear,' said Dad, and I couldn't help thinking that he didn't look quite as surprised as we did when we first saw her. He got a fiver out of his wallet and handed it to me. 'Away to the shops you two, and get something for the tea.'

'Can we get an arctic roll to celebrate?'

'Aye, aye, whatever you want, son,' said my dad, shooing us out the door.

'Who do you think they buried then?' Col's brow was creased as he tried to work this out.

'I dunno. I suppose the hospital gave them the wrong body.' Colin nodded away, but I wasn't convinced. 'Col, you take the money and I'll meet you at the shop. I just want to check something with Dad.' And I took off before Col could complain that he's not supposed to cross Leith Walk on his own.

When I got back to the flat, I didn't go in, but jumped over the wall into the back green. I got down on my hands and knees and crawled along to the kitchen window. I waited a minute or two before cautiously popping my head up and looking in. Dad was making Ma a cup of coffee; she must have been pissing pure caffeine by now. If I stayed really still, I could hear what they were saying. At least I could hear what Dad was saying, 'cause he was shouting, but I couldn't hear my mother's responses.

'We had an arrangement.' My father put an emphasis

100

on the word 'arrangement'. 'It was all agreed, Doreen. And what about the money I gave you?'

I saw Ma's lips move.

'What do you mean he's spent it? And where is he now?'

Ma covered her face with her hands.

'He's left you? After all this? After all that the pair of you put the boys through? Well, you're not coming back.'

Ma was shaking and rocking back and forth again.

'I don't care. You're not coming back.'

By the time I caught up with Col, who was standing nervously at the side of Leith Walk, did the shopping, and got home, Ma had gone. Dad wasn't answering any questions on the subject, so we ate our celebratory meal in silence. We didn't even put the telly on.

We never talked about my mother again. From time to time I tried to raise the issue with Dad but he just got angry. Not just a wee bit annoyed either; he got screamingly, go-to-your-room angry. As a tactic for avoiding discussion this worked well. Col always started to cry, and if I'm honest, talking about my Ma tended to bring tears to my eyes too, and it was difficult to carry on an argument in that state. I made up my mind that as soon as I was old enough I was going to leave home and look for her. As it turned out Colin was the only one who ever saw her again, and what she did to him then was unforgivable.

Colin's conversion to religion came as a surprise to my father and me; our attitude to religion was semi-detached at best. Back in the 1940s Grandad Joe had re-found his religion, mainly to annoy the father of Miss Ailsa Morrison, a dour man who could barely contain his misery at gaining a Polish son-in-law, with or without an anglicised name. As soon as Joe realised that nothing would annoy Mr Morrison more than his daughter having active links to the Catholic Church, he suddenly felt nostalgic for the religion of his youth. He raised the issue with his wife.

'I'm worried that the children are not being brought up in the church.'

Mrs Ailsa Staines (née Morrison) was a little surprised by this. 'But they come to the church with me, Joe. They go to the Sunday School.'

'Is not proper religion.'

Ailsa was getting more confused by the minute. 'Are you saying that you want them to have a Catholic upbringing? I thought you had no time for the Catholic church?'

'I the last of my family, and my children not honouring their heritage.' This was Joe's trump card: his 'last of the family' line was used to get his own way on many different issues relating to child-rearing. Ailsa generally got misty-eyed at the thought of Joe's losses, and gave in.

This time, though, Joe had just brought a whole heap of trouble on himself. Ailsa, being a dutiful wife (and a little bit gullible where Joe was concerned) embraced Catholicism, and took to it with the zeal of a convert, thus ensuring that the two following generations had all the benefits of a full Catholic education, and that Joe never again got a long lie on a Sunday morning. I freely admit most of the educational benefits were lost on me but Col must have been paying some attention.

When Col turned twelve we were living in East Kilbride. East Kilbride had the distinction of being the first Scottish New Town, and was famed for having nearly as many roundabouts as inhabitants. Neither point greatly impressed Col or me, but then we were getting increasingly hard to impress, as this was the fourth town we'd lived in.

Our wandering had started two years earlier, shortly after my mother's reappearance. The first we knew of it was my father interrupting our post-school TV viewing to tell us that he'd got a new job.

'Oh aye,' I said, not moving my eyes from the telly.

'Aye,' said my dad, 'it's in Rosyth.'

'Rosyth? Where's that?'

'In Fife.'

Suddenly Dad had my undivided attention. Col remained oblivious to where the conversation was going, concentrating instead on Johnny Ball, thinking of a number.

'Fife, Dad? That's a long drive every day.'

'Aye, well, I'll not be driving because we'll be moving there.'

This was big news. I did a few quick calculations in my head. Downside, leaving the only home we'd ever known, moving away from Grandad and Florrie, having to go to a new school. On the upside, waving goodbye, hopefully forever, to Lachlan Stoddart. Although I would miss the Stoddarts' house.

Col wasn't taking it so well.

'Moving? What about Grandad and Florrie? And the school? And my pals?'

Dad shifted from foot to foot. 'You'll make new pals.'

It was no use, though. Col burst into tears and couldn't be consoled.

Lachie didn't show much emotion when I said I was leaving. For some reason I was finding it difficult to choose a moment to tell him. I was aware that I was Lachie's only pal, and considering the way he'd treated most of the other laddies in the class I didn't hold out much hope of him making new friends. So I kept the news to myself for as long as possible, and we were only a week away from moving when I raised the subject.

'We're moving house, Lachie. Dad, Col and I are all moving to Rosyth.'

I didn't know what I expected like, not tears or anything, but he just blinked a few times and said, 'Remember to give me back my Star Wars game before you go.'

I didn't.

I wasn't entirely sure what prompted my dad to move. Looking back, he might have been worried about Ma coming back and trying to exercise custody rights, or maybe he'd finally decided to get me away from the influence of the Stoddarts. Whatever the reason was it definitely wasn't a career move. Dad gave up a well-paid job in the Parks Department of the Council to take on some of the shittiest factory work going. The early 1980s weren't exactly boom years for employment so he took what work he could get. This was often on short-term contracts; we were only in Rosyth a few months before we moved on to Port Glasgow, where we lasted the best part of a year. Six months in Paisley, and then our final move to East Kilbride.

To my surprise, given that I'd lived my whole life in one flat in Leith, I found that I didn't mind the moving from place to place. The first few days at a new school were always hard, and I can't say that I made loads of friends, but on balance I still had more pals than when Lachie was running my life for me. Oh, I missed Grandad and Florrie, I even missed Leith some of the time, but every time my father got the suitcases out and said, 'We're moving on, lads,' there was some spark of excitement in my stomach that I couldn't ignore.

Colin, on the other hand, hated the travelling. He was a shy kid, and the constant uprooting wasn't doing him any good. By the time we got to East Kilbride I'm pretty sure he had been beaten up in three different schools. He was probably bullied at school in East Kilbride as well, but I wasn't quite sure what was going on in his head, and to be honest, I didn't ask him. You'd think that being thrust into each other's company would have brought us closer together, that as his big brother I could have provided some stability in his life. Unfortunately, shortly before Col discovered God, I discovered girls, and I was far more interested in what I could get Linda McFarlane to do in the hour between us leaving school and her ma getting home from work, than any crisis my wee brother might be having.

So, the first time I realised that there was anything afoot was when I wakened one Sunday morning to find that his bed was empty. Not that surprising perhaps, but like I've said, Col wasn't what you would call an early bird. I had a hunt round the rest of the flat, which didn't take long, then wakened my dad, who slept on the couch in the living room.

'Col's gone missing.'

'What?' said Dad, opening only one eye. None of the Staineses were really morning people, if I'm honest.

'Col isn't in the flat.'

'Col's not in the flat? Then where is he?'

I should have made the man a cup of coffee before starting on this. 'I don't know Dad, that's why I'm wakening you.'

Both of his eyes were open now and he was looking worried. He flung off his covers and swung his legs to the floor. He was wearing only boxer shorts and I turned my head away in case I accidentally got a flash of his balls.

'He's maybe just gone to the shop,' said my dad doubtfully. 'We'll give him five minutes. Stick the kettle on son.'

We drank a cup of coffee in silence. Dad looked at his watch.

'He should have been back by now. If he's not at the shops, where do you think he's gone?'

I was starting to feel both panicky and guilty. I had no idea where my wee brother would have gone.

'C'mon, Joseph, you must have some ideas.' Dad's voice was raised, and I was feeling a bit aggrieved because it wasn't my fault that Col was missing. 'Think, Joe.'

'I am thinking Dad, but I don't know where Col would have gone. Maybe he's gone to visit Grandad and Florrie?'

'Grandad and Florrie? What would he do that for?'

I was getting really pissed off with his tone. ''Cause he doesn't like being moved about the country every five minutes perhaps?'

Dad looked furious. I know with the benefit of hindsight and two bairns of my own, that the fury was due to him being petrified, but at the time all I was thinking

106

was that if Dad laid a finger on me I was out of there for good. Just then we heard the door open and Col walked in.

'Where the fuck have you been?' we said, almost, but not quite, in unison.

Col looked surprised. 'I've been to Mass. It's Easter Sunday.'

'Easter Sunday?' said Dad, and collapsed back onto the couch.

Now I'm no mind-reader, but I'd hazard a guess that there were a number of competing thoughts going through my dad's head, including various concerns that he hadn't been giving his sons the attention they required, was failing to provide either spiritual or moral guidance, and most pressingly, there wasn't a single chocolate egg in the house.

He looked at us both. 'I'll be back in five minutes, lads.'

Thursday

'I'll say this for you Stainsie, I'm certainly eating better these days.' Father Paul pushes away his empty plate. 'That was the best breakfast I've had in about twenty years.'

I pick up his dish and put it in the pan of soapy water in the sink. 'I'm a qualified chef.'

He raises an eyebrow. 'Really? I never realised you had a trade.'

'Oh aye – I was all round the world on cruise ships doing the catering. I'm an expert on mass catering.'

'Are you?' he says, and I realise I've made a tactical error. He'll have me cooking the old folks' weekly lunch for the rest of my life if I'm not careful. He's obviously filed the information away for future use though, because all he says is, 'Sounds an interesting life.'

A great life if you want to lose your family and drink yourself half to death, I think, but all I say is, 'You get to see the world, certainly.'

'You must have some tales to tell.'

People always do this. They think that life on board a cruise ship must have been one long riot. And, in fairness, it was for about the first year or so: hard work, but plenty of lassies and a staff bar so cheap you could get falling-down drunk and still have change from a fiver. Which was the problem. By my last year at sea I was working from 4 am to 9 am, then again from 4 pm until 10 pm, then going on drinking until the early hours. I was getting so little sleep I started hallucinating that the breakfast sausages were talking to me, which was around about the time the liner and I parted company.

Father Paul's still looking expectantly at me.

'Less stories than you'd think, Father, when you're working an eighty-hour week.'

He looks sympathetic. 'Doesn't leave much time for a social life.'

I wouldn't say that. 'I spent most of my free time in the bar.'

He stares at the table for a minute then looks up at me. 'Not a good thing, Stainsie.'

'Aye.' I'm pissed off at being lectured by a teetotal priest and it must have shown in my face. 'Not that you'd know from first-hand experience.'

He's got an expression on his face that I can't quite fathom. 'I don't drink these days, Staines.'

I nod. I've never seen him with a drink in his hand. 'I know.'

'I can't drink, Staines.' He stares at the table. 'I was a heavy drinker for years.'

This is all news to me. 'What made you stop?'

He smiles. 'God, I'm afraid to say, Stainsie.' He looks almost embarrassed. 'I know you're not a believer.'

'I wouldn't say that exactly...'

He shushes me with his hands. 'I know you're not a believer, Stainsie, but it's true. God made me stop, but it's my own willpower that keeps me from going back to the drink every single day.'

I pick up his coffee mug and land it in the sink next to

109

his plate. 'Aye, well, that's a problem because there may or may not be a God, but I'm pretty damn sure that my willpower doesn't exist.'

He laughs. 'Are you going to go back to the cruise ships?'

I'm not sure they'd have me. 'Naw. I'm hoping to get another catering job, though.'

'Well, no rush from my point of view. I'm enjoying being fed.'

He's certainly changed his tune since I arrived. Amazing how much more people like you if you don't take money off them.

I decide to build on Father Paul's good mood and do some housework. I give the ancient Hoover a dance round the living room and attempt to tackle the dusting. I'm in the middle of ironing some cassocks when Wheezy arrives.

He looks at the pile of washing. 'What are you doing?'

I resume my place behind the ironing board. 'What does it look like?'

Wheeze looks round the room. 'Father Paul away out?'

'Aye – visiting old folk or some shite like that.'

Wheezy picks up one of the cassocks and examines it. 'Did he take your balls with him when he went?'

'It's the twenty-first century, Wheeze – real men do ironing.'

He snorts. 'Not in my house, they don't.'

'Ironing?' I gesture at him with the iron. 'You barely even wash, you clarty bastard!'

'Enough! Have you seen this?' He waves a copy of the *Scotsman* at me. 'There's more about that body

110

up at Isa's development.' He holds the paper at arm's length and, squinting, begins to read. '"Police have identified that the body is that of a woman,"' he pats the paper for emphasis, '"a *woman* aged 14-25, and it is thought that the remains date from around thirty years ago." Blows your Bruce theory out of the water, Stainsie.'

I grab the paper off him. The press is starting to take a real interest in all this. Today the story is on the front page, with a larger article inside. The photo of Mavisview makes it look fantastic, but the story is still the work of some over-imaginative journalist; there's nothing resembling a fact in the whole thing.

I'm not sure where this leaves me. The body is so old it's unlikely to be anything to do with Bruce. There's still the matter of the missing laddie-with-dog but I'm no closer to finding a body for that. It's maybe time to start my packing; I resolve to give it another 24 hours, then it's goodbye Marianne and best of luck.

I fold up the paper. 'Who do you think it is then, Wheeze?'

'No idea.' He takes the paper back off me and reads for a moment in silence. 'Ach – it could be anybody. We've been thinking about this all wrong. We should have known that your key players don't end up stuffed in a cupboard. We've been looking for a Hamlet, and that lassie's a Rosencrantz or a Guildenstern.'

'You think it's a foreign lassie?' Wheezy punches my shoulder. 'What? What are you hitting me for?'

He shakes his head. 'Never mind, you illiterate bastard - have a look at this.'

He hands me a piece of paper. '*North Edinburgh*

Yesteryears Society? You want me to go to some history talk?'

He slaps the top of the page. 'Look at the title of it, man!'

I read on. The original title – an examination of Mary Queen of Scots' residences in Scotland – has been scored out and a new one written in by hand. *'Priests' Holes and Smugglers' Holes: Hidden Rooms in Local Houses.* Well, Wheeze, you've got to hand it to them for responding to the news.'

'Aye, they probably thought they'd get a bigger turnout what with Mavisview making headlines.'

I'm not convinced. I'm not sure I can spare the time. 'They're barking up the wrong tree with Mavisview though – Jimmy said that the place where the body was found was modern.'

'Doesn't mean that there's not other hidden rooms, but. And who knows what's in them?' He taps the leaflet again. 'Maybe this mob know more about the house.'

'So, we're going to this then?'

'Aye, so get your coat.'

I look at the leaflet again. 'It says here the talk doesn't start until 2 o'clock.'

'I know, but I'm not sitting through that pish sober, so let's get down to Shugs for a couple before we go.'

More folk are in the meeting room of Leith library than I had expected. I wonder if it's the usual turnout for a history society talk, or if the change of topic has brought the ghouls out in force. We're a wee bit late and the man's already started. There's not any seats left in the first few rows, so Wheeze and I shuffle our way apologetically to the back of the room. I can't help but notice that Wheeze is swaying a wee bit.

'Come in, come in, gentlemen.'

The lecturer seems pleased to see us at least. He's shorter and younger than I was expecting. I was picturing beards and elbow patches.

'I'm just making a start – defining what we mean by 'hole'.'

Wheezy leans over. 'If he doesn't know that then he can't be getting any.'

I look round in case anyone heard him. 'Shut it, you.'

'I'll be discussing Smugglers' Holes...'

'Sounds like something you need ointment for.'

In spite of myself I laugh.

'...and Priests' Holes.'

I lean over and whisper to him, 'bit of Holy Water sorts that out, Wheeze.'

Wheezy bursts out laughing.

The lecturer stops, pushes his glasses back to the top of his nose, and stares at us. 'Can I help you gentlemen?'

'No, no, sorry, pal.' I try to sound as contrite as possible.

Wheeze pipes up. 'Are you going to talk about the house where that lassie was found?'

The lecturer clears his throat. 'Ah yes, the Mavisview case. I will, of course, be coming on to that in the fullness of time. If you gentleman can contain yourselves until then?'

Wheezy slides down his chair and crosses his arms. 'Wake me when he gets to the interesting part.'

The lecturer's got a kind of slide show set up and he flashes up a picture of a country house.

'Why do people want to hide?' he asks. That's a very pertinent question to my situation. Personally speaking, I find it's generally to avoid a kicking off of somebody.

'Two broad reasons spring to mind. Firstly, persecution. Specifically, religious persecution.'

Like the aftermath of an Old Firm game. When I was fifteen I went to see Celtic play Rangers at Ibrox. I'd tagged along with some laddies from school but managed to lose them on the way back into town. Not being that familiar with the Glasgow landscape I managed to get completely lost, and turned down a side-street off Sauchiehall Street only to walk into a sea of blue and red. I only managed to escape with my life by ducking into a women's clothes shop and hiding behind a rack of ladies' smalls. The shop owner wasn't well pleased, as I remember.

'During the reign of Queen Elizabeth, the Virgin Queen,' he clicks his mouse and a slide of Bessie duly appears, 'Catholics were forbidden from celebrating Mass. This continued through the reign of James the First,' we get a slide of Jamesie-boy, 'especially after the Gunpowder Plot.' He clicks again and we get a picture of a Catherine Wheel, which I think is a nice touch.

'Throughout this period we see a development of 'Priests' Holes' across England, that is small rooms where priests could be hidden, and the trappings of Catholic mass could be secretly stored. Classic examples of priests' holes can be found in Hindlip Hall, Worcester, Braddocks in Essex, and Ashby St. Ledgers, Northamptonshire.' Click, click, click. Wheezy's nodded off by now, and his head's bouncing off my shoulder.

'Now to the second reason for hiding places – crime.

Thievery and smuggling. We see a wide range of tunnels, sometimes stretching all the way from the house down to the sea.' He flashes up a picture of a fireplace and tells us this is the entrance to a tunnel. 'Hidden rooms, interconnected rooms, and secret passageways all helped to keep the smugglers, and their contraband, one step ahead of the customs and revenue men.'

'And now to Mavisview – the reason I suspect many of you are here.' He looks sternly round the room. 'It's likely that Mavisview falls into the second category here – smuggling rather than persecution. We have no strong records of priests being hidden in these parts, and close proximity to the sea makes smuggling a definite possibility. However, I would like to venture a third possibility. The closeness of Mavisview to the village of Newhaven and the Port of Leith meant that young men living there were at risk of entrapment by the Press Gangs, that is, gangs of men employed to 'recruit' men, usually against their will, into the navy. Therefore, these rooms might well be there to hide the young men of the family when rumours spread that the press gang was in town. A kind of forerunner of today's panic rooms.'

He looks round the room again. 'Any questions?'

I stick my hand up. 'See Mavisview, right, what if the place where that lassie was found was actually only put up in, know, the seventies or eighties or that?'

He looks a bit put out. 'There's no evidence that I am aware of that that is the case. Do you have some additional information?'

'Me? No, I know nothing about anything, but, just say, if it was modern, is it still likely that there is a secret

115

room they've not found yet? Could Mavisview be full of wee rooms and passages like some of these other ones?' Here's hoping Mavisview has a couple of hidden rooms full of excise-free whisky. But knowing my luck there's probably a few more old scores of Mrs Stoddart's decomposing behind my fireplaces.

He nods. 'An interesting question, but not one that I can answer, I'm afraid. At least not unless the Police decide to let us historians have a look at the building, before any further damage is done to it.' The way he says it you can tell he's just itching to get in there and have a poke about. I decide that if I do inherit it any time soon I'll make his day and invite him round. 'So, in answer to your question, the room where the unfortunate young woman was found could be the only hiding place, or Mavisview, particularly if it was the work of smugglers,' he flashes us a smile, 'could be riddled with them.'

There's a couple more questions then he winds things up. I wake up Wheezy and as we make our way to the entrance I think that the talk has been a pretty good description of all the times I've hidden in my life: to avoid a sectarian kicking, because I've been up to no good, and the one time I should have hidden but didn't, when I was press-ganged into doing something against my better judgement.

I head back to the Priest's House. Just to spite Wheezy I take my time with the ironing and housework. There's a knock at the door and I'm surprised to see Marianne standing there with some lassie I've never seen before.

'This is Janine. Can we come in?'

116

The three of us sit round the kitchen table. From the look of this Janine lassie I'd say she has a habit: she's skin and bone, with a complexion that's seen better days. She doesn't look at me when I speak to her but fixes her eyes so firmly on a point over my left shoulder that I half expect the Grim Reaper to be standing behind me if I turn round. Aye, I definitely have her down as a junkie, but I can't picture Marianne palling around with an addict so I put the thought to the back of my mind.

'Can I get you ladies a cup of tea or coffee?'

Marianne shakes her head but the Janine lassie says aye. Nobody's saying anything so I try a bit of small talk while I make the tea.

'Did you see that thing in the paper about the body in the house at Trinity? The house is owned by none other than – dan dan da - Isabella Stoddart.'

This statement doesn't meet with the cries of amazement that I was expecting, and when I turn round with the cups the Janine woman is crying.

Marianne sighs. 'That's why we're here, Stainsie. Tell him what you told me, Janine.'

'It's ma cousin.' She's still staring straight past me.

'What about your cousin, hen?' I'm trying to be sensitive but the woman won't stop weeping.

Marianne rolls her eyes. 'For Christ's sake, Stainsie, she means the body in the house is her cousin. Tell him, Janine.'

I look at Janine and she stares over my shoulder. 'See my cousin, right, she disappeared, right, and my mammy always said that she'd been murdered.'

And I'm thinking *Cheers Marianne* for bringing this nutter into my life, but I'm quite keen to get back in

Marianne's good books so I nod in what I hope is a suitably sympathetic manner. 'I see.'

'Marianne said you would talk to my mammy and get her to come through like?'

Good one. 'Uh-huh. And seeing how she's *your* ma would it not be better if *you* spoke to her?'

'Naw, she won't let me in the house these days.'

Probably a good plan judging by the state of her. Janine's not looking well and I wonder if she is rattling. There's something about her that looks almost familiar. I wonder if I knew her way back, and try to picture her a couple of stone heavier, but it's no good. It doesn't dislodge any memories from my brain.

'Janine – are you all right, hen?' She's shaking like a shivery dog.

'Aye Mr Staines, but I need to go and see someone. Could you lend us a tenner?'

I wait until Marianne goes to the toilet, then take the opportunity to hustle Janine out the door without giving her any money. I've not got much tolerance for junkies. Call it snobbery. There's a finely developed hierarchy of dependencies, where the sobriety-challenged such as Wheezy and myself tend to look down on your more hard core addicts.

I slam the door on Janine's bony arse and go back to find Marianne's still sitting in the kitchen. 'What was all of that about? Is your wee pal all there?'

Marianne lights up and rolls a fag across the table to me. 'She's not a friend of mine, I just know her 'cause she lives on my floor in the flats.'

'So, how come she's confiding all of this in you?'

118

'She's not confiding in anyone. She's been shouting her mouth off across the scheme about that body being her cousin, and how she was done in by the Stoddarts years ago.' Marianne gestures at me with her fag. 'She needs to watch herself; Mrs Stoddart might be dead but those laddies that worked for her are still around.'

Damn right they are.

'But I don't see how any of this is your, and now my, problem.'

'But it's not a problem, Stainsie, it might be a solution. I asked my Ma if she could remember Janine's ma and her cousin, and she could. Like Janine says, her cousin did go missing.' She looks at me triumphantly.

So what, I think, but I nod solemnly. 'Aye.'

'According to my ma, Janine's cousin was a right wee tart and everybody thought she'd run off with some laddie or other.'

I make a non-committal kind of noise.

'Just go and see her mammy.'

I sigh. 'I dunno. Having met Janine I'm not that keen to meet the woman that spawned her.'

Marianne looks for something to stub her fag out on, then gives up and drops it into her empty mug. 'But are you not even a bit curious who that body might be?'

'I'm curious about a lot of things, but I think it's pretty rare that the sum of human knowledge has been added to by some heroin-dependent tart. Finding out who this body is isn't going to help us find out who murdered Mrs Stoddart, or for that matter Lachie Stoddart, and I'm...' I'm about to say 'running out of time' but manage to catch myself.

Marianne doesn't say anything, just fixes her big blue

119

eyes on me. I stare back but it's no use. Eyeball-to-eyeball with a good-looking lassie I'm always going to blink first.

'All right, all right, I'll do it. Where am I going?'

She slides a piece of paper toward me and I look at the address.

'Paisley? I've got to go to Paisley?'

1985

Florence Milligan was a forty-year-old divorcee when she met Grandad Joe. I always remember her being quite glamorous when I was a kid. She'd one of those hairstyles where the hair is piled up on top of the head, with a load of Kirby grips and hairspray to keep it in place. She always wore the same combination of clothes: high heels, a straight skirt with a blouse tucked into it, and a cardigan draped over her shoulders. The temperature outside had to be around freezing before she would be seen actually wearing the cardie.

Florrie hadn't had much of a life before she met Joe. Not that I knew this as a kid, but then who does really know their grandparents when they're wee? Most of my knowledge of Florrie's early life came from a conversation she had with Col and me one night when she was babysitting. Well, I say babysitting, but Col was twelve and I was the best part of fifteen, so it was not so much babysitting as youth containment. She'd come with Grandad on a rare visit to East Kilbride, and Dad and Grandad had buggered off to the pub leaving her in charge.

I don't know why she decided to tell us all about her past; probably because Col was always bugging her for information, no doubt looking for sins that he could help her repent. It's never too late to find salvation, or so I'm told. Col kicked open the conversation.

'Have you always lived in Leith, Florrie?'

She nodded. 'Aye, son, Leith born-and-bred. I grew up in a tenement in Cadiz Street.' She always insisted on pronouncing it Kay-deez Street. I took this as the accepted pronunciation, which caused much hilarity on my first Iberian cruise.

Col pressed on. 'Did you have brothers and sisters?'

'Aye, son, six of them.'

'Six?' chorused Col and I in mutual horror.

'Aye, two lassies and four laddies, and my Ma and Pa, and all of us living in a three-room flat.'

This sounded like hell to me. It was bad enough sharing with one brother. 'Wasn't it a bit cramped?'

'Aye, son, but not that uncommon back then.'

Neither of us could think of anything more to say, and our minds were beginning to drift toward that night's TV when Florrie carried on.

'My father was a bastard.'

This was unprecedented. We'd never heard Grandad or Florrie swear before; even my dad tried, although mostly failed, not to swear around us. We were fascinated.

'Sorry, lads, but he was. He was a tyrant, always one for using his fists or a belt on you. We were all scared of him, me the most 'cause I was the eldest. He'd go for my ma and I'd try and protect her, not that it did her much good in the long run, God rest her soul.'

I looked at Col and I could see his tiny brain was about to explode.

'What happened to your ma?' I asked.

'Och, she never kept well, living off her nerves all the time. I think we all knew she wasn't going to make old bones, but it was still a shock when she died. I was

122

only fourteen and I had to see to my dad, the house, my brothers and sisters, everything.'

The two motherless Staineses exchanged a glance. Florrie carried on.

'It wasn't much of a life, lads. I had to leave school...'

'At fourteen?' Col said in disbelief.

'Oh aye, son, you could do that then. But it was a damn shame. I was top of my class in most subjects and I could of had a good job in an office or something, but instead my life was on hold until my wee brothers and sisters were old enough to look after themselves. There were no nights at the dancing or courting for me.'

I was confused. 'But you did get married?'

Florrie stiffened. 'Aye, well, that's another story. You lads'll be wanting to watch the telly, not listen to me rabbit on.' And with that she put the TV on and the subject was closed.

It was the best part of a decade before I found out the story of Florrie's first marriage. The information came to me via my wife, as a result of a conversation she had with Florrie one night when they'd had a bit too much to drink. This was back in the days when my wife, my ex-wife, still enjoyed a drink, before she went all teetotal and self-righteous on me.

Anyway, Florrie's wee brothers and sisters did grow up, and got jobs, and got married and moved out. In her early thirties she found herself alone in Cadiz Street with just her dad for company, who was as evil-tempered as ever, although a good deal less handy with his fists than he was when he was younger.

It wasn't all gloom and doom though. Despite her lack of qualifications she managed to get herself that office job that she had always wanted, in a shipping firm based at the side of the Links. She started work at Galloway, Thornton and Ryan Shipping Co as a typist, but after many years' hard work her talents had been recognised and she was now the secretary to the senior partners. This netted her an office to herself, a higher salary, and most importantly, the envy of all the girls in the typing pool.

She had a bit of financial independence, and a lot of responsibility, yet it wasn't enough. £600 a year and sole custody of the key to the stationery cupboard was all very well, but it didn't keep you warm on a cold winter's night. She was still a handsome woman, not ready yet to qualify as one of God's unclaimed treasures. But she had to face the harsh fact that she was 36 years old, and time was running out. She was on the point of giving up hope when Charlie started work in her office.

Charles Bosworth Smith was employed as a shipping clerk, on the strong recommendation of his former employer in Liverpool, England. He was in his late twenties, tall, and had hair that reached almost to his collar. This was as close as Galloway, Thornton and Ryan got to the Swinging Sixties, and with this air of danger added to his lovely English accent, all the lassies in the typing pool took an immediate fancy to him. Florrie rose above all this nonsense– she was in a position of authority now, and in any case, he wasn't going to look twice at her, so why bother? But if she was honest with herself, when she was drifting off to sleep at nights her thoughts did turn to a pair of brown eyes, and the soft Scouse tones of C B Smith Esq.

As a senior and trusted member of staff (and one

without a spouse or child to make demands on her time) it often fell to Florrie to lock up at night. She took her responsibilities seriously, and one night in October she was half-way home when a terrible thought struck her. She couldn't remember whether she locked the petty cash away in the safe. Florrie ground to a halt. Every night she put the petty cash away and there was no reason she wouldn't have done it tonight. Reassured she walked on for a couple of streets.

But then she stopped again. What if she didn't? The faith of the senior partners in her would have been misguided. She could be demoted back down to the typing pool, and she couldn't bear the smug faces on the other typists if that happened. So Florrie turned tail and hot-footed it back to her work.

When she got there there was a light on in the office. She was taken aback, not sure whether one of the partners had popped back, or if there was someone up to no good. Florrie wasn't easily scared so she marched right into the office, only to come face-to-face with Charlie Smith, who was hovering around her desk.

'What are you doing here?' she demanded, too shocked to comply with the usual secretary/Shipping Officer deference.

Charlie looked shocked but quickly recovered himself.

'Looking for you,' he said, 'or at least, looking for your desk to leave you this.' And he opened his jacket and shyly handed her a rose.

('How romantic,' said my wife.

'What a cover story,' snorted Florrie.)

Now, Florrie had seen enough romantic features at the Saturday matinee to know how the heroine is

125

supposed to react in these situations, but under the circumstances all she could do was stare at him. His big brown eyes stared back at her in silence for a minute, then he muttered an apology and turned on his brogue-encased heel. Florrie sat in silence listening to his footsteps disappear, before checking that the petty cash was locked away. It was.

Over the next few weeks Charlie kept out of her way; he couldn't even look her straight in the eye.

('Was he too embarrassed?' asked my wife.

'Naw, he was just worried that I was going to jump on him.')

Unfortunately, the damage was done. Florrie was smitten. She couldn't stop thinking about him, and the shy way he had handed over the flower. And here the situation would have stayed, with Florrie mooning after Charlie, and Charlie keeping a low profile, if they hadn't been overtaken by events. Florrie's dad died.

It was an unexpected death. Mr Milligan was barely into his sixties, and had been in good health as far as everyone knew. The old man must have had other ideas though, and only a month before his death he'd been to the lawyers to put his affairs in order. It turned out his death was not the only surprise that Florrie got. Milligan, for all his other faults, wasn't a spendthrift, and he had got a tidy sum set away in the bank. And he'd left all of it to her.

Florrie was amazed, first at the amount of money, and then at the fact that from beyond the grave her father was acknowledging the work that she'd done for him.

Word got round the office that she was now a woman of independent means. Mr Thornton, one of the senior

126

partners, called her into his office. Mr Thornton was in his fifties, unmarried, and possessed of halitosis so strong that at least two of his former secretaries had resigned their posts rather than continue to take shorthand for him. He had always taken an interest in Florrie, in what she hoped was a 'friendly uncle' manner.

Mr Thornton stared at her for a minute or two before speaking. 'I just wanted to let you know how sorry I was to hear about your father's death.'

He died six weeks ago and you're only mentioning it now, thought Florrie, but she managed to nod her thanks.

Mr Thornton cleared his throat and fiddled with some paper clips on his desk. 'I hope this is not an indelicate enquiry, Miss Milligan, but I do believe that you have inherited some money from your father?'

'Yes,' she said, wondering where this was going.

Mr Thornton had got a little chain of paper clips now. 'Are you... would you be considering giving up your position?'

'Of course not,' said Florrie, 'I'm dedicated to my work here'. And anyway, it's not that much money, she thought to herself, although she didn't say it.

Mr Thornton looked relieved. 'Good, good, very glad to hear that.'

She rose to go and had her fingers round the door handle when Mr Thornton called her back.

'If you need any investment advice, Miss Milligan, you've only to ask. I'd be happy to discuss stock opportunities one lunchtime or, eh, over dinner if you would, eh, prefer that?'

She smiled in what she hoped was a grateful manner and opened the door without answering.

She was backing out of his office when she bumped, literally, into Charlie.

'I was so sorry to hear about your father.' Even under the circumstances she couldn't help noticing how handsome he was. She felt guilty at even thinking about men, when her old, surprisingly affluent, dad was only just in the ground. She pulled herself together.

'It was a sad business.'

Charlie nodded sadly. 'I lost my father a couple of years ago. He'd been ill for a good few years but still, when it happens...'

He looked so upset that Florrie laid a reassuring hand on his arm. Charlie jumped and, embarrassed, Florrie turned to go. She felt a hand on her shoulder.

'Miss Milligan?'

'Yes?'

'If it's not an inappropriate moment to ask, would you like to join me for coffee one evening after work?'

Florrie was so overcome she could only nod her acceptance.

Coffee led onto dinner, and within weeks they were a couple. Charlie said they had to keep it a secret from the people at work because he suspected that the partners wouldn't approve of the fraternisation between the ranks. Florrie knew for sure at least one of the partners wouldn't like it. She didn't mind that they had to meet in out-of-the-way places, it just made it more exciting. And of course now she had a flat to herself. Not that anything untoward happened, she was at pains to point out.

('You never...' said my wife.

'No.'

'Not even...'

'No!')

Three months and six days after their first coffee date, they had dinner at Florrie's flat. Florrie was worried that Charlie was off his food because he had hardly touched his meal. Charlie sat toying with his uneaten peas, then suddenly cleared his throat and announced, 'I've something to ask you.'

'Yes?' said Florrie, every inch of her 36-year-old body willing it to be the right question. It was.

'Will you marry me?'

'Aye, Charlie, aye I will.'

It was a Registry Office affair. She was a wee bit disappointed when Charlie suggested that they tie the knot in front of a Registrar instead of a Minister - she would have loved to see the faces of the girls from the typing pool when she walked down the aisle in off-the-shoulder white taffeta. She was so disappointed, in fact, it led to their first argument.

'But, sweetheart, you know I'm not a religious man.'

'Can't you just cross your fingers and pretend?'

Charlie shook his head and laughed. 'Anyway, if we have a big church do there's more danger of people at work finding out.'

Florrie was shocked. 'You mean we're still not going to tell people at work even though we are married?'

Charlie was avoiding her eye. 'They wouldn't understand.'

'Nonsense,' said Florrie. 'You're ashamed of me.'

129

'Sweetheart, no. I love you.' Charlie was on his knees at her side now. 'I don't care about those people, and I don't want to listen to their opinions. We'll both be leaving there soon enough.'

This was news to Florrie. 'We will?'

'Oh yes. I'm not wasting my life in a place the size of Galloway, Thornton and Ryan. I've got plans for us.'

Florrie was getting interested and began to forget her annoyance. 'Like what?'

Charlie took her hand and kissed it. 'Well, children, obviously, and they're not cheap. A car. And of course, a mortgage.'

Florrie wasn't sure. She didn't know anyone with a mortgage, and she'd got a good landlord with her – their - flat. But Charlie was insistent that it was the next logical step for them.

'What is the point of giving your money to a landlord? He's the one that benefits, and he benefits twice over. He's got your money coming in, and he can sell the flat and keep the profit on that.'

Florrie mulled this over. 'I hadn't thought about it like that.'

'And he can put you out of the flat whenever he wants.'

'I've got a lease.'

Charlie stood up. 'Well, we're going to have to move anyway. In a couple of years this place won't be big enough for us.' He leaned over and playfully patted Florrie's stomach.

Florrie was sold on the idea. Any doubts she had were completely outweighed by the thoughts of children. Being the most senior secretary in Galloway, Thornton and Ryan was all very well, but she couldn't wait to give it all up and stay at home playing mummy to two or three little Smiths.

They started looking at flats. The first two weren't up to much, but the third one made Florrie's heart skip a beat. A bay-windowed living room, two bedrooms ('one for the little Smiths,' said her husband) and a beautiful back green.

'Well' said Charlie, 'what do you think?'

She looked up at the cornicing and the ornate ceiling rose. 'Oh Charlie, I love it, but can we afford it?'

Her husband smiled. 'Leave it with me.'

He made some calls, claiming a slight connection with the lawyer that was selling it. She heard the phone being put down, and Charlie bounded into the room. 'I've some good news.'

'Yes?' Florrie could hardly contain her excitement.

Charlie gave a smug smile. 'I've managed to get the lawyer to knock 10% off the cost of the flat.'

Florrie leapt from her chair and hugged him. 'Oh, that's wonderful.'

'But he wants the deposit in cash.'

Florrie stepped back. 'In cash? What does he want that for?'

'My dear, sweet, naïve girl. So he can keep a small bit of it for himself, and tell the seller this was the best offer he was able to get.'

Florrie didn't like the sound of this. 'I'm not sure.'

Charlie twisted a lock of her hair round his finger. 'How much did you love that flat?'

Florrie thought again about the bay window, and the bedroom for the little Smiths. 'All right then, love, let's do it.'

Next day at lunchtime they took all the money out of Florrie's account. Florrie couldn't concentrate that afternoon, worrying about Charlie having all that money on him. What if he got robbed on the way to the lawyers? They met up after work and she told him about her second thoughts. He laughed at her and kissed her on the brow.

'Don't you worry about a thing.'

Charlie didn't come home in time for dinner. That's fine, thought Florrie, it's a business deal, albeit a shady one, so maybe he's had to stay a bit longer. By nine o'clock he still wasn't home, and all her previous worries about him getting robbed come back to the surface. By midnight she was frantic, and she thought about going out to find a phone box to call the Police. She reluctantly decided to wait until morning.

Charlie didn't turn up for work the next morning. 8.30 passed, then 9 am, and by 9.30 am she was scared stiff. She went in to see Mr Thornton, and explained that she was worried that Charlie had had an accident.

Mr Thornton leant across his desk and patted her arm. He seemed surprisingly unconcerned about the whereabouts of his employee. 'There, there, Miss Milligan, I'm sure you don't need to upset yourself about our Mr Smith.'

Florrie burst into tears. She explained everything – about their marriage and how he hadn't come back last night. Mr Thornton turned white and then red in quick succession. He emptied his container of paper clips onto the desk and pushed them around with his pen. Florrie couldn't bear the silence, but just when she was about to

132

speak Mr Thornton asked her something that surprised her.

'Did you give Mr Smith any of your inheritance?'

'Yes,' she said, 'I gave him all of it to put the deposit down on a flat.'

He put his head in his hands. 'Oh dear, oh dear, oh dear.'

Florrie was really worried now, but also quite confused about what was going on.

'I have some very bad news for you, Miss Milligan.' Mr Thornton gave a deep sigh. 'Mr Smith's work has been of concern to us for quite some time. We've actually begun to suspect that he has been stealing money from the company.'

And it all suddenly became clear to Florrie. It was obvious why the handsome Mr Smith was interested in her, all the big talk about flats and children. Her money was gone.

Mr Thornton coughed and looked embarrassed. 'I'm afraid I've more bad news. Mr Smith's wife has also been in touch with us.'

'His wife?' said Florrie, her heart breaking.

The look on Mr Thornton's face could have been compassion, or pity, or even love. Whatever it was Florrie couldn't bear it, and she resigned her post on the spot.

Florrie got a new job, on a lower wage, in the office at a Bond Warehouse. There she met a widowed Pole, with a hapless son, an alcoholic daughter-in-law, and two toddler grandsons. She must have been delighted to meet someone even more down on their luck than she was. Six months later they got married.

And it was a great story, it really was, but I couldn't help wondering where her siblings were in all this. She gave up her life to bring up her six brothers and sisters, and none of them stood by her in her hour of need?

Years later I was having a drink in a pub on Easter Road. I noticed another of the drinkers kept looking over at me, a guy in his sixties who looked like he'd drunk a pint or two in his life. Being technically underage by four months, I was a wee bit worried by his interest. He sat down beside me and ordered himself another pint.

'Can I get you one, son?'

So it was obviously not my youth that was bothering him. I was now worried about his interest for a host of other reasons, but then I thought, a free drink's a free drink so I nodded. 'A pint of 80 please.'

'You're Joseph Staines' grandson aren't you?'

I nodded. 'Aye.'

'He was married to my sister.'

'Florrie?' I was delighted to meet one of her siblings at last. I put my hand out to shake his. He didn't take it and I noticed that he was a bit the worse for wear.

'That bitch ruined my life.'

I thought I'd misheard him. 'What?'

He stared into his pint. 'She had my father wrapped round her little finger. She made life miserable for all of us growing up - always slapping us around, or telling my dad that we'd done stuff and getting him to belt us.'

I couldn't believe this. 'Florrie did this?' I wasn't having my step-grandmother spoken about like that and I stood up to go. The man put his hand on my arm to stop me.

'And then, to cap it all, when my dad dies and leaves

her the money to divide up between the family as she sees fit, instead of giving it to us she passes it all on to her fancy man.'

I didn't linger over my pint after this.

Florrie must have been delighted to meet Joe and his dysfunctional family. The one and only time the Staineses have ever offered anyone a shot at redemption.

Friday

I know Paisley a wee bit. We lived there for six months or so, in a tenement block not far from the station. Janine's mother, Mrs Jardine, lives on the outskirts of the town, a world away from where we stayed.

I find her address no problem. It's a sturdy wee bungalow, set behind a front garden of grass surrounded by flowers and heather. I go to open the gate but something holds me back. The woman's obviously got a good life here. She can probably live without me and her junkie daughter stirring up the past. But the curtains twitch – she's seen me so there's no going back. I just hope that Janine has sent me on a wild goosechase.

'I'm Joseph Staines – we spoke on the phone?'

She nods and stands aside so I can step in. I walk down a narrow corridor and turn, as directed, into a pastel-painted living room decorated with photos of her grandbairns. Mrs Jardine follows me in and I get a chance to look at her. She's a handsome woman in her fifties, full-figured, with greying brown hair cut in a neat bob. I don't see too much of Janine in her.

'Thanks for agreeing to see me, Mrs Jardine.'

'Call me Sheila.'

Sheila insists on making me tea and I take the time to look at her family photographs on her mantlepiece. There's a wedding photograph of a young couple, and

136

school photographs of three gap-toothed bairns.

'Your grandchildren?' I ask as Sheila comes in carrying a tray.

She nods. 'Ross is seven, and the twins are five. I'm a very proud granny.' She reaches behind the grandchildren's pictures and pulls out a framed photograph of a little girl playing on a beach. She's a pretty wee thing with blond ringlets. 'My niece.' She passes me the picture. 'That was taken in 1980. She'd have been about eight.'

The telephone rings and Sheila excuses herself. She leaves the living room door open, and I can't help but overhear her half of the conversation. I get the feeling it relates to my being there. I gently push the door shut and wander over to the window. Her back garden is every bit as lovingly cared for as the front. I'm so busy staring at it that I don't hear Sheila comes back into the room.

'I have to say, Joseph, that my husband's not very happy about me speaking to you.'

I don't blame him. 'Oh – why not?'

'He thinks I should let things lie. Everything that happened to me connected with Leith was bad, and he's just worried for me if you bring it all up again.'

I feel really rotten but I don't try to put her off. She pours out the tea and hands me a china cup.

'So, you're a friend of Janine's?'

'Not really, to be honest.'

She smiles. 'You're certainly not like some of her other friends.'

'Aye.'

We sit in uncomfortable silence for a minute or two while I try to think how to start. Sheila speaks first.

'If you're not a friend of Janine's, why are you here?'

137

It's a good point and I'm not really sure I can explain that to myself never mind her. I try a half-truth.

"Cause I'm worried about your Janine. She's shouting her mouth off round the scheme and she's going to get herself into trouble.'

'What's she saying?'

'Did you hear about that body that was found in a house in Trinity?'

She shakes her head. 'No.'

I sigh and think how best to summarise what's happened. 'Well, developers smashed through a wall, or something, and found the skeleton of a young lassie. Janine's been going round and saying it was her cousin and that she was murdered.'

Sheila's staring straight down at her tea, and I notice that that cup's shaking a bit.

'Sheila?'

She looks up.

'Do you think your niece was murdered?'

There's a long pause. She eventually says, 'I don't know. But I do know that's what my sister thought.'

'Why?'

She sighs. 'My sister had her kids far too young. She wasn't even out of her teens, and she wasn't capable of looking after them properly. Her laddie was completely out of control, always in trouble with the Police, and Shee-Shee...'

'Your niece?'

She nods. 'Aye, that was our daft name for her cause when she was little she couldn't pronounce her own name and that's what it sounded like when she tried. Anyway, Shee-Shee was a bit wild, always hanging round with the

138

laddies. Not that I'm in any position to criticise anyone else's parenting, not with the way my Janine turned out.'

I give an embarrassed nod.

'When she was just into her teens she took up with this laddie Stoddart. The laddie was no looker but he'd plenty cash, which was enough for our Shee-Shee. Anyway, she'd been knocking around with the laddie for about six months, when one night she just doesn't come home.'

This story is bringing back some memories for me, and they aren't memories that I want to confront. I try to focus on what Sheila is saying.

'Mags, my sister, goes round to the Stoddarts' house to see if she's there, and the father, Guthrie I think he was called, laughs in her face and says that his son's not seen that 'wee tart' for weeks.' She stops and takes a drink of her tea.

'Mags knows this isn't true, and starts shouting the odds, saying she's going to the Police and that, and Guthrie flips and throws her out. That night I'm round at Mags' when a man comes to the door.'

'Guthrie?' I ask. 'Or was he a young laddie called Bruce?'

She shakes her head. 'No, he says his name's Meikle, and that Guthrie's sent him to apologise and give us some news about Shee-Shee, and can he come in? We let him in, and as soon as he's inside he starts laying into Mags, saying all sorts of stuff that'll happen to her if she goes to the Police. I try to help her and he pulls a knife and starts threatening me as well, saying that he knows I've got kids, and he knows where he can find them.'

I wince. 'So, you never went to the Polis?'

She snorts. 'We never even reported her missing. What could we do?'

She's right. If they'd grassed up the Stoddarts they'd all be under the floorboards of Mavisview. 'Is Mags still in Leith?'

'No. About four years after Shee-Shee disappeared' - the tea cup's shaking again - 'my sister killed herself.'

I'm not sure whether to say anything but I figure she ought to know.

'The house where the body was found was owned by a member of the Stoddart family.'

'Oh Jesus.' She spills her tea all over her skirt. I lean forward to help but she pushes me away and goes out of the room. It's a good ten minutes before she reappears, wearing a different outfit and a forced smile.

'So, it looks like we were right then' she says.

I nod. 'Looks like it. Are you going to go to the Polis?'

She picks up the picture of her niece and stares at it for a moment, before putting it back on the mantlepiece. 'No, son. Not after all this time.'

I'm not sure if that's the right decision or the wrong decision for her. 'It might give you, what's the word, closure?'

But she shakes her head. 'No, son.'

As she's showing me to the door she stuffs a twenty pound note into my hand and asks me to pass it on to Janine. I wonder if she knows what Janine's into but she must have read my mind and says, 'I don't need to know what she spends it on.'

And as I leave her lovely wee house, I think of her there with her man and her job, surrounded by her grandbairns, and I wonder if she's ever known a minute's peace in her life.

I'm just closing her garden gate behind me when the door opens again and she calls me back.

'I don't know if this is any use to you but you might as well take it.'

She hands me another photograph. 'It's the most up-to-date one I have.'

I take a good long look at the picture.

I know the face. I thought I would.

Shee-Shee. Shirley-Anne Jackman.

1985

My dad and I weren't really getting on. The usual teenage stuff – staying out late, drinking too much, smoking. Oh aye, and me being a seething cauldron of hatred, due to him killing my mother off probably didn't help matters between us either. In five years my dad had never mentioned my mother. Col and I had discussed it, but neither of us has had the nerve to actually confront Dad about what was going on. No wonder Colin found God.

By the time I was seventeen I had four O-grades, two Highers and an almighty chip on my shoulder. Salt'n'sauce for your grievance, Mr Staines? Oh, I was mad at Dad for everything: my ma, the moving about, you name it. When he came home one day and mentioned a new job in Helensburgh I decided I was out of there.

'I'm not going,' I said, geared up for a fight.

Dad nodded. 'I wasn't sure if you'd want to.'

This took the wind out of my sails. I hadn't entertained the possibility that he was just as fed up of me as I was of him. I immediately felt hard-done-to.

'I know when I'm not welcome.'

'That's not fair, son.' He patted his pocket looking for his fags, then he remembered he gave up smoking a couple of weeks ago. I think he got fed up of me stealing them. 'Everything I've done, it's been for you and your brother.'

With hindsight, this would have been the time to bring up the issue of my missing mother, but like any seventeen-year-old laddie I wasn't coping well with the emotional turn the conversation was taking. So I shrugged.

My father sighed and said, 'You could go to college.'

I hadn't thought of that, but as soon as he said it, it seemed a perfect solution.

I did some extensive research about my career options, which consisted of me asking Linda McFarlane's opinion while she lay on her bed leafing through *Just Seventeen* magazine. She'd undone the top three buttons of her shirt and her tie was hanging loosely round her neck. Every so often she threw her red curls back over her shoulders and when she did that her skirt, which was already two inches shorter than the length approved by St Kentigern's Academy, rode up further. I reckoned she had two more moves before I could see her pants. It was an image that's got me through many sleepless nights since.

'What do you think I should study at college, Linda?'

She looked at me over the top of her magazine.

'Do you want to get rich?'

I shrugged. 'Maybe.'

'Or do you want to meet lassies?'

I didn't answer that one 'cause I knew it was a trap. To my surprise she went on.

''Cause if you want to meet lassies...' She turned her magazine round to face me and pointed to an article *The Top Ten Sexiest Professions for Men*, 'here's your answer.'

I wasn't sure that this was the most scientific way to

make a decision affecting the rest of my life, but I was intrigued nonetheless.

'What's at number one?'

'Architect.'

I could see the glamour in that but I wasn't going through six years at university just to improve my chances of getting laid.

'And number two?'

'Doctor.'

Six years at university *and* you have to deal with sick people. I gestured to her to go on.

'Professional athlete. Right up your street.'

I threw one of her soft toys at her. Gratifyingly she wriggled to avoid it and revealed another inch of her upper thigh.

'Fireman.'

'Too dangerous.'

'Lawyer.'

'Too much like hard work.'

'Pilot.'

'Don't you have to be gay to be a pilot?'

'Naw – that's air stewards. You've got to be dead bright but, so that rules you out.'

I looked for another soft toy to throw at her but she carried on before I could lay my hands on one.

'Musician.'

'I'm not very musical.'

'Model.'

'You definitely need to be gay for that one.'

'Oh aye – that's all that's stopping you, Stainsie. Teacher.'

'Away you go – nobody finds teachers sexy.'

'It says so here! *Just Seventeen* doesn't lie. Anyway, last one. Chef.'

Chef. I couldn't immediately think of a reason why not. Couple of years at college, then a lifetime of lassies falling at your feet, assuming there aren't any doctors or firemen in the vicinity.

'Aye, a chef would be all right.'

Linda laughed. 'You – cooking? You could burn water.'

'Is that right?' I couldn't find anything to throw at her so I leapt on to the bed and started tickling her. She was laughing so hard my hand was in her knickers before she could push me off.

My dad pulled a face when I mentioned the idea of catering college, but he didn't say no.

'I'll help you out, you know, financially and that.'

I shrugged.

'Have you thought where you'll go? There's plenty colleges in Glasgow.'

And I don't know what made me say it, maybe I knew it was the thing that'd annoy him most, but I said, 'I was thinking about going back to Edinburgh.'

He stared at me for a minute. 'No.'

'You can't stop me.'

'I'm not paying for you to go back to that place. It's nothing but bad memories.'

I was really losing it now. 'Not for me it isn't. I've got plenty of good memories of living there.'

But I still couldn't bring myself to mention my mother. I wanted to ask him if she was still living there, if that was what all this was about but I didn't have the nerve.

'Over my dead body,' he said, and walked out. Next time I saw him, he'd got a fag in his mouth.

But he'd got me over a barrel. Even if I studied part-time and got a job I wasn't sure that I could afford to go to college without any help from him, not when you factored in renting a room, food, and travel. I was on the point of giving in and getting the bus to Glasgow to get some prospectuses when Florrie rang.

'How are you doing, son?'

'Not bad, Florrie. How are you?'

There was a slight pause. 'Not bad, son. Taking it one day at a time.' It'd been three months now since Grandad died. 'How's school?'

'I'm thinking about leaving, Florrie, and going to college.'

'Oh, aye, son. In Glasgow I suppose.'

'I was thinking Edinburgh...' and I swear I was about to add, *'but my dad's not keen,'* when she jumped in.

'Edinburgh! Oh, that would be great, son. Remember I've got a spare room here if you need somewhere to stay.'

By the time my dad got home from work I'd got an interview arranged with Telford College and my bag half packed.

It took him a long time to forgive me.

Friday

When I get back to Edinburgh I head straight for Shugs to tell Wheezy about my meeting with Mrs Jardine. Before I get a chance to open my mouth he starts talking.

'Some bloke's been asking about you round the scheme.'

I close my eyes and hope for the best. 'Polis?'

'I don't think so.' Wheezy's playing with a beer mat. He only does that when he's worried about something, so now I'm seriously fretting as well. He carries on. 'Anyhow the Polis know who you are and where to find you. Naw, this laddie wasn't Polis. He was in here about an hour ago. Big chap and handy-looking with it.'

'Aw, Christ.' All I need is another hard bastard looking for me. 'Did he say what he wanted?'

He shakes his head. 'Naw, but he was flashing his cash about, hinting that he'd see anybody right that could point you out to him.'

'Did anyone help him out?' Considering how many people gave my name to Danny Jamieson I'd be surprised if there wasn't a queue of people waiting to cash in, but Wheeze shakes his head again.

'Naw, not with me sitting right there. But I don't know if anyone else has said anything.'

This isn't right. I go out of my way to avoid trouble

and it's still finding me. Some bastard's bound to tell him where I am when Wheeze isn't there listening. I wish we still lived in the days when living in a church meant sanctuary.

'Right.' *I've had it with Leith.* 'Enough is enough. I'm leaving until all this quietens down.'

Wheezy throws his beer mat at me. 'No, you are not. You're not going anywhere until you've put my Marianne in the clear.'

Sod that. 'Marianne and you can sort it out yourselves. I've done my bit.'

And I push my chair back and take off, with Wheeze throwing curses at my back.

I've got about fifteen quid left, which is just enough to get me a bus ticket to Glasgow. I'll drop in on my brother and see if he can put me up for a few nights. It's not ideal but social embarrassment is better than a kicking any day. With him and his wife being big into religion the chances are they'll feel obliged to help me out. After all, I'm family.

There are a few minutes to spare before my bus leaves and I could use a drink, so I head round to one of the basement bars on York Place. The pub has just had a delivery from the brewery and a large chap is rolling the barrels into a trap door. I hover on the steps for a minute wondering whether to cut my losses and try somewhere else, when I realise that the big man looks slightly familiar. I'm halfway down the stairs before realising that the last time I saw him he was trailing six feet behind Isa Stoddart, holding a pit bull on a leash. It's Bruce's sidekick. Apparently not dead.

I'm trying to back quietly up the stairs when he sees me.

'You!'

For a big man, he's quick on his feet and before I can get up the stairs he's got me by the collar.

'I want a word with you.'

'Aye, no problem, big man, but just let us go for a minute.' I realise with horror that he's pulling me toward the trapdoor. 'Come on now, pal...'

I'm airborne. The drop isn't too bad, only about six feet and I land on the sacking that they have in place to cushion the fall for the beer. I barely manage to roll out of the way before the big chap jumps down.

'You owe me!'

'I owe a lot of people, or so I'm told.' Although I'm not sure exactly what I'm due this chancer.

'I lost my job when Lachie died.'

'I'm sure you'll get another one.' To be honest I'm not sure what the prospects are like in the whole henchmen industry. 'Anyway, you've got a job here.'

He walks toward me and stands looking down, one foot either side of my legs. 'This...' he waves round the room, '... is shite. And they took my dog.'

We look at each other. He leans toward me.

'I lost my job.'

'Aye, you said that.'

He extends his arms, grabs a handful of my jacket and slowly pulls me toward him. 'And my dog.'

I'm beginning to suss that Bruce was the brains of this particular operation. I gently tug at his arm, and to my surprise he lets me go. I stay sitting on the floor; I don't want to push my luck by standing up.

149

I decide I might as well get his side of the story. 'So, how come you're not working with Bruce anymore?'

He looks as if he's about to start crying. 'They said I wasn't needed anymore.'

They? Bruce, I assume, but who else? 'Who said that?'

'Bruce and the Spanish laddie.'

This is new. 'Who's the Spanish laddie?'

'The laddie that came over from Spain.'

'Of course.' I'm beginning to think the pit bull was further up the chain of command than this guy.

Bruce's accomplice suddenly sits down on an upturned barrel. 'I lost my job. You owe me.'

I take a chance and get to my feet. 'I'm sorry you lost your job, big man, but I don't see how it's my fault.'

''Cause you killed Mrs Stoddart, and 'cause of that the laddie from Spain turns up.' He starts to cry. 'I miss my dog.'

Jesus. This is all I need. A sensitive, animal-loving thug who wants to kill me. Well, he can join the queue.

'Here's what I'm going do – sorry I don't know your name?'

'Duncan.' He sniffs.

'Right, Dunc. Here's what I'm going to do. I'll find this Spanish laddie and put in a good word for you. How does that sound?'

He doesn't look convinced. 'Do you think that'll work?'

I nod vigorously. 'Oh aye, absolutely.'

I'm sidling toward the stepladder and he's not trying to stop me so I figure I'm free to go.

'I'll be in touch, Dunc.'

He nods, miserably.

150

I scale the ladder, and push open the trapdoor which takes me out behind the bar, much to the surprise of the lassie serving there.

So, Bruce has been bullshitting me. But just 'cause he isn't a murderer doesn't mean that he's not up to giving me a kicking when his tallybook doesn't materialise.

I leg it to the bus station as fast as I can, and my heart doesn't stop racing until I've left Edinburgh far behind.

'See that chap that was looking for me, Wheezy, is there any chance that he was Spanish?'

There's a pause at the other end of the line while he thinks about this. 'Naw, he had a bit of an accent but I'd have said Irish if anything. Where are you?'

'I'm on the train to Newcastle.'

There's silence at the other end of the phone and I almost feel bad for lying to him, but I wouldn't put it past the crafty bastard to come looking for me.

'Are you coming back, Stainsie? We need your help here. Marianne's relying on you.'

My stomach lurches at the thought of Marianne. 'Aye, well.'

There's another silence.

'I'll be in touch, Wheeze.' I'm not even convincing myself.

'Aye, well.' He hangs up on me.

My brother and his family live in a flat in the West End of Glasgow. It's a nice bit of town, and I suppose it suits them location-wise, with him working at the Council, and her at the uni, but still I'm surprised that Col's gone for a flat. After all the years we spent living in crappy tenements I thought he'd make for the country as soon as he had any money. That's what I'd do. Nice wee cottage with a garden.

I left in too much of a hurry to check Col's address so I've had to find his place from memory. The first couple of flats that I try are full of students, then I get some mad old bat who won't even open her door. Eventually I find a stair door with a 'Staines-Highfield' nameplate.

'All right, Colin?'

He's looking older than I expected, but then it's been a good few years since I last saw him, and I guess I'm not aging too well either. He's cropped his hair to try to cover up the fact that it's receding at the temples. This gives me a brief moment of pleasure. He might be the one that ended up six foot tall, but I'm the one with a full head of hair.

From the look on his face, Col isn't too pleased to see me. His two lassies come running out to see who is at the door. I'm surprised at the age they are; I'd put them down as about ten or twelve now. The living room door is open and I can hear the sound of some kids' programme on the TV.

'Hello girls.' I can't mind either of their names, which isn't going to go down well with my sister-in-law. 'Remember me? Your nunkie?'

They both stare at me. The bigger one pipes up. 'Who's that man, Daddy?'

There's the briefest of pauses. 'That's your Uncle Joe, Catriona.'

'So, Col, are you going invite me in then?' I'm trying to sound jovial but I can hear my heart echoing in my head. If he doesn't help me out, I'm sleeping at the station.

He opens the door a fraction wider and I take that as an invitation.

'Place's looking nice, Col. You been having work done on it?'

My attempt at small talk seems to be pissing him off even more. 'Aye, Jackie's been dealing with it.'

'Is she in?'

'No, no at the moment.'

Thank God.

He points to the kitchen. 'Come through. Away to your programme, girls.' With that he ushers his daughters back into the living room and closes the door firmly behind them. I'm sensing that he's none too delighted at the family reunion.

Their flat really is lovely, I wasn't lying. It's the kind of thing you'd see on a property show. Stripped pine floor boards, pale pastels colours throughout, and just enough kids' toys littered about to look like the place is lived in. Jackie's obviously got an eye for the interior design, but I haven't really got a chance to take the place in properly before I'm shepherded into the kitchen.

Col starts making us a drink.

'So Col, how've you been?' I slide into a kitchen chair without waiting to be asked.

Colin puts down the kettle and speaks without turning round.

'What do you want, Joe – is it money?'

I feel lousy. 'Aye. Aye it is. I'm in a bit of bother. I'll pay you back, obviously, but...'

Colin's back sighs.

'Honestly, Col...'

153

He turns toward me with a look of fury on his face.

'What kind of fool do you take me for, Joe? Ever since we were bairns you've caused me grief – you and that pal Stoddart of yours. Well, after the last time we gave you money...'

'Which I will pay back as soon as I can.'

He ignores me. 'After the last time, Jackie and I agreed that we wouldn't be helping you out no-strings-attached again.'

I try another tack. 'Well, if you are a bit short of cash, if you could at least put me up for a couple of nights.'

He shakes his head and turns back to the kettle. 'No.'

I'm getting desperate. 'Col, you don't realise quite how much trouble I'm in. If I go back to Leith the now I'm a dead man, and I don't have any money to go anywhere else.'

Col shakes his head with a little disbelieving smile on his face. This isn't boding well for me getting any cash out of him.

'Come on, Col. I've got nothing. You're living here in a bloody paradise, with your lovely home and Jackie and wee Catriona and... eh the other one.'

Colin's still smirking. 'Catriona and who, Joe?'

He's got me there. He slams my cup down in front of me but doesn't sit down, preferring to drink his coffee standing up and leaning against the sink.

'Though I'm not surprised that you don't remember my daughter's name. I'd be surprised if you can even remember your own bairns' names.'

This is a surprisingly mean comment for my wee brother. I'm almost impressed. 'That's not fair.'

'Isn't it?' There's a pause while he has a sip of his

coffee. 'When was the last time you even had contact with them?'

I want to tell him to piss off, but I do need the money so I decide to be honest. 'My lassie sent me a Christmas card last year.'

Col looks surprised. 'Really? How did she know where to contact you?'

'She sent it care of the pub.'

'That was clever of her.'

It was; I was proud of her initiative and ashamed at how well she knew me. 'Aye – she always was a smart lassie. Got her mother's brains, fortunately.'

He almost laughs. 'Did you write back?'

'Naw.' I laugh. 'What was I going to say to her? Hope you are all having a fantastic time out there in Brussels. By the way, is that prick your mother married still running the whole of the European whatsit? Oh, and seeing as you ask, hen, yes I am still the same loser I was when your mother left.'

He looks at me for a moment and says softly, 'You're still her dad.'

Not much of one.

Colin finally sits down opposite me. 'I'm making you one offer, Joe, take it or leave it. There's a community in France – I've a leaflet somewhere.' He leaps up again and roots about in one of the kitchen drawers. He passes me a leaflet with a lot of happy-clappy types in brightly coloured clothes on the cover. It's not looking good.

'A 'therapeutic community'?'

He's nodding so hard he almost bounces up and down in the chair. 'It's run by the church but you don't have to be practising to go there. They don't ram religion down

155

your throat or anything, it's just a space for you to go and get your head together.' He pauses for a minute to think of the least judgemental phrasing he can come up with. 'You know – work out your problems.'

Ten minutes later I'm outside the house with £500 of Col's money burning a hole in my pocket, and directions to a hippy commune on the outskirts of Lille. It's a testament to my wee brother's naïvety that he gives me the money just on my solemn promise that I will actually get myself on the next *Easyjet* to France. And it's a testament to how shite my life is at the moment that I decide that I will actually give the godbotherers a go.

1986

Edinburgh was working out just fine. Florrie kept me fed and watered without ever asking for a penny in rent, and while *Just Seventeen* might have overstated the sexual magnetism of your average trainee chef, I wasn't doing too badly with the lassies. Oh aye, and the course was all right too.

Since I'd turned eighteen a world of employment opportunities had opened up to me, and I was now employed as a glass collector in *Raiders*, one of the vault bars in the centre of town. Edinburgh isn't the type of place to waste space in its city centre, and when a viaduct was built across the city it made good use of the arches. The South Bridge vaults had been used as workshops and slum housing, before settling on their current recreational use as pubs.

I was interviewed for the post by the Manager, Rob, an amiable Geordie in his early twenties.

'So, have you worked in a bar before?'

Obviously I hadn't, but I'd been well coached by the Careers Guidance Officer in the Student Services Office at college. 'Not as such, but I have a range of transferable skills that I have learned both through my college course and through my personal life,' I quoted from memory.

'Yeah? Like what?' Rob was looking amused at this.

I list them on my fingers. 'Communication skills, customer relations, catering.'

157

'And in your personal life?' He was still looking entertained, but unfortunately I hadn't really prepared for this one. I improvised.

'Well, I've drunk in a number of pubs.'

Rob burst out laughing. 'OK – you can start on Friday as a potman and we'll see where your transferable skills take us.'

As I was leaving the pub he shouted after me, 'Watch out for ghosts on the way home!'

I was wondering what he meant by that when I walked straight into a six-foot-tall apparition, with a pure white face, a top hat, and a long black cloak. The other use of the Edinburgh vaults – haunted walks for tourists.

After my birthday I took a good look at my life. I was enjoying the catering course, and I couldn't say I was too upset at not being in my dad's good books. Life should have been good. Yet there was a little voice nagging me that I had unresolved business here. I needed to find out what had happened to my ma.

Florrie, while usually willing to give opinions on every topic under the sun, was tight-lipped on this one. I'd waited for what I thought was a suitable time to introduce the subject. It was Sunday evening and I'd made us a full three-course meal using all my new-found culinary skills as an attempt to soften her up.

She finished her French apple tart and put down her fork with a sigh of satisfaction. 'I don't know what they're teaching you at that college Joseph, but they're doing something right. That was smashing.'

I picked up her plate and put it on top of mine. 'Thanks very much. It's the least I could do, know, with you letting me stay here and everything.'

She took the plates back off me and stood up to take them through to the kitchen. 'You're very welcome, you know that.'

I followed her through. 'I'm really enjoying living in Edinburgh again, but...'

She took the bait. 'But what, son?'

I looked as troubled as possible. 'But I keep wondering if I'm going to bump into my ma...'

'Oh Joseph.' She put the plates into the sink.

'... is she still living in Edinburgh?'

Florrie didn't say anything. Her lips had formed into a tight, straight, line.

'Florrie, if you know anything please tell me.'

She shook her head and reached for the washing up liquid. 'I'm in enough trouble with your father for inviting you to stay here. I'm not getting involved.'

'But Florrie...' I could see my one chance slipping away.

'I mean it, Joseph, don't ask me about your mother. And if you've any sense you'll leave the past well enough alone.'

She wouldn't be drawn any further on the subject, which is maybe not that surprising, considering her relationship with her own family. Perhaps she didn't know anything, or didn't want to see me getting hurt, but either way she wasn't giving me any assistance in tracking down my ma.

Without Florrie's help I wasn't quite sure where to start looking. A ring round the half a dozen Staines in the Edinburgh phone book didn't reap any rewards. I hadn't any alternative but to look up Ma's side of the family, and I wasn't sure what reaction I would get.

159

I started with Ma's brother, Uncle John. A check through the Stevensons listed in the phone book showed a J Stevenson living in the bit of town where I remembered visiting Ma's family. I decided to visit in person rather than risk a phone being slammed down on me.

Uncle John lived in a council scheme on the other side of Edinburgh. It looked pretty much as I remembered it, though he was obviously having some work done on it because the front door had been taken off its hinges and was lying in the front garden. I took a deep breath and pushed the bell. A lassie appears in the frame wearing skin-tight jeans and a perm that put about three inches on her height. It took me a minute to recognise her.

'Kirsten?'

She looked me up and down. 'Maybe.'

'It's me – your cousin Joe. Joseph Staines.'

She looked a bit confused which wasn't surprising seeing as she was probably about eight last time she met me. 'Dad!' she shouted back into the house.

Uncle John appeared. He was stripped to the waist and was carrying a drill. I hoped he was going to be pleased to see me.

'Uncle John – it's me, Joe. Doreen's laddie.'

His face rippled. He put down the drill and stepped toward me. For a moment I thought he was going to hug me but he seemed to change his mind at the last minute and held out his hand instead. 'How are you doing, son?'

'Not bad.' I shrugged.

'Come in, come in.' He ushered me into the house and sent Kirsten off to get him a t-shirt and me a cup of coffee. There was an awkward silence.

'You doing some work on the place, Uncle John?'

He nodded and leaned back in his chair. 'Aye son, I've just bought it off the Council and I'm making a few changes.'

I followed his lead and made myself comfortable. 'I didn't realise you could do that.'

He laughed. 'Aye, son, God bless Mrs Thatcher.'

I didn't have to respond to this, fortunately, because Kirsten arrived with the coffee.

I smiled at her. 'How old are you now, Kirsten?'

She smiled back, a wee bit shyly. 'Fifteen.'

'Aye, and thinks she's twenty-one.' Uncle John pulled on his t-shirt. 'Can you give us a minute to ourselves here, hen?'

Kirsten looked surprised but didn't argue.

Uncle John took a long gulp of tea. 'Are you still living in Paisley?'

Now I was surprised. 'No, I'm living in Edinburgh these days. How did you know I lived in Paisley?'

'I bump into your granny from time to time.'

There was a pause while I tried to work out who he meant. 'Florrie?'

He nodded.

I was a bit confused but kept the conversation going. 'I'm living with Florrie now.'

'Really?' He got out his fags and offered me one. 'So, what can I help you with son?'

I took a deep breath and hoped that my nervousness didn't show. 'I've left home and I think it's about time that I made contact with my ma. I know my father doesn't want me to...'

Uncle John nodded. 'Well, he has his reasons.'

This stopped me in my tracks. I'd assumed that Ma's

161

family hated Dad as much as I did for taking us away. I wasn't anticipating them taking his side.

'What reasons?' I said, with the tone of indignation that only a teenager can carry off.

Uncle John sighed. He was playing with his fag and still hadn't got round to offering either of us a light. 'I was half expecting you and your brother to turn up here one day, but I'm still not sure what to say to you. You know your mother liked a drink?'

I started to get angry. 'She was a good mother.'

'I know that, son, I'm not saying otherwise.' He held his hands up to calm me down. 'But after you and your Dad moved away she started drinking even more. Your aunties and I tried to give her some support but she's had money off of all of us, and stolen stuff from us when we wouldn't give her money. She's caused all sorts of scenes and although I wanted to help her, I had to think about my kids, and my sisters' kids, so we all agreed that we couldn't do anything else for her...'

I couldn't believe what I was hearing. 'So, you just chucked her out? Pretended she didn't exist?'

He shook his head. 'Not entirely, son.'

'But more or less?' He didn't respond to my accusation but he finally got round to lighting his fag, although he forgot about mine.

'I know that you want to find her, son, and catch up on all that you've missed out on but it's not going be a happy reunion, take it from me. I couldn't have it on my conscience if I put you in that situation. Anyhow, I'm not even sure if I could help. It's been over two years since I last saw her.'

'Thanks for nothing,' I said and stormed out, throwing

162

my unlit fag back at him. I regretted it later when I got on the bus and found out I'd no fags of my own left.

Two weeks later a letter arrived for me at Florrie's.

Dear Joseph

I've discussed your visit with your Auntie Viv and Auntie Eileen. We've thought long and hard about what to do, but we've decided that it's not up to us to decide if you should meet your mother or not.

The last known address we have for her is a hostel on Vine Street. If she's not still living there the staff might be able to help you with where she's gone.

Look after yourself son and if you want to get back in touch your aunties would love to see you.

John

I read the letter three times then set fire to it with my lighter. I never followed it up.

Friday

It's late by the time I get back to Edinburgh. I need to go to the Priest's House to get my stuff, not least my passport, but I don't fancy wandering round there in the dark. I can't be sure that there's not some hard man waiting for me with a plan to kick my head in, but I'm not spoilt for choice with other options.

I reluctantly make my way to the rathole that Wheezy calls home. I press the buzzer to get in to the block, but there's no reply. I hang around for a couple of minutes, until a young couple come out. I smile politely and they hold the door open to let me in. The door to Wheeze's flat is so manky I pull my jacket over my hand before I knock on it. There's no answer. I try again with my naked knuckle but there's still no response.

Kneeling down I take a look through the letter box. Through the open door of the living room I can see Wheezy fast asleep on the sofa. He's snoring his head off, with an empty polystyrene chip packet going up and down on his chest. I don't stand any chance of attracting his attention.

As a last resort I decide I'll try my luck at Marianne's. She'll probably tell me to sling my hook.

I knock gently.

Hearing her come to the door I stand back so that she can see me through the spy-hole. I hope to God she's not armed with a mop.

164

'Stainsie.' She opens the door wide, and to my surprise, throws her arms round me. 'I knew you'd come back.'

I'm thinking on my feet here. 'Well, I heard you were relying on me.'

An hour later I'm luxuriating in a bath that Marianne has run for me. Only lassies do baths properly – you know, bubbles, and fancy soap, and all that shite, and I think she must have cracked open her finest bottle of relaxing bath salts with added God knows what, 'cause as I lie there I can feel the tension flooding out of me. Of course, I can feel it flood back every time I hear a noise outside, thinking that I've been tracked down by Bruce, or the Irish stranger that's been asking after me, or maybe even the Spanish laddie who may or may not be a figment of Duncan's imagination.

I haven't gone into the ins and outs of why I'm here instead of at the Priest's House and fortunately Marianne doesn't ask any questions. As I smoke the last of the fags that she's given me, I can smell sausages cooking. So far, as a host Marianne is totally outstripping Father Paul. I decide reluctantly that I better get out of the bath, but I can't face getting back into the clothes that I've had on all day so I wander back through to the living room just in a towel. I sit staring at Marianne's lava lamp, watching it run through its palette of colours. I jump when she comes in with a couple of sausage rolls on a plate.

'I thought you might be hungry.' She places the sausages on the coffee table and sits down beside me on the sofa.

'Thanks.' I reach for the rolls carefully, making sure the towel is still wrapped round me. I'm starving. Through a

165

mouthful of sausage, I say, 'I really mean it. Thanks for looking after me.'

'It's the least I can do.' She's nursing a cup of coffee. 'Uncle Mick said that you'd had some bother and had to leave town again.' She stares into her coffee and laughs. 'I was gutted.' She looks me in the eye. Damn, but she's a good-looking woman.

'How come?'

She stares into the coffee and gives an embarrassed little laugh. ''Cause I got it into my head that you were going to sort out all this mess that I'm in.'

This is a lot of pressure. 'Marianne, I think I can safely say I have never sorted out anyone else's mess. I'm bad enough with my own mistakes.'

'I know, but…'

'But what?' There's an edge to my voice; I don't really want an answer.

She rests her head on her hands. 'But I am in so much trouble, Stainsie. What if I did kill Mrs Stoddart?'

'I'm really pretty sure that you didn't.' I finish off the last of the sausage roll and hope she drops the subject. She doesn't.

'But if I didn't kill her, who did?'

I sigh. 'Aye, well, that is the question. And I'm not a detective.' And every theory I've had so far has been wrong.

'But you *are* going to find out who did it?'

I chew the last bit of my sausage roll. I take my time eating because I really don't know what to say to her. 'Marianne…'

She interrupts me with a sigh. 'I know, Stainsie, you're not a detective.'

She looks so miserable and I've not got any false promises that can make it better, so I put my arm round her and give her a hug. 'It'll work out Marianne,' I lie. 'You'll see.'

She rests her head on my shoulder for a moment, then pulls back. She turns her head and kisses me gently. I find this a little bit surprising and my brain's telling me that it isn't gentlemanly conduct sleeping with a lassie when you are planning to leave the country early the next morning, but unfortunately my brain is a couple of minutes behind the rest of my body. Within a minute we're at it hammer and tongues.

She leans back. 'I'm working in the morning, but if you want to...' She leaves the sentence unfinished but I get the drift.

'What happened to you'd rather go to prison than sleep with me?' I ask Marianne, stroking her lovely soft hair.

I never get an answer to my question, because at that minute the living room door flies open, and in the gloom I can see the unmistakable outline of a hand holding a gun.

1986

I was picking up a round of empties from a table in *Raiders* when somebody kicked a barstool into the back of my legs.

'Oi,' I said, turning round.

'Oh, it is you. I thought it was.'

It was a laddie about my own age, chubby, wearing a leather jacket and a sneer. He'd got longish hair, a bit on the greasy side, and a smattering of teenage plukes, finished off with a very misguided attempt at a goatee beard. It took me a minute or two to figure out who it was.

'Lachie?'

He held his hand up in a kind of are-you-serious gesture. 'Aye, you tube, who else?'

I suppose my luck was bound to run out sooner or later. I'd thought so long as I kept out of the pubs in Leith I'd probably be OK. He was staring at me, so I thought I'd better make some conversation.

'So...are you here on your own?'

'No, loser.' He smirked. 'Who sits in a pub on their own? I'm here with my girlfriend.' He gestured over his shoulder. 'She's gone to the bog.'

Lachie had lost none of his charm in the past five years. My heart was racing and I had to put down the glasses that I was carrying, because my hands were shaking. I knew I should tell him I was busy and get back to the bar before he could ask me too many questions, but despite my nerves I was overcome with curiosity to see what kind of girl Lachie had managed to pull.

He waved to a lassie who was winding her way between the tables. 'This is Shirley.'

Shirley was tottering between the tables in the highest heels I'd ever seen, which still didn't make her more than five foot tall. She had a mass of blond curls, which she threw back over her shoulder in a gesture that made me think nostalgically of Linda McFarlane, and she had obviously spent a good hour or two doing some intricate make-up thing before she came out. The lassie was way out of Lachie's league. She also looked about four years too young to be in a pub.

'Hiya.' She gave me a little wave and turned to Lachie. 'Are we going on somewhere now?' She slipped her hand into his, while I looked on in disbelief. In what upside-down universe did Lachlan Stoddart manage to pull a lassie like this?

'In a minute.' Lachie fixed me with one of the stares I remembered so well. I needed to put the glasses down again before I dropped them. 'You working here tomorrow night?'

'Eh...' I couldn't think of any way to put him off.

He smiled. 'Right – I'll see you then.'

The next night he was sitting there, nursing a pint. He nodded when he saw me.

'All right?'

The good-looking lassie wasn't with him. 'I thought you said only losers drank on their own?'

169

He threw me a dirty look. 'I'm not on my own, I'm here to see you. Anyhow Shirl and her pals will be here any minute.'

I kept my head down for the rest of my shift trying to look too busy to sit and chat to Lachie. Rob was amused by my unusually hard graft. My transferable skills had never been more in evidence as I scurried round *Raiders* picking up glasses and being as attentive as possible to customer needs. I volunteered to deal with a blockage in the Ladies' toilets, and when I came out Rob called me over.

'OK – I take the hint.'

I didn't grasp what he was on about. 'What hint?'

'I realise that your range of customer care skills are not being used to the fullest. Let's give you a go on the bar on Sunday.'

This was great news and usually I would be delighted, except every time I looked over at Lachie he was still sat on his own, scowling into his pint. I wasn't quite sure how to deal with this apparition from the past; I came back to Edinburgh for many reasons but taking up with the Stoddarts again was definitely not one of them. I decided I would just play it cool and hope he got the message.

'Oi, Loser!' I heard Lachie summoning me but when I looked over this time he wasn't on his own anymore. Shirley had arrived and she'd brought some seriously fine-looking pals with her, who, I was happy to see, looked a good deal older than her.

'What time do you finish work?'

I made some non-committal sounding noise, partly 'cause I didn't want to go anywhere with Lachie, and partly because I was distracted by the lassies, who were even better looking close up.

He flicked a thumb in the direction of the girls. 'They want to go clubbing.'

I looked at Lachie, and the tiny blonde, then past them to the other lassies with big hair and short skirts. 'I can be ready in twenty minutes.'

And that was me, back in the fold. The temptation of colour TV and Pong of our youth had been replaced by the temptation of good-looking women, and I was totally prepared to put up with Lachie's haverings if that's what it took to hang around with Shirley and her mates.

Guthrie was delighted to see me again. I suspected that Lachie wasn't inundated with friends, so he was, no doubt, glad to see that his son had got someone to pal about with. But beyond that I think he was genuinely glad to see me; he asked me loads about my college course and my job at *Raiders*.

Lachie and I settled into a routine with him coming round to the pub at weekends, and both of us going on clubbing after closing time with Shirley and her pals. A couple of times a week I hung out at Lachie's gaff; Guthrie'd bought him his own flat on Albert Street. It was a cracking wee pad, marred only by Lachie's run-ins with the neighbours over the constant noise he created. I'd have probably hung out there more – he had a fantastic range of computer games – but Mrs Stoddart had a habit of calling round to see her son and she'd lost none of her power to creep me out.

I couldn't figure out the deal with Shirley. She was round Lachie's day and night, usually with some of her mates. The lassies she hung around with were all nice-looking, but Shirl was in a class of her own. She was the kind of lassie that you never saw without her make-up on, and her hair done. I would be the first to admit I was smitten with her, although I wouldn't have dreamed of even hinting that to Lachie.

The only problem with Shirley was that I couldn't shake the feeling that she wasn't as old as she was making out. When I asked Lachie how old she was he shrugged and said, 'Seventeen, eighteen?'

Aye right, I thought to myself. 'Is she working then?'

'Naw - she's on the dole.'

No, she's not, I thought. *She's a bloody schoolkid playing truant.*

But it was none of my business so I didn't push it with him. Shirl was nice as well as pretty; she was funny and always ready with a smart answer. She'd got Lachie wound round her little finger, and I didn't blame him – I'd have given her the shirt off my back if she'd asked.

Yet, for all I'd made my mind up to keep out of it, I was worried about the situation. For one thing, I was pretty sure that Lachie was committing a crime that he wasn't aware of. But more than that I was worried about Shirley. A young lassie like her shouldn't be around all the booze and drugs that Lachie had easy access to. It wasn't just drugs that I was worried about either: Guthrie's laddies-with-dogs were in and out of Lachie's flat and I'd seen both of them leering at her. And, here's the thing that I couldn't get my head round: I'd seen Guthrie eyeing her up as well.

Guthrie was round at the flat all the time, and if the lassies were there he always had a laugh with them. The lassies all thought he was wonderful; he was still a fine-looking man, and he wasn't above bunging us all some money to get a drink or two when we were going out. Whenever he visited there was always one or other of the lassies sitting on his knee, and another one running back and forth getting him food and drink.

I often wondered about Guthrie. I couldn't imagine that he was faithful to Mrs Stoddart, but it wasn't exactly a topic I could ask Lachie about. I had high hopes that Guthrie was going to make his son see sense about the age of his girlfriend, but he didn't appear to have noticed it, although he'd noticed plenty other things about her. But then looking's not a crime, is it, even if it is your son's lassie?

I usually worked at *Raiders* at the weekend, so my big nights out with Lachie tended to be on a Thursday night. Our usual routine was that I headed over to his flat after college and we had a few joints and beers, then went for a few more drinks in one or other of the pubs on Leith Walk, before we headed up to the clubs on Lothian Road. Shirley and her pals joined us in one of the pubs. Lachie ended up paying for most of the drinks, which helped to explain his sudden popularity with the lassies.

. One night Lachie'd got himself in a worse state than usual. One of the laddies-with-dogs had given him some coke so he was being even more obnoxious than usual, which wasn't going down well with the bouncers in the club. Inevitably we got thrown out, and Shirley, Lachie and I got a taxi back home. Lachie was raging all the way down Leith Walk but by the time we got up to the flat he was crashing. Shirl and I settled down in the living room with a couple of beers while Lachie disappeared off to the bathroom. After half an hour he hadn't reappeared and we realised he'd taken himself off to bed. Shirl stuck her head round the door of his room and saw that he was snoring away. She came back and made herself comfy at the other end of the sofa from me.

'I'd better be off then,' I said, getting up.

'Stay,' said Shirl. She started rolling a joint. 'Share this with me.'

I didn't take much persuading. She stretched out on the sofa and I slid down onto the floor and sat at her feet. I looked up at her and thought how young she looked. I knew I shouldn't but I couldn't leave well enough alone.

'Don't you have to be up for work in the morning, Shirl?'

She was concentrating on the joint but gave a tiny shake of her head. 'Naw – I'm not working at the moment.'

We sat in silence for a minute.

'Shirl?'

'Aye?'

My heart was beating really fast. 'Can I ask you something?'

She laughed. 'What?'

'How old are you?'

'Nineteen.' She smiled and kicked the back of my head with her foot.

I snorted. 'Aye right, Shirl. How old are you really?'

'Nineteen!' She laughed again, and threw me her handbag. 'Check my ID.'

I delved in and took out her purse. Sure enough her

Young Scot card had her birthday as 4th May 1967. I turned it round to show her. 'Sorry, pal. Shouldn't have doubted you.'

I was about to hand her the bag back when I caught sight of the edge of her bus pass. I wriggled it out of her purse.

She caught sight of what I was up to. 'What are you doing, Stainsie?'

The bus pass had a picture of Shirley, without makeup and in her school uniform. The birth date on the pass was 4th May 1972.

'You're fourteen.' For once in my life, I was right.

Shirl sat up and snatched the bag off me, scattering ash as she did so.

'You aren't going to tell Lachie, are you?'

I didn't know what I was going to do. 'Shirl – you're too young to be hanging around with Lachie, and taking drugs and that.'

'Don't say anything, Stainsie.' Shirl swung herself off the sofa and onto the floor beside me. 'Please.' She placed her hand on the top of my thigh, and got onto her knees. 'Say you won't tell him.' I didn't say anything, and after a few seconds she leant over and kissed me, and her hand moved on to my belt.

'I'm going home' I said, pushing her away. This was too weird for me.

Shirl gave me the cold shoulder after this. I wasn't sure if it was because she was worried I'd tell Lachie, or because I'd rejected her. Maybe a bit of both: hell hath no fury and all that. Guthrie on the other hand, couldn't get enough of me – always asking how I was doing, how I was enjoying the job, his dark eyes gleaming as he nodded at my answers.

And I was quite proud of the achievements I had to tell him. I'd passed all my catering exams so far, and I'd been moving rapidly through the ranks at *Raiders*. I'd graduated from potman, to substitute barman, to valued member of staff with responsibility for cashing up on the quiet nights when Rob was off.

Guthrie obviously thought I was showing promise because he started confiding in me about some of the problems he was having with his empire. To be honest, I wasn't that keen on hearing about the problems of running a protection racket, or in fact any of Guthrie's anecdotes that ended with him joking about breaking somebody's legs, but I was flattered that he bothered to talk to me. He didn't even attempt to interest Lachie in his business affairs.

'That bar on Great Junction Street is late with their payment again.' Guthrie struck up a conversation one night in the flat, after Lachie'd fallen asleep on the sofa.

'Oh. Right,' I said, nervously.

'I'll have to get round there and break both the bar manager's legs if I'm not paid double this week.'

I couldn't think of a single thing to say to this so I offered him a fag and lit up myself. Guthrie laughed at my discomfort.

'I'm just kidding you, Stainsie, I'd never break both a man's legs.'

'Really?' I said with a feeling of relief.

'Aye. I'd only ever do one. A man can't work with two broken legs, so I've even less chance of getting my money. And it always leaves me another leg to come back for.'

176

He winked at me. I wasn't sure if I was imagining it but it felt like Guthrie was sounding me out, seeing if I was deserving of a place in his little empire. He steered the conversation round to *Raiders*. I wasn't happy about this but I was obviously not going to say so, so I just nodded.

'They're one of my clients.'

'Oh, aye.' I took a long swig of my lager. I really didn't want to know any of this.

'Not one of my better-paying clients it has to be said.'

I shrugged. 'We're not that busy a lot of the time.'

Guthrie laughed. 'That's what they said, and I didn't believe them either.'

My stomach was doing back-flips. I had a mental picture of Rob lying in the lane behind *Raiders* with two broken legs.

'Stainsie, son, do you fancy helping me out with my little problem?'

Not really. 'How's that?' I said reluctantly.

'See one night when you're locking up, just leave one of the doors, or windows unlocked, eh? Could you do that for me, son?'

There was no way I was getting involved in this but I didn't know how to say so, so I said, 'Can I think about it?'

There was the briefest of pauses, then Guthrie laughed and said, 'Of course you can, son,' and on his way to get us another couple of cans he ruffled my hair like I was five years old again.

I spent a sleepless night at Florrie's thinking what to do. I pulled back the curtains of my room and watched the night sky gradually lighten. I swung from one point of view to another. I didn't want to get *Raiders* turned over, but if Guthrie got his money that way, maybe he'd leave Rob in peace. Or maybe not. By the time the sun crept over the tenement roofs I'd decided I'd tell him that I couldn't do it; he wasn't going to be pleased but I reckoned seeing as I was his son's best friend, in fact his son's only friend, he wasn't going to do me too much damage.

I headed round to the Stoddarts' to tell Guthrie. The door was open but there was no one in the front office. It'd been many years since Mrs Ainslie sat at reception, chain-smoking and helping Guthrie to cook his books. Her desk was still there though, and Shirley's pink handbag was sitting on it.

I hesitated for a minute. If Lachie and Shirley were here, then I wasn't really going to get a chance to talk to Guthrie. But if I didn't talk to him today, it was another night watching sunrise over Cadiz Street for me. I needed this over with. In a flurry of resolve, I chapped the door and without waiting for an answer pushed it open.

I should have waited; if I'd learned anything in life it's not to walk in uninvited. Don't walk into your own cabin without knocking in case your roommate is abusing himself, don't walk into your mother's bedroom in case she's got a bottle on the go, and don't ever, ever, walk in unannounced on Guthrie Stoddart. Shirley was bent over Guthrie's desk and he was standing behind her, giving it to her good and proper.

'Staines!' cried Shirley. Guthrie had one of her arms pulled behind her back. She didn't get a chance to say anything else cause Guthrie clamped his hand over her mouth.

'Son...' said Guthrie, but I didn't wait to find out what

he was going to say. I was straight out of the house and across the Links. I took the stairs to Florrie's flat two at a time.

Three days later I jacked in my course and signed up as a kitchen assistant on a cruise ship sailing out of Newcastle.

Saturday

I realise now that I'm not a man of deep philosophical leanings. I always thought that if I was staring death in the face I'd be thinking meaningful thoughts, or at least have selected scenes from the life of Stainsie going through my head. Although with the way my life has panned out it would probably make me glad to go.

But no. Even as I'm staring at the gun, the main thought going through my head is, if I die with a hard-on will I stay that way? Does all the blood rush away from that region or does *rigor mortis* set in right away? I'm not saying that it would be an entirely bad way to go, but I'd definitely have a closed casket. I'm not having Wheezy and the lads down the pub taking the piss even when I'd dead.

'Who is it?' I say, pulling my towel firmly into place to preserve what's left of my dignity. 'What do you want?'

There's no answer, but the door opens slightly. The lava lamp is illuminating the gun a neon yellow, then purple, then green. I don't want to die a psychedelic death. I look round for something to hide behind, but the only thing within reach is Marianne and even I can't bring myself to hide behind a lassie.

There's a noise and I realise that my front feels wet.

'Jesus, fuck!' I stagger back, looking to see how much blood is on my chest. There isn't any.

'Liam,' shouts Marianne. 'What have I told you about playing with that water pistol in the house?'

'Water pistol? You little bastard.' My hands are round Liam's throat before my brain kicks in with a warning that I'm unlikely to ever shag his ma if I throttle him. I decide I don't care. 'You little prick!'

'Stainsie!' Marianne manages with some difficulty to prise my hands off her first born. 'Liam – get to your room.'

He scarpers, and Marianne and I look at each other. The mood has been killed, even if nothing else has. 'I'll get you a sleeping bag,' she says.

I nod. 'Fair enough.'

I sit down on the sofa. As I start to calm down I think it's probably for the best; after all I'm out of here tomorrow. And I can't entirely blame Liam; I mean no laddie wants to walk in on his Ma doing a Govan curtsey in the living room.

Roll on morning.

I wake on Marianne's sofa. A number of factors have combined to ensure I had a crap night's sleep. For one thing, the sofa isn't long enough for me to stretch out, and I have a new-found respect for my father, after all the nights he spent sleeping on sofas in the one-bedroom flats of my teenage years. No wonder he was always in such a bad mood. In addition to the physical discomfort, I kept waking up thinking that I'd find the tiny, irate, figure of Liam standing over me, waiting to drop his ma's TV on my head.

But the main reason I couldn't sleep was that my conscience was killing me. Tell me, Jiminy Cricket – what have I done wrong this time? The usual? Drunk too much and got myself into a situation I can't handle? Met a nice lassie that I could maybe have something good with and then run off at the thought of responsibility? Gee, if I stay and face the music will I turn into a real, live, boy? Or will I still be a liar with a wooden heart?

I sit up, yawn, and stretch my arms. I'm not alone; there's a real, live, boy in the room. A pair of speccy eyes are staring at me over the top of the armchair where I'd dumped all my clothes the night before.

'Morning, Liam.'

He doesn't reply. He sweeps my clothes onto the floor and plonks himself down on the chair.

'Are you going to try to strangle me again?'

'I don't know, Liam. Are you going to soak me with a water pistol again?'

He doesn't answer my question. 'When are you leaving?'

'Soon enough, don't you fret. Where's your Ma?'

He yawns. 'Still asleep.'

I get up and pull on my trousers. 'Right, Liam, tell your mammy I had to go, but I'll give her a ring later on.'

Liam stares at me and doesn't say anything. I wonder if I should slip him a tenner, then I remember that he nearly gave me a heart attack last night and I decide I won't bother.

'Just tell her, right?'

I manage to get in to the Priest's House and pick up my stuff without wakening Father Paul. Fair play to him – the man deserves a long lie now and then.

All the way to Waverly Station I'm looking over my

shoulder but it's an uneventful trip. Jiminy Cricket is still nipping my head, but, well, Wheezy and Marianne should know by now that I'm a reliably unreliable bastard. If I'm their best hope, let's face it, they were fucked anyway.

'Where to, pal?' says the man at the ticket desk.

'How much is it to Newcastle?' and I dig into my jeans for the wad of Colin's cash. It isn't there. I try each of my pockets in an increasing state of panic.

'Single or return?'

I take off my coat and start rifling through it, but I know that I'm not going to find it. That money was never out of my jeans pocket. I've either dropped it or been dipped.

'Single or return, pal?'

I run both my hands through my hair. 'I can't find my money.'

'Can't help you there, pal. We're strictly cash only. No credit.' He laughs at his joke and I want to kill him.

I lean on the counter with my head in my hands, and moan quietly to myself. The ticket man takes pity on me.

'Try reporting it at the Supervisor's Office, pal. You'd be surprised at what people hand in.'

My head snaps up. 'Really?'

'Oh, aye. There's a lot of honest people out there.'

Not surprisingly the supervisor's office is no use. But then if *I'd* have found a wad of 500 notes lying on the concourse I'd have been straight into the station bar with it and hard luck on the rightful owner, so I suppose I don't really have karma on my side.

I sit on one of the station benches and try to make sense of all this. Could I have had my pockets dipped? But I still had the money on me last night, and I'd kept an eye out for neds on the bus this morning. Maybe I dropped it, maybe even now the money is lying on the floor at Marianne's. Then I remembered waking this morning to a pair of eyes staring back at me from right above where I'd left my clothes.

Liam.

'Marianne? Are you in there? Open the bloody door!' I give the door a kick for good measure. I can't believe that they are not in at quarter to nine on a Saturday, then I remember that Marianne had said something last night about working the next day.

'Liam? Are you in there?' I give the door another booting, and the old bat from next door sticks her head out and tuts at me. I'm not in the mood for tact. 'Oh, fuck off.'

'They're not in. And I'm calling the Polis.'

Better and better. 'Don't bother. I'm out of here.'

I can't even begin to think where Liam might be. Marianne said he stays with his dad sometimes, and with her ma, but I don't know where either of them live. What I *do* know is that with every hour I spend wandering round Leith I'm more likely to run into somebody that wants to have a one-to-one chat between their boot and my face.

I want out. It's time for desperate measures. I head over to the one place I know I'll find money.

'Father Paul?'

He doesn't answer so I drop my rucksack on the kitchen floor of the Priest's House and think where I'm

184

most likely to find some cash. I've already pocketed any spare cash left lying round the place over the past week, so I reluctantly decide to try Father Paul's bedroom.

'Father Paul?' There's still no answer so I gently push the door open. Jeez, but his room is depressing. There is the bare minimum of furniture that you could have in a room and still call it a bedroom. I know the man's dedicated his life to God but I'm not sure why that stops him having a few home comforts. I stop worrying about Father Paul when I see a couple of brown envelopes lying on his bedside table. They're the contents of the collection plates for the last two Sundays. I pick them up and hope the congregation has been generous enough to get me to France.

Taking the stairs two at a time, I bounce into the kitchen and bend down to pick up my rucksack.

'Hello, Stainsie.'

I jump about three feet in the air. 'Jesus, Father, I didn't hear you come in.'

A pint of milk and the papers lie on the kitchen table. Bloody good timing on his part; another five minutes doing his shopping and I'd have been gone. There's no disguising the fact that I'm standing there holding all my worldly goods in one hand, and all his money in the other. I can't talk my way out of this one so I sling the rucksack over my shoulder and step toward the door. Father Paul steps in front of me.

'Father, I don't want to hurt you but I need this money.'

He smiles, his lips a grim line. 'And my church doesn't?'

I push him out the way.

'Won't you be needing this, Stainsie?'

I turn and he's standing there with my passport in his

185

hand. The bastard's been through my bag. I make a grab for it but he gets hold of my arm and forces it up my back. Next thing I know my head's resting on the Saturday *Guardian* and I've a searing pain in my collarbone.

'Don't want to hurt me indeed!' says Father Paul and lets rip with a few phrases that he didn't pick up in any seminary.

'What are you doing?' I say through gritted teeth. 'You're a priest – not bloody James Bond.'

'You know what they look for in the modern priesthood, Stainsie?' he asks, increasing the pressure on my arm slightly. 'Life experience. I spent four years in the army in my twenties.'

'Was that before or after you turned into a jakey? Ow!' Don't antagonise a man that's got you in an armlock.

He lets me go and I drop to my knees.

'I should never have offered you that money before. I should have known that your sort never go away, you just hang around trying to get more and more. Well, you can piss off. You've had the last cash you're getting out of me or my parishioners.'

'But...' I try to protest but I can't think of what to say. He isn't going to believe me if I try to tell him now about Bruce's threats to Marianne.

He isn't done with me yet. 'It would have been better for everyone if you had stayed out of town. It would have been better if you really had...' he stops suddenly.

'If I really had what?'

He ignores me. 'Just get your stuff and get out. Whatever trouble you're in you can get out of it without the Church's money.'

I pick up my rucksack and passport with my good arm,

but have to put them down again in order to open the door. I linger on the step.

'Father, I'm sorry about all this,' I say, but he ignores me and picks up his paper. 'I only intended to borrow the money Father. I'd have paid it back when I got on my feet.'

A loud snort of disbelief comes from behind the *Guardian's* sport section.

God save my rotten soul, and my lying, wooden, heart.

I decide to sound Wheezy out about where his great-nephew is likely to be of a Saturday lunchtime. All I have to do is find Wheezy, which shouldn't prove too difficult as he is generally a creature of habit, most of them bad. My first guess at his whereabouts turns out to be a double whammy, 'cause not only is Wheezy sitting in the back room of Shugs, but he's got Liam for company.

Wheezy catches sight of me over the top of his pint. He lowers it slowly. 'So, you're back in town?'

'Yeah - I realised you couldn't live without me and all that.' I'm not in the mood for discussing my change of plans. I point at Liam in what I hope is an intimidating manner. 'What's he doing here?'

'We're celebrating.'

I could do with a quiet word with Liam outside. 'Are children even allowed in here?'

He gives me a look, and says, 'I said – we're celebrating,' as if that overrode any licensing requirement Shugs might have. Suddenly I'm suspicious.

'What are you celebrating?'

'The boy here's won £500 in a Spelling Bee.' Liam's staring into his coke.

'Oh really?' This isn't good. 'No wonder you're celebrating.'

'That's not all. This wee man' – he breaks off to ruffle Liam's hair – 'this wee man, instead of wasting it all on skateboards or whatever, uses it to pay off his mammy's back rent. Have you ever heard the like?'

'Oh, God.' *I'm a dead man.*

'What's the matter with you?'

'Nothing. Here – take this.' I dig into my pockets and throw my last remaining coins on the table. 'Get us a round to celebrate, Wheeze.'

He doesn't need to be asked twice, and pisses off to the bar.

'Right you little bollox, get my money back.'

'I can't. The Housing's got it now.'

'Oh, God.' I fold my arms on the table and put my head on top of them. 'Oh God, oh God, I'm dead.' I sit up. 'And it's all your fault, you wee bastard.'

Liam looks defensive. He's keeping a good table's width away from me, and has one eye on where his great-uncle's got to. He doesn't need to worry. The state my arm is in since Father 007 finished with it means it's going to be some time before I'm choking anything.

'My ma needed it more than you did. She's got nothing and you're wandering round with big wads of cash.'

'That was all the money I had in the world, you wee prick.' I put my head back in my hands. 'What am I supposed to do now?'

Wheezy appears back with two pints, and a coke and packet of crisps for Liam. 'Drink up, Stainsie. I've got a plan.'

Wheezy's rabbiting on to Liam but I'm not even listening to what they're saying. I sip my pint and try to think. I've run out of options. I'm Gary Cooper in *High Noon*. I'm Ripley in *Alien*. I've no money and nowhere to go so I'm going have to stay right here and get enough information to point Danny Jamieson in the right direction. I lean forward and cut across the conversation.

'You said you had a plan?'

1986

The *Elisior* cruise ship had five decks, twelve bars, three pools, a cinema, a gym, and a theatre. Not that I got to see any of them, with me working 70-hour weeks in the depths of the ship's kitchen. Kitchen Assistant was the lowest of the low in the cruise ship pecking order. I was a fairly streetwise eighteen-year-old, with my dad's policy of moving us to a new town every six months to thank for that, so I managed to avoid the worst of the practical jokes. Nobody succeeded in sending me off to get a long weight, or a sky hook.

What I wasn't prepared for was the freely available sex. In fact, sex that was downright hard to refuse at times. I was officially the freshest meat in the kitchen, and, as is traditional, was propositioned by just about everybody. And in fairness to me, I could see why they were interested. Over the past few months I'd begun to fill out, and started looking like a man, instead of a skinny teenager. My hair was dark, long, and styled with the best 1980s feather-cutting that the trainee in one of the hairdresser's on Leith Walk could manage. My only real gripe about my appearance was that I seemed to have stopped growing at 5' 9" rather than the 6" I was hoping for.

The first time I was propositioned I had only been on the

ship a couple of weeks. It had taken me a fortnight to get up the nerve to go into the staff bar. I was sharing a room with Pers, a Swedish guy in his forties who was a veteran of the cruise ships, and was none too pleased to be rooming with me. I didn't know who he was hoping to be sharing with. I didn't think Ingrid Bergmann was likely to be needing a bunk up on a European cruise ship. However, after some bouts of shouting and swearing in the first week about keeping out of his stuff, he'd pretty much left me alone.

I'd been spending my spare time in the cabin on my own, but for some reason, I think involving a hangover, Pers was staying in one night and made it clear that I should get out of his space. Which was also of course my space, but he was about three stone heavier than me and a lot more aggressive so I decided the time had come to check out social life at sea.

The bar was pretty full but I couldn't see a single face that I knew. I kept my head down and made for the bar.

As I was ordering my pint a voice said, 'hello' and I turned to see Michael, one of the soux chefs, standing there. I had learned just enough in catering college to know that soux chefs were several rungs up the food chain from kitchen assistant so I was pretty pleased that he was bothering with me.

'All right, Michael – can I get you a drink?'

He shook his head and waved his full glass at me. I wondered what he was drinking; it looked like gin and tonic. *Sophistication.*

He didn't say anything, just leant back against the bar, scanning the room. I tried my best to get the conversation going.

'So, have you worked on the liners for long?'

He shrugged. 'Maybe four years?'

I found his accent quite difficult to follow. I thought he was Italian or Spanish or something like that. He didn't say anything else and there was a long pause while I tried desperately to think of conversation. I was just about to ask him where he was from when he leant across to me.

'Do you like me?'

'Do I like you?' I wasn't expecting this. 'Well, aye.'

He shook his head impatiently. 'Do you like *men*?'

I wasn't entirely sure what was going on here, but he clarified it for me.

'Wanna fuck?'

I wised up quickly. The approaches from blokes were surprising but basically ok, 'cause I could just tell them where to go. But the approaches from women were harder to ignore. Older women. Attractive women. And I wasn't about to turn any of them down.

I wasn't on the ship very long before I had my first crush on a lassie. Claudette was from London. She was in her late twenties, gorgeous, and black. This was exoticism such as I had only imagined. The nearest St Kentigern's had had to an ethnic mix was a Filipina nurse, who weighed about twenty stone and had never to date figured in any of my erotic fantasies. I couldn't believe my luck when Claudette started showing an interest in me.

Her and the other waitresses all took the piss out of me anyway, which I wasn't that averse to – I could handle a bit of banter – but I started to notice that she was going out of her way to be rude to me. Always a good sign.

The waitresses had a particular interest in finding out about my sexual history.

'So, are you a virgin then, Scottie?' asked Tessa, one of the American waitresses, picking up plates of entrées for the evening buffet.

'No,' I said with as much scorn as I could manage, seeing as Linda McFarlane, for all her bright red curls, had failed to assist me on that particular issue. 'Of course not.'

'Lots of women then, Jock-boy?' said Claudette with an arch of her eyebrow, offering me a pile of dirty dishes.

'Enough women, thank you very much.' I took the dishes from her and crouched down to start loading the dishwasher. Over my shoulder I said to them, 'But I'm the kind of gentleman that doesn't kiss and tell.'

They staggered about laughing.

That night I was in the kitchen on my own. It always fell to one of the kitchen assistants to give the area a late night clean, in preparation for the following morning's breakfast, so I was down on my hands and knees scrubbing the floor when I heard somebody come in. I stood up to see Claudette standing there with a drink in her hand. She was swaying slightly which made me think she was a bit the worse for wear.

'So, how much of a gentleman are you then, Jock?' she said, coming toward me. In spite of myself I took a step back. She pushed me into the corner between the wall and the fridge and started to undo my flies.

Travel is educational.

I think I fell a little bit in love with Claudette after that. Not that she was remotely interested. She twigged that I'd got a crush on her, so she dropped the banter and kept out of my way. Eventually in an act of desperation

193

I attempted to corner her in the kitchen, much as she'd cornered me earlier, except when I took a step toward her she moved to the side and said, 'Get over it, Jock.'

'I can't. I think I love you.'

She laughed, then put her hand over her mouth, with a look of slightly amused pity.

'I'm sorry, Joe, but it was just a fling. There's plenty more women on board – you'll get over it.'

Which I did. With Tessa. And half the other waitresses. And the occasional passenger that I managed to seduce, although this was strongly frowned upon by the management.

I was feeling quite The Man, what with the growing notches on my bedpost (or fridge) until I realised that my technique, or apparent lack of it, was the topic of discussion throughout the kitchen. I overheard a conversation between the waitresses noting a few of my shortcomings, which at least, thank God, concluded that I was improving.

Travel *is* educational.

On my first shore leave I'd a bit of money in my pocket, so I decided to give Florrie and my dad a bodyswerve, and check out how Linda McFarlane was getting on. We'd kept in touch over the past couple of years while I'd been sailing the seas and she'd been studying at St Andrews University. Our chosen menthod of communication was the postcard: just enough writing space for some mild flirtation without having to go into the details of either of our lives. I'd had my hair cut and bought some new clothes. I was hoping to show my favourite curly-haired red-head a few of the techniques I'd picked up in the Caribbean.

My first impressions were, frankly, a disappointment. She met me off the bus. The red curls were gone, replaced by long light-brown hair, tied back in a ponytail. ('My hair? Oh, I was always doing mad things to it at school, Stainsie – perms and dyes and that.') I wasn't expecting her to be dressed in a St Kentigern's uniform (not in public anyway) but I was hoping for more than jeans and a t-shirt that came half-way to her knees. And to cap it all, she was with some limp-dicked bloke called Sebastian that she hadn't bothered to mention in her recent correspondence.

The pair of them showed me to my B&B. They were wandering along hand-in-hand and every time we met someone coming in the opposite direction I had to step off the pavement to let them past. Three was definitely a crowd, and I wasn't a fan of crowds. I was half-thinking about jumping ship, and Linda could see that I was put out. I let her talk me into meeting up that evening. When she turned up at the pub, I was pleased to see I'd made the right decision. She'd ditched the limp-dick and brought one of her pals instead.

'You remember Paula from St K's, don't you?'

'Oh aye, of course' I said, though I could swear I'd never seen the woman before. She was slim, with dark hair and eyes, pale-skinned but with a smattering of freckles on her cheekbones that just cried out to be traced. I should have remembered her. But then at school I could never see further than Linda's bra strap.

A few drinks later and my earlier moodiness was just a distant memory. The Paula woman was smart as well as pretty, and I wasn't even that bothered when Sebastian turned up and sat with his arm round Linda's shoulders.

195

The lassies managed to smuggle me into their Student Union's disco, and after a couple more lagers served in plastic glasses, I managed to manoeuvre Paula into a dark corner for a snog. We ditched the others and headed back to her hall of residence, where I finally got a chance to use the knowledge I gained at sea.

I woke up the next morning, slightly cramped in Paula's single bed.

'So, this is a student hall of residence then?'

She rolls onto her side. 'Yeah – is it better than a cabin?'

I cuddle into her. 'Better than a cabin you have to share with a 40-year-old Swede with hygiene problems.'

Paula burst out laughing. I really liked this girl. She was pretty, she laughed at my jokes, she thought I was a god in the sack (probably)... I really couldn't have asked for more.

I ended up spending the whole two weeks of my leave staying in the David Russell Halls. I pottered about in the library and the Student Union while she was at classes, then we met up for walks on the beach, lingered over hot chocolate in cafés, and of course, had lots of single-bed sex. I couldn't help but ponder that this would have been my lifestyle if I hadn't been so keen to get away from home. Even then, if I'd stayed on at college I could have done my HND then transferred to university. That is, if I hadn't walked in on Guthrie Stoddart committing statutory rape.

I wondered what happened to Shirley. I still wasn't sure what it was that I saw, whether it was just Guthrie doing the dirty on his son, or something worse. I left Edinburgh without telling Lachie I was going, and I hadn't been in touch with him since, so I didn't know if he'd found out about Shirl and his dad. I couldn't say I was missing Lachie but I did feel kind of sorry for him. I'd run off, and Shirl was going to dump him for somebody richer, and even more gullible, one of these days. I was glad I was out of it all.

On the last day of my leave Paula came with me to the train station at Leuchars to see me off.

We held hands and I thought I could see a tear or two in Paula's eyes.

'This is sad, isn't it?' I said and she nodded miserably.

'Paula?' I decided to try my luck. 'Do you think you could write to me while I'm at sea, and then maybe we could meet up when I next have leave?'

To my amazement she agreed.

And I did write. In fact I surprised myself with what I wrote. Paula brought out something in me, and I found I was writing not just about what happens on the ship, but also about my feelings for her, and my hopes and fears for the future. In short, I found myself writing love letters, and I ended each of them with a note of the number of days until I got to see her again.

I didn't knock back any of the offers of knee tremblers behind the freezer that came my way, but I told myself that it was all educational, and that Paula would benefit from it. The only downside to life was that I had a sneaking suspicion that Pete from the Bursar's office was steaming open Paula's letters before he passed them on to me, and the whole Bursar's office was having a good laugh at my expense.

My next shore leave was even better. I headed straight

to St Andrews and spent two fantastic weeks with Paula, although if I'm honest I think I was half in love with Paula, and half in love with university life. I even sneaked a prospectus into my bag to read at my leisure when I was back at sea.

On our last night before I went back we spent the night with Linda and Seb at the Student Union disco. Paula was a bit drunk and suggested that we go for a late night walk on the beach. Linda and Seb weren't up for it, so Paula and I headed off on our own. It wasn't really the weather for a beach walk and the West Sands were deserted.

'Jesus, but it's cold.'

'It'll be warmer when you get back to the Canaries and forget all about me.' She gave me a playful punch on the shoulder.

'As if.' I decided it was now or never. 'Paula, I love you.'

She stopped walking and looked at me. 'I love you too, Stainsie.'

We fell into a sand dune, wrapped up in each other, and forgot about the cold.

It was hard being back at sea. I missed Paula so much I considered jumping ship, but this plan was scuppered when I realised I didn't actually have enough money to get home. I was sitting in my cabin composing a letter to Paula ('179 days until we next meet') when I got a phonecall from the Bursar's Office. It was Pete.

'So, you're going to be a daddy?' he said conversationally.

'No, I'm not,' I said. I wasn't falling for that one.

'Well, I've got a letter here says different. That night on the beach you never used a condom, blah, blah, blah... got pregnant, blah... opposed to abortion on religious grounds, blah...'

I dropped the phone and set off to kick the shit out of Pete from the Bursar's Office.

It was a church wedding. Not what I would have wanted, but I wasn't really in a position to make too many demands. My job was just to turn up, say 'I do,' and keep well out of the way of Paula's dad. It wasn't exactly the wedding Mr Peterson had been dreaming of for his wee lassie: a nineteen-year-old bride who was obviously six months gone, a father of the groom in a suit that last saw an airing in 1979 and a best man that was wearing his school uniform 'cause he didn't own any formalwear. And as for the groom himself...

I met Mr Peterson for the first time at the rehearsal. Paula'd already told me that I was being introduced to him as late as possible in the proceedings in order to minimise the chance of him killing me before the big day. The Staineses had managed to arrive late at the rehearsal so Mr P had a face like fizz before I even opened my mouth. Mrs Peterson, a lovely woman, dragged him over to be introduced to us. He managed to shake my hand without incident, but it all went wrong when he decided to make polite conversation.

'Is your mother not with you, Joseph?'

The Staineses really should have seen this one coming and agreed a strategy but instead my father said, 'She's unfortunately unable to make it;' I said, 'She's out of the country at the minute;' and Col said, 'She's dead;' all at the same time.

Mr Peterson looked at us like we were insane and walked off. It was the second longest conversation I had with him throughout my married life.

Saturday

'It'll never work.'

'Aye, it will.'

'It's immoral, and probably illegal, and, more to the point, I look a right prick.' I look at my reflection in the mirror. 'Nobody is going to believe that I'm a priest.'

Wheezy tucks in my dog collar. 'You look more like a priest than Father Paul ever does.'

He's got a point there – Father Paul is more often to be seen in jeans and jumper than a black suit and dog collar.

'Well, Wheeze if I'm really going to do this I better get going.' I've never been more keen to get out of the Priest's House. I made Wheeze search the premises for about fifteen minutes before I would set foot in the place. I wouldn't put it past Father Paul to be hiding behind a doorway waiting to get me in a half-nelson and tell me about his exploits in the SAS.

'I'll come with you.'

'Really?' I'm surprised. Wheezy has not shown much interest in hands-on investigation up until now.

'Never let it be said I'm not pulling my weight around here.'

I snort. 'Perish the thought.'

The Marrot Muir Nursing Home is only a couple of streets away from Isa's development. The home is a converted manor house, with a nice set of grounds. The management have installed some kind of summerhouse, and there are a couple of old dears and their relatives sitting in it, enjoying the weak sunshine. All in all, you could see your days out in worse places than this.

We buzz the intercom, and a woman in her forties opens the door to us. I get a nostril full of institutional smells: vegetables cooking, pine disinfectant, drying washing. For a moment it seems unbearably sad but I recover myself. I flash her my dog collar and my best smile. 'We're here to visit Agnes O'Neill.'

She frowns, screwing up her eyes behind her dark-rimmed glasses. A lock of hair falls loose from her hairband, and she pushes it back irritably. 'I thought Father Paul usually visited Agnes.'

'Yes, yes he does, but unfortunately there's been a bereavement in his family, so I'm replacing him. Just for today. Not long term. Or anything like that.'

'And this is?' She gestures to Wheezy.

'This is my... assistant celebrant.'

She scowls for a futher minute then gives in. 'Very well. I'll show you to her room.'

On the way there she asks us how much we know about Agnes' condition.

'Not much, to be honest. Father Paul was called away quite suddenly.'

She sighs. 'You'll see for yourself that Agnes is quite confused. She can't walk unaided and she suffers from dementia.

'Does that mean she's lost her memory?' Wheezy pipes up.

'Not entirely.' She shakes her head, and pushes open

202

a set of double doors. She gestures for us to go through. 'Her recent memory is impaired, but she does have good recall of her younger years.'

'Good-o.'

'She'll be glad to see you; she's not had many visitors since her niece died.' She knocks gently on one of the doors. 'Here we are. Agnes – there's a priest here to see you.'

The room is small and overheated. In the middle of the room an old lady is sitting in front of a TV.

'Jesus – how old is she?' whispered Wheezy.

'Agnes.' The nurse bends down and speaks to her loudly, 'This is Father...' she breaks off and turns to me, 'Sorry, Father, I didn't ask your name.'

'Joseph' I say, 'Father Joseph', then kick myself for using my real name.

'Father Joseph is here to see you, Agnes.'

She stands back up and nods to us. 'Good luck.'

Now we are here I don't know what to say to Agnes. I look at Wheezy for help but he grimaces at me and whispers through gritted teeth, 'Say something then.'

'So, Agnes, how are you today?'

She half nods but doesn't take her eyes off the television.

'Shall I just turn the TV off for a minute, Agnes, while you and I have a chat?'

I press the off button and the TV screen turns black. Suddenly it seems very quiet. Agnes turns to look at me.

'How are you today, son?'

I take her hand. It's like parchment. 'Not bad, Agnes. How are you?'

She smiles and I can see she hasn't got her teeth in. 'Not bad, son.'

'Do you like living here, Agnes?'

She nods. 'Aye, son, but I'm just here for a few weeks.'

'Is that right?' From the state of her that seems unlikely.

'Aye, son, just until Isa's got my house sorted out.'

'Isa?' Both Wheezy and I speak together. I remember what the nurse had said on the way in. 'Is Isa your niece, Agnes?'

'Aye, son.' Agnes sounds surprised. 'Isa's a good lassie.'

'See this.' Wheezy sidles over to me with one of Agnes' photos in his hand. 'Don't you think that woman could be Isa thirty years ago?'

It certainly looks like the Mrs Stoddart I remember from my youth. I take the picture. 'Agnes – is this Isa in the picture?'

She stares fondly at the picture, then starts to scowl and pushes it away.

'Isa's a good girl, whatever you lot say. She had that one bit of bother, and her just a young lassie, and you know what men are like. Men are pigs.' She looks up at me.

'Aye, they are that, Agnes.' She doesn't need to tell me that. I'm practically wearing a snout.

'Ask her about Mavisview,' Wheezy whispers helpfully over my shoulder.

'Agnes, did Isa ever come and visit you in your house?'

She looks at me as if I'm stupid. 'Of course she did, son, her and Guthrie and wee Lachie.'

'Did Isa ever bring other people with her when she came to visit?'

She stares at me and I'm not sure if she understands. 'Isa's a good lassie.'

204

'Well, that was a waste of time,' I say. We're walking back to Leith. 'Apart from finding out someone got Isabella up the duff way back when.'

'I always suspected the young Isa was a wee hoor. Anyhow, it wasn't a waste of time. While you were chatting up old Senga there I took the opportunity to have a shufty at her papers and see what I found?' He takes a sheaf of papers out of his pocket.

'Wheezy – you can't go stealing things from an old wife! I'm supposed to be a priest for Chrissakes!'

He smiles. 'So, you don't want to know what it says then?'

'I'm confused.'

'What about, Stainsie?'

'Well, to be honest, all of it.'

The papers Wheezy lifted are spread over a table in the back room of Shugs. Wheezy sighs.

'OK, Brains, let's start again at the beginning. This,' he says, waving a bit of paper at me, 'is a Power of Attorney allowing a James Meikle to run Guthrie Stoddart's affairs. Are you with me so far?'

'Eh... not really.'

Wheezy looks at me, despairingly. 'Guthrie must have gone gaga or be in a coma or something, and is letting this Meikle fellow run the show. This,' he waves the paper again, 'says he can legally do that.'

I've heard the name Meikle before, but it takes me a minute to realise where. 'Remember that women in Paisley I went to see, Wheeze? The one who thinks it's her sister's lassie that ended up under the floorboards in Mavisview?'

He nods. 'Aye.'

'Well she mentioned a man named Meikle.' I try to remember what she'd said. 'I think she said he was a nasty bastard.'

'That figures. So Meikle and Guthrie Stoddart have been working together for years then.' He folds his arms and stares up at the ceiling. 'Interesting.'

'Wheeze?'

'What?'

I point to the paperwork. 'You were going through these papers?'

'OK, OK. Exhibit B 'Companies House Form 288a – Appointment of director or secretary'. Form is filled in with the name of the company – ST Enterprises Ltd – and with the details of one James Anthony Meikle. All that remains to be added is a signature from a remaining Director to authorise the appointment – and look! There's a little cross made in pencil to let Agnes know that's where she needs to sign. Are you following?'

I shake my head. 'Not entirely, no.'

'Right, you need at least two people to set up a limited company, OK?' He picks up two pens to illustrate his point. 'So, say those two people are Isa,' he waves a red pen at me, 'and Agnes.' Agnes is blue.

I point at the blue pen. 'Not just a daft old wife Mrs Stoddart's taking advantage of then?'

'Maybe not. So, now Isa's dead, Meikle thinks he can get old Senga to sign the form, probably not understanding what she's doing, and he can take control of Isa's company.'

I take the blue pen off him and start doodling on the back of an envelope. 'But she hasn't signed it?'

206

He smiles. 'And now I've accidentally walked off with it, she's not going to sign it either.'

Meikle isn't going to be chuffed if he ever works out where all his paperwork went to.

I think of something. 'I've got another idea, Wheeze. What if Isa and Guthrie have remained business partners all these years, and what if Isa, Guthrie, and Agnes were the directors?' I put the blue pen back next to the red one, and add a teaspoon. 'If Meikle's got Guthrie's vote, and he gets Agnes to appoint him as a director, wouldn't that give him overall control of the company?' I put the teaspoon and blue pen into an empty cup.

Wheezy takes them both back out. 'But Guthrie's already got a vote, and I'm sure Agnes would do whatever he told her. He doesn't need Meikle as a director to get his own way.'

I start doodling again, with the red pen this time. 'Aye, but what if he isn't really doing this on Guthrie's behalf – what if he wants Isa's company for himself?'

Wheeze sits back and contemplates this. 'He's after the money?'

I have another theory. 'The money, but maybe also revenge.'

'Revenge?'

I lean forward. 'It's a long shot, Wheeze, but what if Meikle is Isa's illegitimate son? She leaves him in Ireland when she comes over here to live with Auntie Agnes, then, when he's all grown up, Guthrie finds him a place in the family firm. But Isa's got another son by then, hasn't she, the apple of her eye, and Meikle harbours a grudge for the rest of his life at how he's been treated.' I'm making it up as I go along now. Eat your heart out,

Daily Record. 'He probably has a good life with Guthrie but he's jealous of missing out on his mother's love. So, he sees a chance with Guthrie's decline to get his hands on Isa's money, and comes over here, bumps her off, and does her idiot son in for good measure.'

Wheezy's looking unconvinced. 'But if Meikle's her son he would inherit all her money anyway.'

'Only if he's been recognised as her offspring. I wouldn't put it past Isa to have farmed him off on some cousin or somebody back in the old country.'

'That's speculation.'

I nod. 'Aye.'

'And conjecture.'

'Aye,' I say again, though I'm not quite sure what Wheezy means.

'And none of this helps us prove that it was Meikle that killed Isa and not my Marianne.'

He's right. 'It gives us a motive for Meikle to have killed her.'

'What – that she's got money and he fancies a bit of it?' He goes to take a mouthful of lager then realises his glass is empty and puts it down in disgust. 'Half the scheme would have that motive.'

I'm running out of ideas. 'Well, you think of something then.'

Wheezy winks at me. 'Already have, my son.' He holds up the third bit of paper. 'Exhibit C – covering letter from J Meikle, explaining that he is the *bona fide* representative of Guthrie Stoddart, enclosing some paperwork, blah blah blah, and most importantly, giving his local contact details if she wants to get in touch.'

I don't like where this is heading. 'Meaning?'

'Meaning somebody needs to get over to his office and have a quiet look around.'

'Meaning me?' I sit back on my chair and fold my arms.

'Aye.'

I pick up our empty glasses and put them on another table. 'Naw. No way. Naw.'

'Why not?'

'I've got a bad arm for one thing.' I make a show of waving my right hand. 'What if he comes back while I'm there and I can't defend myself?'

Wheezy laughs loudly. 'Even with two good arms you couldn't defend yourself! You've just been beaten up by a priest for Chrissakes!'

'A priest that used to be in the Marines!'

He picks up my packet of crisps and helps himself. Through a mouthful of cheese and oninon he says, 'Whatever. Anyhow, are you going to look at this place, or have you got a better idea?'

And I have to admit that I haven't.

Wheezy insists we go back to the Priest's House so that he can advocate on my behalf to Father Paul. I haven't given Wheeze the whole story, obviously, skipping over the part about wanting the money to leave town. I painted it more as a misunderstanding between the two of us, which Wheeze thinks will be sorted out by him explaining about our investigations.

I use the walk back to the Priest's House to try to get Wheezy to see sense about the Meikle plan.

'It isn't safe, poking round the property of a man like that.'

He gives a dismissive hand gesture. 'You'll be fine! In and out under the cover of darkness.'

'We aren't even sure what I'm looking for.'

He sighs. 'We're looking for anything that proves he had it in for Isa.'

'Like what?'

Wheeze thinks for a minute. 'You'll know it when you see it.'

When we get back to the Priest's House, I'm surprised to find Marianne waiting on the doorstep.

'All right, hen?' says Wheeze and gives her a hug, while I let us in. 'Were you looking for me or for Father Paul?'

She extracts herself from his embrace. 'Actually I was after a quiet word with Stainsie.'

'Don't mind me, hen,' says Wheezy, picking up a newspaper and heading for the living room. Two minutes later I hear the TV being turned on.

'That's your uncle making himself at home.'

She laughs, then looks miserable again. I pull out a chair for her, and stick the kettle on.

'Where's Liam?' I ask. I wonder what he's said to her.

'At his grandma's.' She's looking pretty uncomfortable, and sits twisting her hair round in her hand. She's creating a little row of ringlets. It's like looking at Shirley Temple. 'He's the reason I'm here. I know he took your money.'

So the little bastard 'fessed up. 'He told you then?'

'He had to – I went into the Housing to pay my rent and they told me it had been paid off in full.' She looks down. 'You should have said something.'

'What would have been the point? It's not like you could pay it back.' *Believe me, hen, if you had anything worth stealing I'd have been round for it in payment.*

210

The ringlet-twisting is getting more and more frantic. 'I will pay you back. I could take out a loan.'

'For Chrissakes, no more loans!' I slam a mug down next to the kettle and spoon some coffee into it. 'That's what got us into all this trouble in the first place.'

She stares at me with those lovely blue eyes of hers. 'I will pay you back, Stainsie, I promise.'

I try for some humour. 'Aye, I've first claim on your next Lottery or Pools win.'

She looks down again and I'm hoping that she isn't about to cry, but fortunately Wheeze appears at this point, intent on me making him a cup of tea.

'And after that you better get going Stainsie, son, 'cause it'll be getting dark soon.'

'Where are you going?' asks Marianne dabbing at her eyes, and Wheezy fills her in on our visit to Agnes O'Neill.

She looks at both of us. 'Isn't that a bit dangerous to do on your own?'

'I won't be doing it on my own,' I say and hold my hand up to silence Wheezy, 'and don't give me any of that 'it's not a two-person job' nonsense, because it definitely, absolutely, is.'

He looks offended. 'I was just going to say that I am not ideal as an accomplice, what with the asthma making it difficult for me both to warn you, and to run away, should the need arise.'

Unfortunately, he's right.

'I'll go,' says Marianne.

'No!' say Wheeze and I at the same time.

'I want to, though. You're doing this to try to keep me out of trouble, and between that and Liam taking your money, well, it's the least I can do.' And she stares at

211

me again with those lovely eyes, and I'm all of a sudden less focused on the matter in hand and more thinking about what might have happened last night. She takes my silence for consent. 'Right, that's settled then, I'm coming with you.'

'But...' starts Wheezy.

She silences him with a wave. 'Shush, Uncle Mick. I'm doing this.' She looks back at me. 'I'm going home to get changed – meet me at my flat in half an hour.'

With that, she picks up her bag and leaves.

Wheeze and I look at each other.

'If anything happens to her, I'm holding you responsible.'

'Cheers, Wheeze.' Now I'm responsible for Marianne, on top of everything else. If I can get myself in and out of Meikle's offices without getting a doing it will be a miracle, never mind looking after my female accomplice. 'Now give me a tenner. There's some things I need to get.'

Marianne opens her door dressed head-to-foot in black, holding a matching woollen hat in her hand.

'What are you dressed as – a cat burglar?'

She looks down at her outfit then back at me. 'I thought I should wear something dark.'

'You should wear something that makes you look inconspicuous, not like a bloody mime artist that's lost her gloves.' This is never going to work.

She glares at me. 'How do you know so much about what you wear when you break in somewhere?'

A good question. 'Never you mind.'

Meikle's offices are in Leith docks, part of the ongoing

regeneration of the shore. The docks were once the heart and soul of Leith, the very reason the town existed. Mary Queen of Scots came ashore here, which we like to boast about because God knows things worked out well for her. John Paul Jones tried to sail a flotilla of ships into Leith, but was put off by the weather, thus continuing the popular trend of turning back at the sight of Scottish rain started by the Romans and maintained by your more lightweight overseas tourist in the present day.

When Grandad Joe was working here, back in the forties, the docks were already past their prime. The great days of shipbuilding, enhanced by a couple of world wars, were over, and the demand for the wet docks of Leith was in terminal decline. A few years after Joe moved to the Bond, the main activity taking place in the docks was late night prostitution, which the Leith Police dismisseth-ed in an unofficial policy of tolerance.

What saved the docks was the same thing that saved seafronts across the country, that is, an increased interest in the leisure potential of waterside developments. What is it about the British public that they like to sip their lattes by the side of a refurbished canal or a decking-entombed dry dock? The graves of Leith seafarers, from merchant navy men to Arctic whalers, must be echoing to the sounds of rotating, as first the Seamen's Mission building becomes a boutique hotel, then a state-of-the-art shopping centre is built at the Western Harbour.

The streets leading up to the docks are full of over-priced flats, again a common feature of dockside devel-opment in my experience. People pay a lot of money for the privilege of not being able to find a parking space, and having nowhere for your bairns to play. The area has

213

been under development for a while, and it's a mixture of recently completed flats, and work that's still underway. The streets are deserted.

We manoeuvre our way through the double-parked cars in silence. Marianne hasn't said a word since we left her flat, which makes me think she's having second thoughts. I make up my mind that if it looks the slightest bit dodgy I'll send her home, and sneak back here on my own later. We walk through the housing and into the docks proper.

'I think this is it.' I point to a two-storey stone building. It's one of the original dock buildings which has been done up recently and rented out as office space.

Marianne looks at me nervously. 'How do we get in?'

I look up and down the street. 'Not through the front door, anyway.'

We head round the side of the building, me leading the way. The back door's overlooked by a newly built block of flats, but I don't see any lights so it's odds-on they're not yet occupied.

'You stand here and let me know if you hear anybody coming.'

It's an old-fashioned window, one of the ones that are divided up into little panes. It's the best result we could have hoped for. I put my gloves on and get out the newly-purchased glasscutter and suction pad I've brought with me. Some jiggery-pokery and the whole of the top middle pane pops out into my hand. I reach in and open the window from the inside. It's a bit on the stiff side but I manage to get it open about a foot.

I gesture to Marianne. 'I'm going in.'

'What if there's an alarm?'

214

'Then I'll be coming straight back out again and we'll be legging it.'

I climb through the window, and it doesn't seem to set off any sensors or alarms, which makes me think we aren't going find anything of value here. Marianne struggles to climb in so I grab hold of her waist and pull her through. Even under the circumstances I feel a flicker of desire. *Later, Stainsie.* The window's obviously not used to being open and shut. It refuses to close again, but after a minute or two of frantic battering it suddenly falls shut with a thump. I leave the pane of glass on one side, to be replaced when we leave.

We're in an office, but a quick glance at some of the paperwork lying around makes me think it isn't Meikle's. The door is locked, but a quick ferret about in the top drawer of one of the desks produces a key. I go out into the hall and Marianne follows as close behind me as she can. She isn't too happy to be here; that makes two of us.

There's another three offices on the ground floor, but none of them match the name on Agnes' letter. As we go past the front door to the office block, I put the chain on the door.

I turn to Marianne. 'You wait here. You let me know if you hear anyone coming.'

'How?' She looks slightly panicky.

'Shout, and then get yourself back out that window.'

She still looks a bit uncertain so I try some reassurance. 'Look, the chain's on the front door. If anyone tries to get in that gives you time to shout up to me then get yourself back out the window.'

She frowns. 'Aye, but what about you – how will you get out?'

I look up the stairwell. 'I'll worry about that when it happens.'

Meikle's office is on the first floor. The door is locked, and I won't able to get it opened without him knowing somebody's been here. I'll knock off his petty cash while I'm here and he'll maybe think it was some junkie looking for easy money. Also, the moolah would come in handy.

The door takes a while to open. I'm not an expert lock picker, but it's an old door with the original lock and eventually it yields to brute force. God bless the developer's commitment to original features. At the risk of sounding like Jimmy Gillespie, I don't understand why you'd spend money doing up an office and not bother to put in half-decent security. Architects – living in another world.

I take a minute to find my bearings. The office is to the front, so that puts the kibosh on putting the lights on. There are blinds, but they're the crappy Venetian type so you would still see the light from the street. I use my torch instead.

There isn't much in the office. Meikle can't have been using it long – there's no files or piles of paper lying around. There are a couple of large cupboards and a desk, which is a beauty. It's a massive mahogany affair, at least five foot wide, with a green leather top held in place by a series of little metal buttons. True to form, there's nothing lying on top of it.

I try each of the drawers in turn, and each one of them opens. This confirms what I've been thinking – this isn't an office, it's a postal drop. In the bottom drawer there's a pile of papers. I sit down on the chair, also a fetching mahogany/green leather combination, and start leafing through them.

They all look quite recent. A letter catches my eye, because it's got the logo of Miss Spencely's law firm. The letter is addressed to Meikle, and is confirmation of his firm being appointed as security consultants to the Mavisview project. I'm not sure what a 'security consultant' is, but I can ask Miss Spencely next time I see her, seeing as she signed the letter.

I fold the letter up and stick it in my pocket, and decide to check out the cupboards. The first one is completely empty. I open the second door, expecting to find it equally bare. I'm wrong. The cupboard is full of men's suits. Never wanting to miss an opportunity I pat down the pockets but find only loose change. My foot bumps into something squashy. I bend down and pull out a sleeping bag; it looks like I'm not the only one dossing down. This strikes me as funny for about thirty seconds until it occurs to me...

'Staines!'

...that Meikle might come back at any minute.

I can hear Marianne running up the stairs. 'Staines – there's someone at the front door. He's trying to get in but he can't 'cause of the chain. He's trying to kick the door in.'

Shit. 'You were supposed to go out the back window.'

She grabs hold of my arm. 'I know, but I panicked.'

There isn't time to do anything. I shove Marianne into the empty cupboard. 'Stay in there and don't come out for any reason.'

She nods, terrified.

There are footsteps on the stairs. 'I know you are in there.'

217

The voice has a soft southern Irish accent. I've always liked the Irish accent, but I'm guessing the owner of the voice isn't going to be as pleasant as his dulcet tones would suggest. The door to the office opens and the lights are flicked on. I blink in the unexpected light and freeze; what goes through a rabbit's mind when he sees the car headlight and knows he's going to die?

The first thought that went through my mind was, 'at least he isn't holding a gun', which was rapidly replaced by the realisation that Meikle's a big bastard. His head's just about scraping the top of the doorway, which must put him at 6'4" at least. He's a handsome laddie; in his fifties but well maintained, with dark hair streaked with silver, and he's wearing a nicely fitted suit.

He gives me the once-over. 'What have we got here, then?'

I decide it's time for a bit of play acting. 'I'm sorry, pal, but I was desperate for a hit, right, and I was hoping I could get some money out of these offices, right...'

I didn't get any further with my drug addict imper-sonation because he steps forward and punches me. I tip backwards, mahogany over leather.

It hurts. Really, really hurts. This is the first time in my life that I've actually been hit. My father never laid a hand on me, although he occasionally threatened to. I went through school without challenging anyone to a fight. I've never spilled the wrong man's pint. I've made it through a long association with Lachlan Stoddart, rammy-starter *extraordinaire,* without either of us getting battered. I'm the guy who breaks the tension with a joke, who slides out the pub door at the first sniff of trouble, who hides behind the magazines while the shopkeeper gets abuse. So, why isn't it me hiding in the cupboard?

218

He waits for me to get back on to my feet, and I can see he's got a knife in his hand.

'So, some wee junkie scumbag thinks he can help himself to my money? Is that it?'

'I'm really sorry, pal.' I reach into my pockets and grab a handful of coins. 'Look – I'm putting the money back.'

He grabs me by the throat and pushes me up against the wall.

'Sorry doesn't quite cut it.' He holds his knife to my face. 'If you'll excuse the pun.'

He slides the blade slowly along my cheek and I can feel it bursting open. That's the thing about professionals. Like musicians and that. A quite-good guitar player can make beautiful sounds and all, but he's always going to have that look about him that says, 'see this - it's difficult, man, but I'm doing a great job.' But the real professional, your Jimmy Page or whoever, does it with a look that says, 'piece of piss this. I'm not even trying'.

And now I'm here I can see Bruce, the laddies from the scheme, Isa Stoddart herself, for the fucking amateurs that they are. This guy's the real deal – Jimi Hendrix and Eric Clapton all rolled into one. He's cut me from nose to ear and he isn't even sweating.

'Is that tears in your eyes, son? Is that you crying?'

Aye, I'm bawling, you bastard, I've just lost half my face.

He takes a step back to look at me, but doesn't release his grip on my throat. 'Now a smart laddie like you will see sense. Take this as a warning. I don't want to see you round here again, cause if I do…' he takes the knife and starts jabbing me very gently at the top of my leg, '… I'll kill you.'

I believe him.

He takes out a handkerchief and wipes down the knife. 'Let me see you to the door.'

He grabs my arm and hauls me down the stairs. The front door is still open, with the busted chain lying on the floor. He pushes me out, but just as he is about to close the door behind me he stops.

'I don't suppose you know a man by the name of Staines, do you?'

I wonder if this is some kind of trap but I shake my head anyway.

'Just a thought. If you do bump into someone of that name, be sure to show him your face.'

I slide down the wall until I'm sitting on the pavement. I can't bring myself to touch my cheek but I can feel the blood pouring down my neck. All of a sudden I think I'm going to be sick but can't bear the thought of retching so I roll over on to the pavement and lie flat on my back.

I don't know what to do. Marianne is still in there and I don't fancy her chances if she's found. Considering what Meikle's just done to me, what he'd do to a lassie on her own doesn't bear thinking about. She must be sitting in the cupboard saying a thousand Hail Marys.

I can't go back in and get her, cause in my present state I'm no match for Meikle. In fact, in any state I'm no match for him. I can't stay here either though, in case Meikle decides to leave and finds me still here. I take my jacket off and wrap it round my head to try to stop me leaving a trail of blood, and holding onto the side of the building I half walk, half crawl, back round to where we first climbed in.

'Oh Christ, Stainsie.' I think I must have passed out. Marianne's kneeling over me, tears pouring down her unblemished cheeks. She gets out her mobile. 'I'll phone an ambulance.'

I put my hand out to stop her dialling. 'Meikle?'

'He got a phone call and left about half an hour ago but I was too scared to come out until I was sure he wasn't coming back.'

I try to sit up. 'You can't phone from here. We need to get away.' This is big talk 'cause I'm not sure if I can stand. 'Help me up.'

'Oh Christ, I'm gonna be sick.' Marianne doubles over and heaves up. 'I'm sorry, Stainsie, but your face...' She heaves again.

This is the last time I ever do any dirty deeds with a woman as a sidekick. Or at least a good-looking woman. If it has to be a lassie, I'm going for Velma next time instead of Daphne.

'C'mon you.' I help her up. 'Time enough for that when we've got me to a hospital.'

I pick my jacket up and hold it against my face again. The pain when I touch it is overwhelming and I think for a minute I'm going to faint.

'Oh Jesus, Stainsie, there's so much blood.'

She isn't wrong. 'Aye, it's going to be quite a treat for the office workers on Monday morning, but let's just get out of here. Come on.'

We stumble back round the side of the building. I'm terrified that Meikle will be waiting for us but there's no sign of him, so we stagger round to Commercial Street.

We can't get a taxi to stop. Which is strange because I would have said a weeping lassie and a guy with blood pouring from his face was a good fare these days. Three

221

taxis slow down when Marianne waves at them, then pull away when they catch sight of me in all my glory.

I'm beginning to feel cold; I think this is what shock must feel like. I'm starting to rethink the ambulance idea when a van pulls up beside us.

'Staines - is that you?'

Manny leans across and opens the passenger door. He looks at us in horror. 'Christ! What happened to you two?'

Marianne pulls me to my feet and I fall into the passenger seat. 'Can we tell you on the way to Accident and Emergency?'

Dr Evelyn Murray is on duty at A and E.

She smiles when she sees me. 'Mr Staines. It's been a while since I last saw you in here.'

Dr Murray is gorgeous. Every time I'm here I have these fantasies where she takes off her white coat and lets her hair loose, and tells me she's very attracted to men from Leith. Unfortunately, she's knocked me back every time I've asked her out and I'm beginning to think she doesn't see me as a catch. Admittedly I've not been at my best when she's seen me, but I could teach her a thing or two about life that she wouldn't have learnt at medical school.

She touches the side of my face with a latexed hand and I wince.

'That's a beauty of a shaving cut, Mr Staines. I'm afraid it's going to need stitches.'

'Will you need to knock me out first?' *Please put me under. Let me get away from all this for a few hours at least.*

She shakes her head. 'No, no. I'll just use a local anaesthetic. You'll not feel any real pain but it might be enough to bring a tear or two to your eyes.'

And this reminds me of Meikle, and what's just happened and this time I really do start crying, humiliating myself in front of the two lassies. This sets Marianne off again, and Dr Murray sends her off to get a cup of tea.

'I don't suppose I can persuade you to talk to anyone?'

I think I get the inference. 'About my drinking? I'm not drunk at the moment.'

She nods. 'I know. And that's what worries me. I can understand you arriving here with mysterious cuts and bruises while under the influence, but from my experience of Friday night in A and E,' she tilts my head back for another look at my cheek, 'I'd say someone had cut you.'

Good-looking and smart.

'No, no, I just...' I can't think of a single reasonable explanation.

'You could talk to the Police.'

We both look at each other. I can feel the blood still dripping down my neck.

'Just a thought. I'll get the anaesthetic.' She turns to leave and then stops. With a smile she says, 'You take care, Mr Staines.'

I think I'm in there.

1988

My mother's second death was a good deal more permanent than the first. Colin suffered the most from it. The poor laddie spends years wondering where our Ma got to, and why we weren't allowed to contact her, and then when she finally does get in touch with him... it's just as well Col had God to fall back on.

It took Col a good couple of years to tell me the full details of what happened and some of it I had to piece together for myself. But we can both agree that it started in the run up to Colin's eighteenth birthday. Over the past few years he had become quite settled in East Kilbride. He'd got a group of friends that he'd made through the church, although no girlfriend yet as far as I was aware. I hadn't seen much of him since I'd left home, so we'd kept in touch mainly by letters and through Florrie, as my dad and I weren't really talking. In our limited contact Col and I were getting on pretty well, although much to my annoyance the lanky wee bastard had reached the dizzying heights of being 6' tall.

Dad and Col had a nice wee flat, and Dad had a second job driving a taxi of an evening; Col was off to university in the autumn so Dad was trying to make a bit extra to see him set up. When the phone rang at eight o'clock at night, my brother was in the house on his own. He didn't recognise my ma's voice.

'Is that you, Joseph?'

'No, this is Colin.'

He could hear what he thought was a woman crying at the other end of the line, and his first thought was that something had happened to Florrie.

'Is it Florrie? Is it bad news?'

The crying stopped. 'It's Mammy, sweetheart. It's your Ma.'

Colin put the phone down on the hall table while he thought. He wasn't good at dealing with complex emotional issues. He had an unconditional offer to study maths at Glasgow University in the autumn; give him a set of numbers over a disappearing mother any day. Momentarily he wished he had a pen and paper so he could do a graph of his feelings, with one arm measuring how pleased he is to hear from her, and the other arm measuring how pissed off Dad is going to be.

'Colin, darling?' said the phone. He picked it up again.

'Aye, Ma?'

'How are you, son?'

'I'm OK. How are you? Where are you? Are you in East Kilbride? And where have you been living?' Col had eight years' worth of questions he wanted answered. Ma chose to ignore them.

'I know it's your birthday soon, son – can I take you out to celebrate?' Col had to think about this for a moment. He would obviously have to meet her without telling my dad, but he wasn't entirely sure he could cope with all this on his own. Curiosity overcame him, and, not being the most exciting of eighteen-year-olds he suggested they go to the cinema.

Dad didn't suspect a thing. Col's birthday fell on a

225

Saturday, and keen as my dad was to mark the occasion, he'd also got the offer of covering a taxi shift, and Saturday night was good money that he didn't want to miss out on. He assumed when Col said he'd be going out anyway that it would be with some of his friends, and wee bro didn't say otherwise.

All the way into town on the bus Col worried about the evening. What if he didn't recognise her? What if she was three sheets to the wind? Worst of all, what if she didn't turn up? He didn't think he could bear that. But when he got to the cinema she was standing there, smaller, thinner, and greyer than he remembered, but unmistakeably Ma.

They went for a pizza before the film, and had a great time reminiscing about when we were wee (I have to admit to a moment's jealousy when I heard that). Ma didn't have a glass of wine with her meal, going instead for the fizzy water option. Col was too polite to mention it though he was dying to ask if she was off the booze. There were a couple of tearful minutes when Ma started talking about how she'd let us all down, but Col steered the conversation back to the positive – and probably on to God, if I know my wee brother.

Ten minutes into *A Fish Called Wanda,* Ma was getting a bit agitated. Col kept asking if she was OK, until the people behind him kicked the back of his chair and told him to shut up. Ma whispered to Col she was going to the toilet. When she wasn't back half an hour later he was a bit worried, but he wasn't the kind of laddie to make a fuss, especially one that involved the Ladies' toilets.

The film ended and John Cleese and Jamie Lee Curtis rode off into the sunset, but Ma still hadn't reappeared.

Col hung around in the corridor outside the Ladies' toilets in an increasing state of agitation until the cinema staff started to take an interest in him.

'Can I help you, sir?' said an usher who was about two years older than him, and was putting all the sarcasm he could manage into the word 'sir'.

'Eh...' Col wasn't quite sure how to put this. 'My ma went into the toilets about two hours ago and she hasn't come back.'

The usher didn't look impressed. 'Two hours ago and you're only looking for her now? It must have been a good film.'

'*A Fish Called Wanda.*'

The usher nodded solemnly, as if this did justify Col's tardiness, and shouted over to an usherette.

'Julie – take a look in the Ladies' bogs for us. This chap's lost his mother in there.'

Julie the Usherette wasn't in the toilets for very long. The door flew back open and she ran out looking more than a little pale.

'There's a pair of legs sticking out of one of the cubicles.'

'Shit,' said the usher.

'I think she's dead,' said Julie.

'Shit' said the usher again and ran off, Col assumed, to phone for an ambulance.

Two other usherettes came running up to see what the excitement was, and Julie repeated her story.

'Poor you! Finding a dead body like that – it must have been dreadful.' They whisked her away in a blur of sympathy through a door marked 'Staff only'. Nobody noticed Colin. He was left on his own wondering what to do – should he go in and see Ma, or wait for the

227

ambulance? He used the time to think of another graph: one arm with how much he didn't want to see a dead body, and the other with how much he had to see for himself that Ma was really dead.

He pushed open the door and walked slowly into the bright lights of the Ladies'. The usherette was right. In the second last cubicle there was a pair of brown Clarks shoes sticking out in the ten to two position.

'Ma?' said Col tentatively.

She didn't answer and Col couldn't bring himself to touch the legs, so he went into the next stall and balanced on the toilet seat in order to get a view into Ma's cubicle. He looked down and saw her lying there, her skirt and her face both twisted at the same unnatural angle. Ever the maths student, he admired the symmetry of her death.

He was still standing there when the medics turned up. They did their best, but it was no good. Ma had had a heart attack and no amount of medical intervention could disguise the fact that this time she was really dead.

My father, of course, was under the impression that Col was out with a bunch of God-fearing teenagers, and he wasn't even aware that Ma had reappeared. When he got a hysterical phonecall at the taxi firm at 12 o'clock at night, it took him a while to grasp the situation.

'Ma's dead,' said Col, and burst into tears.

My dad wasn't quite sure how to react to this; he was under the impression that both Col and I realised that she wasn't technically dead, just dead to us as a family. He knew that Col had always been the sensitive one, but he thought he was bright enough to understand the situation.

'Actually, son,' he said in as soothing a tone as he could manage, 'Your mother is still alive.'

228

'No, she's not,' said Col, 'I'm at the hospital.'

Shit, thought my dad. Col's finally worked out what's going on, he's flipped, and he's been sectioned. It must have been the worst few moments of my dad's life.

Serves him right.

The funeral was in Edinburgh, where Ma was from. It was an even smaller affair than her previous imaginary burial. My father, as next of kin, had ended up paying for the funeral so pretty much every expense had been spared. The only luxury he'd coughed up for was an announcement in the *Scotsman*, in case Ma's family wanted to attend. Let's be charitable and say that they weren't *Scotsman* readers, because they didn't make an appearance.

So, it was just Dad, Col, Paula and me. Paula was pregnant again, much to the annoyance of her father. It was typical of Paula to make the best out of a situation. To her way of thinking, getting pregnant at eighteen wasn't a disaster, it was 'a good opportunity to get having kids out of the way' so she could get back to having a career. She was hoping for a boy and I was hoping for a miracle that allowed me to actually support all four of us.

The Church was cold. There weren't enough of us to act as pallbearers, so Dad had the undertakers wheel Ma's coffin in and leave it down the front for us all to stare at while we waited for mass to begin. It wasn't a pretty sight. Dad had ordered the cheapest coffin the funeral parlour had on offer, and he hadn't splashed out on any flowers, so all she'd got in the way of flora to see her into the afterlife was a 'Ma' made out of white carnations, which Col and I had gone halfers on. I looked round the church in the hope that someone else was going to turn up. Paula was taking up two seats to herself, and we'd parked the wee one's buggy at the end of the pew. But despite spreading ourselves out as much as possible we didn't take up more than one row in church. Not a great reflection on my mother's life.

Father Power did his best to construct a positive eulogy out of the barbed comments that my father had given him. There was a lot of talk about sheep returning to the fold, and merciful Gods. I started wondering if Ma was given the last rites when she was lying on the floor of the cinema bogs, and whether she was still practising by that point in her life anyway. I made a mental note to ask Col after the service; I was sure Col wouldn't have made it through a whole meal without asking her if she was a regular churchgoer. He couldn't spend two hours with a complete stranger without asking them that.

Father Power was lingering over the challenges of my mother's life when we heard the door of the church open. We were all so surprised that we gave up any pretence of listening to him and all five of our heads swivelled round to look at the newcomer.

It was Lachie. He hadn't changed over the past few years. A bit fatter, and he'd lost the goatee, thank God, but recognisable. Even from the other end of the church I could see that he was wearing a suit that would be way out of my price range. It looked like he was working in the family business.

'Who's that?' whispered Paula.

'An old pal of mine, I suppose.' It wasn't really the time or place to try to explain Lachlan Stoddart.

Father Power broke off from the eulogy and coughed politely. We reluctantly turned round to listen.

Lachie mooched up to me at the end of Mass. He was kind of subdued.

'Sorry to hear about your ma.' If he was bearing any grudge about me disappearing off without a goodbye he was keeping it in check, for the duration of the funeral at least.

I put my hand out and shook his. 'My ma and I weren't that close in the last few years, you know, but your ma's your ma, right?'

He nodded.

I couldn't stop myself trying to find out if he knew about Guthrie and Shirley. 'You still seeing that Shirley lassie?'

He shook his head. 'Naw – ended a few years back. Bitch stole some money off my old man and I never heard from her again.'

So that was the cover story. I nodded slowly. 'Shame but – she was a nice looking lassie.'

'Aye.' There was a bit of a pause and I wondered if I should ask after his folks, but he got there first. 'Did you hear my ma and dad split up?'

'No, no, I didn't know that. Sorry to hear it.'

'Yeah, well.' He looked me in the eye for the first time in the conversation. 'Fancy coming round to mine later?'

Maybe it was the stress of the day, or maybe it was me reverting to being a stroppy seventeen-year-old and wanting to piss my dad off, but whatever the reason I heard myself say: 'Sounds good.'

231

'Was that Guthrie Stoddart's laddie?' My father wasn't looking too happy at this.

I nodded. Dad and I had barely said two words to each other since I got back. He was probably still pissed off that I hadn't written to him once in two years. If Paula hadn't made the effort to let him see his granddaughter, he wouldn't have been able to find me for the funeral.

Dad scowled at me. 'I didn't think you were palling around with him these days. You've no invited him to the reception have you?'

I shrugged and Dad could barely contain his irritation.

'The Stoddarts are bad news. Even you must know that.'

'Can we maybe discuss this when I'm not burying my mother, Dad? Though it is nice to have been invited to at least one of my Ma's funerals.' I'd been dying to use that line all day. He walked off in disgust.

I looked toward the pub, where my pregnant wife and wee brother were sitting surrounded by sandwiches and sausage rolls for twenty, and at Lachie's figure disappearing into the distance.

'Lachie! Wait up!'

Saturday

We get into a taxi outside A&E.

The driver turns round. 'Where to?'

Marianne and I look at each other. I wonder whether Father Paul or Liam has the bigger grudge against me. I'm coming down on the side of Liam being the marginally better bet when Marianne tells the driver to head to the Priest's House. I'm a little hurt and turn on the sarcasm.

'I wouldn't want to be a burden to you, Marianne.'

'I'm sorry, Stainsie, but I just need to get my head round everything that's happened tonight.' She looks like she's going to cry. 'And I don't want Liam to see you looking like that.'

'Fine,' I say and we spend the rest of the journey in silence.

I get the taxi driver to drop me off a couple of streets away from the Priest's House. I find a discreet doorway and light up a fag, then scroll through my phone's address book.

'Danny?'

'Yeah.' He sounds tired, and I feel bad about wakening him. I know he needs his beauty sleep.

'It's me, Staines.'

'Oh, aye.' He suddenly sounds more awake. 'Have you got something for me?'

'Eh, no, sorry.'

'Then what the fuck are you wakening me for?'

I have a drag on my fag while he abuses me. 'Aye, Danny, the thing is, can you remember the very first person to tell you that it was me that done Mrs Stoddart in?'

There's a silence then he laughs. 'Well, this *is* a coincidence. The very first person to grass you up has just been back on the phone to remind of his suspicions a mere two hours ago. What's going on, Staines?'

I ignore his question and put one of my own. 'So, Danny, who was it?'

There's a pause, then he confirms my suspicions.

Father Paul's watching the footie highlights when I go in.

'I should have had that key back off you, Stainsie,' he says, without turning round. He's not looking quite as murderous as he was last time I saw him. I walk in front of the TV so he can get a proper look at me. He stares for a minute then picks up the remote and turns the football off.

'So, what happened to you?' he says quietly.

'You want me to start at the beginning?'

He nods. 'Aye.'

'Well this idiot priest got me involved in something that was nothing to do with me and pretty much ruined my life.'

Just for a second he looks guilty, then he comes out fighting. 'Nothing's ever your fault is it, Stainsie? Working for the Stoddarts – not your decision? Going to Newcastle – not your decision?' He picks up the *Coke* can he's been drinking from, squashes it and throws it in the direction of the bin. It rolls round the edge of the basket then drops

234

in. 'Never refused a drink ever – not your decision?' He squashes up his fag packet and throws it after the *Coke* can. Another direct hit; the man could be playing for the *Boston Celtics* if he wasn't a priest. 'You and Mick are two of a kind, aren't you? Every mistake that the pair of you have ever made has been due to someone else.'

'Aye, that's fair comment, Father, but what about the mistakes I didn't make but everyone seems to think I did, like you know, murdering Isa Stoddart? Any idea why everyone thinks that?'

He squirms in his chair. *Busted*.

'Why did you tell Danny Jamieson that I killed Mrs Stoddart? You knew that I didn't.'

He's run out of things to throw in the bin. He goes to stand up, then sits back down again and looks at me. 'All this has got a bit out of hand, hasn't it, Staines? I mean, I just dropped a few hints to people that you might have had something to do with it, and then suddenly everyone on the Scheme is talking about it as if it's Gospel.'

I'm almost buying this when I remember his phone call to Danny earlier this evening. 'Aye well, after your recent call to DS Jamieson I'm sure he'll be around to arrest me any minute. Or did he tell you I had an alibi?' He's looking increasingly uncomfortable. 'Why me, Father? Why did you give him *my* name?'

He jumps to his feet and starts shouting. 'Because people like Marianne always end up in the shit, and scum like you get away with everything.'

I take a couple of steps back. He seems to calm down a bit. 'You were leaving town, Staines...'

'They do have Polis forces in England – they could have found me.'

He laughs abruptly. 'I wouldn't have cared if they did, Staines. You had it coming.'

'Why – 'cause I like a drink?'

He looks at me like I'm stupid. 'Because you worked for the Stoddarts! You were part of the whole Stoddart machine. Half my parishioners owed Isa money, and there's you, wandering round bold as brass with her tallybook, trying to find which one of them you were going to turn over to Lachlan and his thugs.'

I grunt.

He pushes me. 'What do you think would have happened to Marianne if you'd grassed her up to Lachlan?'

It doesn't bear thinking about. Lachie was very attached to his mammy. I remind him of the most relevant point. 'But, I didn't grass on her.'

'And why was that, Staines? Was it because deep down you're a decent, kind-hearted soul, or was it because we gave you £1,700 not to?'

I stare at the floor and for a horrible minute I think I'm about to start crying again.

He walks over to me and looks at the scar. 'So, what did happen tonight?'

I shake my head. 'Can I tell you in the morning, Father? I need to get some rest.'

He says nothing, but he makes no attempt to stop me when I head for the stairs. As I climb I wonder exactly how far Father Paul would go to protect his parishioners. I'm definitely putting a chair under my door handle tonight.

Father Paul doesn't put the TV back on, and a few minutes later I hear him turn in as well.

1998

The beginning of the end for Paula and me was the Open University degree. By the time the kids were toddlers, Paula was going stir crazy stuck in the flat and she was looking for something to keep her mind occupied. She had had the prospectus for six months, but she was suffering a crisis of confidence and hadn't managed to send her application off. Like a fool, I encouraged her.

'You've already done a year at university – of course you could handle it.'

'I dunno Joe – that was five years ago. What if my brain's turned to mush in the meantime?'

I leant over and kissed her hair. 'Don't give me that, Paula. You can do this. Now come on – get that application filled in.'

In the end I stood over her until she filled in the forms for 'An Introduction to the Social Sciences'. I should have checked the rest of the course content; the 'Women in Society' course nearly killed us. They might as well have renamed it *All Men Are Bastards And What Were You Thinking Marrying One?*

Yet against all odds Paula and I made it to our tenth wedding anniversary. It fell when I was home on leave, and Florrie volunteered to babysit so we could have a night out. Paula didn't like leaving the kids for long so we went for a meal at the pub in the village. We'd moved to

Aberlady, a village in East Lothian; Paula grew up in the country and fancied the same lifestyle for our children.

I poured us each a glass of wine. 'Here's to us. *Slainte.*'

We clink glasses. 'Ten years. We've been busy.'

'You have anyway – you've got your BA, and your job.' She'd recently been employed as a researcher in the Scottish Executive.

'And you've been all over the world.'

'And you've raised two kids single-handed while I did that.'

She laughed. 'I'm not complaining, Joe.'

Looking at her sitting there, slightly flushed from the wine, I thought how much I loved my wife. And as always, when I admitted to myself how happy she made me, I then immediately got feelings of panic because I couldn't understand why she was still with me. Every time I went back on the ships I convinced myself that she wouldn't be waiting when I got home. I tried not to show anything, and reached over and took her hand.

'I love you, hen.'

Two weeks after our anniversary I started sleeping with one of the waitresses on the liner. Donna was in her early twenties, small and slight, with long brown hair. She wasn't outstandingly pretty, but I knew I was knocking on a bit, so all-in-all she was a bit of a catch. She was also a dyed-in-the-wool bunny-boiling lunatic, but I wasn't aware of that at the time. She'd got me at a disadvantage: she knew all about me from what the other waitresses had said, but this was her first trip so nobody knew anything about her.

It started the same way it always does, with a bit of

banter, and meaningful glances over the dirty dishes. I'd worked my way up to chef by this point, with my on-the-job vocational training certificates safely under my belt. I was glad of the distraction that Donna presented because the trip hadn't got off to the best of starts. I opened my cabin door to find that I was sharing with Pers the Stinky Swede again, and in ten years he hadn't got any better-tempered or sweeter-smelling.

Donna knew that I was married but I didn't think that she was too bothered. The second time we slept together she tried to figure out what my situation was.

'So – your wife?'

'Aye,' I said cautiously, not really liking where this was heading.

'Are you separated?'

'Naw! What makes you say that?'

She leant across me to get her fags off the bedside table. 'The fact that you're shagging someone else?'

I didn't say anything. This was a delicate situation and I feared for my balls if I told her the truth, told her that this didn't really mean anything to me.

She lit two fags and handed one to me. 'So, are you just staying together for your kids?'

I thought for a minute. 'No, I wouldn't say that.'

'You still love your wife?' she asked, with a look of disbelief.

I shrugged, and she lay still staring at me.

It was turning into the trip from hell. We were short of kitchen staff so I was doing more shifts than I should be, and was taking speed to get me through my shift, and having a drink or several to bring me down again at the end of the day. But my biggest problem was Donna. She turned out to not be quite as relaxed about my marital status as she made out, and she'd started pressuring me about where I saw our 'relationship' going.

I tried to take it down a notch or two, but it wasn't that easy to avoid someone on ship. If Donna'd noticed any change in my manner she wasn't letting on. She'd got my rota memorised, and every time I finished a shift she seemed to be waiting at my cabin door for me.

I reckoned I was down to around two hours sleep a night by now, which wasn't doing my paranoia any good. I'd got all these thoughts about Paula going round in my head. I thought that if a loser like me can find someone to sleep with, what offers was she getting? Why, with all her qualifications and that, would she even want to be with me? The older she got, and the more she improved herself, the more I could imagine her thinking that she could do better for herself and the kids.

I started phoning her at odd hours. Except I didn't realise that I was phoning at odd hours, I just phoned every time my paranoia got out of control, then realised that it was actually three in the morning where she was. She dealt with it pretty well, considering she'd got to get up in the morning.

'Joe – what's the matter?'

The phoneline crackled and hissed while I tried to think of what to say. 'Nothing. I just wanted to talk to you that's all.'

'At 3 am?'

'Shit. Sorry. But you're OK? There's nothing you want to say to me?'

There was a pause while she tried to work out what

240

the hell I was on about. 'Like what? Joe – are you OK? You're not working too hard?'

'No, no. Sorry. I'll let you get back to sleep.'

I hung up and turned round to see Donna standing behind me. I tried to smile. 'You OK, hen?'

She didn't say anything.

It was no wonder I ended up with the sausages talking to me. After a particularly sleepless night (due to Donna who seemed to be powered by *Duracell*) I got up at 5.30 am to get the breakfasts started. I was staggering around due to the lack of sleep when I heard a voice. I looked round the kitchen but nobody else looked up.

'Over here.'

I looked in the direction of the voice. It was coming from the frying pan.

'You shouldn't be here, pal. You need to be with your wife and bairns.'

So, I jacked the job in and caught the next available flight to Edinburgh from Alicante. It was nice to be home. On my previous visits I hadn't really had a chance to explore Aberlady fully. It was a bonnie place, bang on the shoreline, a real wee tourist trap. I was back a week when I popped in for a pint at one of the pubs and got chatting to the manager. He was looking for, wouldn't you know it, a qualified chef, and a couple of drams later a happy arrangement had been arrived at.

I couldn't believe that everything was falling so neatly into place. I'm not just saying that – I really couldn't believe my luck and immediately started looking for things to worry about. I didn't have far to look.

241

Paula wasn't as delighted to have me around full-time as I had hoped she'd be (and neither were the kids, but that was another matter.)

'I wish you'd talked to me first,' she said. 'I wasn't pressuring you to come home.'

Which was true, but started me wondering why she wasn't keen to have her husband at her side. 'Don't you want me around?'

She looked impatient and shook her head. 'No, no, I didn't mean that, it's just that I've got used to being here on my own, and doing my degree and that.'

I reached over and held her hand. 'Well you've got your degree now – we can spend our spare time doing family stuff.'

She didn't look too thrilled at the prospect. 'But the thing is these days you really need a post-grad qualification to get anywhere. I was thinking about doing a management course or something like that.'

Post-grad qualification? She was moving further and further away from me.

I started getting suspicious that she'd found someone else. It was nothing I could really put my finger on, just a couple of phone calls that I overheard that I couldn't quite make sense of, and, oh yes, my rampaging paranoia.

Seeing as the poor lassie didn't get much of a social life between working full-time and bringing up the kids, I guessed that she'd met someone through work. One morning I noticed her making an extra effort with her appearance. Usually she wore a black or a navy suit, with minimal make up and flat shoes, a no-nonsense look.

This day, however, she was wearing a skirt and heels, and spent about half an hour doing her hair and make-up. Right, I thought, this is it, if I wanted to know, it was now or never.

I called in sick to the pub and got the bus into Edinburgh. I had to hang around outside the Scottish Executive for two hours before I saw her, but it was worth the wait. She was with some older man and they were laughing and joking together. She didn't see me and I followed at a discreet distance and saw them go into a restaurant. I didn't know what to do. Half of me wanted to follow her in there and accuse her, and the other half didn't want to know. Maybe if I ignored it she'd get over it and we could go on as before. I could get a better job, maybe, or go back to college. Whatever it took.

But the inquisitive half of me won and I pushed open the door to the restaurant. I marched up to her table, and she jumped in surprise.

'What are you doing here?'

I ignored her and focused on the Suit Guy.

'Are you sleeping with my wife?'

The Suit spluttered into his drink, which I couldn't help but notice appeared to be a soft one.

'What?' he said, and started to laugh.

'Right you – outside.'

'Oh, for God's sake, Joe.' Paula buried her face in her hands. 'Brian, can you give us a minute?'

'No problem,' said the Suit and disappeared off to the bar, no doubt for another fresh orange and lemonade.

'You are having an affair though, Paula, aren't you? I mean look at you – all done up to the nines.'

She glared at me. 'I had an interview this morning, Joe,

243

and I got the job. Brian's my manager and he's taking me out for lunch to celebrate.'

I slumped into the seat vacated by her boss, and my relief began to be overtaken by embarrassment.

'I'm sorry, love.'

Paula didn't respond, and sat swirling her wine round the glass.

'I can change, hen, get a new job, whatever you want me to do.'

'Joe...'

She said my name softly which made me start to panic. She should have been yelling at me. I kept talking to try to stop her saying anything. 'Go to college, anything.'

'Joe, the job is in Brussels.'

'But...' She'd never mentioned this before.

'The kids and I will be moving.'

I was confused. If she was expecting me to move country she could have given me some warning. Then I realised. 'And I am not invited.'

She took a gulp of the wine. 'There's someone else, Joe. He's already got a job out there and I'm going out to be with him.'

I grabbed the remains of her wine off her and downed it. 'I'll pack my bags tonight. I wouldn't want to stand in the way of your new life.'

'*My* new life?' She picked up her handbag and rummaged around in it. She pulled out a letter which she slammed down in front of me.

'What's this?'

'Read it.'

I slid the letter out of the envelope and started to read. *Donna.*

244

'Paula, this doesn't mean anything...'

She laughed. 'Finish the letter Stainsie – the second paragraph from the end is a particularly interesting dissection of your sex life. Good to see that this Donna woman has done both primary and secondary research.'

I wasn't quite sure what Paula meant by this but I turned the letter over and saw that Donna'd left no stone unturned, detailing not just every sexual encounter I had with her, but everyone I'd ever slept with on board. Not for the first time I cursed the gossip-mongering bastards I'd had to work with.

The waiter arrived in the middle of the pregnant pause that followed.

I stood up. 'I better let Brian have his lunch.'

The first couple of months at Lachie's passed in a stupor. True to my word I'd moved out of Paula's that night, and not having anywhere else to go, I turned up on Lachie's doorstep. He looked at the state of me and the bags I was carrying and gestured me in without a word. The next few nights passed in a haze of drunkeness, and I dedicated the days to sleep. After about a week I pulled myself together and started thinking about getting another job and finding somewhere more permanent to live. When I told Lachie this he laughed.

'What's the point of getting a job?'

Because we've not all got rich mammies, I thought to myself but all I said was, 'Well, aside from the need to eat, I need to start paying Paula some child maintenance.'

He snorted. 'Let your bitch wife look after herself. She's got a new man on the go – let him pay for the kids.'

I was about to object to him talking about Paula like that when he carried on:

'I'll get you some work, cash in hand. And you can stay here as long as you want.' He passed me another can of lager, and somehow it was a done deal. You'd think a Catholic boy would know better than to sell his soul so cheaply.

Of course, it wasn't really within Lachie's power to give me a job. Mrs Stoddart was running the show now. Lachie was a wee bit vague on the details of where his dad was these days, but he'd dropped a few hints about Spain. Whatever the circumstances of Guthrie's departure, Mrs Stoddart was definitely in charge of hiring and firing. She didn't look too impressed when Lachie suggested putting me on the payroll, and I couldn't really blame her. An unemployed, alcoholic chef is no one's solution to an HR problem.

But she couldn't refuse her Number One Son anything, so she compromised by giving me a few quid on a retainer for some unspecified duties, and I kipped at Lachie's for nothing. Oh aye – and all the free booze and pills I could stomach, from Lachie's endless supply.

The situation was an insult to my dignity. I'd no money, no friends, and Paula hadn't left any forwarding address, which showed a remarkably realistic view about her chances of getting any child support. I should have picked myself up there and then and slept rough, or if things got really bad, gone back to my dad's. Instead I stayed at Lachie's for the next nine years.

And it wasn't like living with him was easy. I was completely dependent on him, and it would take a bigger man than Lachie not to take advantage of that. Living with Lachie was like being back at school; we still spent most of our days sat in front of the TV bickering, the only difference being the number of channels to choose from. Lachie wanted me to be the enforcer that I never was at school. When we were out he still picked fights with people, and expected me to sort it out. But this wasn't school anymore; we weren't dealing with schoolkids who were frightened of his dad, and I spent most of my life in serious danger of a kicking.

The flat was a bloody midden. Whatever else Ma Stoddart was forking out for, it wasn't for a cleaner. There was a pile of dishes in the kitchen that had a crust that was halfway to being penicillin, and there was a layer of dirt round the bath an inch deep. The only thing in the flat that ever moved was the pile of boxes that took up half of the floorspace in the living room. When I first moved in I made the mistake of asking what they were.

'Merchandise,' said Lachie, through a mouthful of Mars bar. He hadn't lost any weight recently.

'What kind of merchandise?'

Lachie just smiled. 'What are you looking for?'

Within the week a couple of laddies-with-dogs arrived to pick up the boxes, and a week later brought another set. I put the boxes to the back of my mind and spent the time cleaning the kitchen. I wasn't the greatest chef in the world, but I did have some standards.

I tried to leave, I really did, but I'd burnt my bridges. After I'd been at Lachie's about a year I phoned my dad. Well, I tried Florrie first of all but the number I had for her wasn't working. My dad answered on the first ring.

'Hi Dad, it's me, Joseph.'

There was a long pause, and I realised this wasn't

going to be a prodigal-son-welcomed-back-into-the-fold situation. He finally spoke. 'I wondered when you'd be in touch.'

'Dad...' I wanted to ask him if I could come and stay with him, but I didn't have the nerve.

'What, Joe? What do you want? Because if it's money I've none to spare, seeing as I'm covering your responsibilities to your children.'

That was humiliating but he wasn't done yet. 'Are you staying with that Stoddart laddie now? Are you on the payroll of that mob?'

'Sort of,' I mumbled.

'Well, you can stay away from me, and from your brother. And leave Florrie alone too.'

There wasn't much I could say to that, so we both held on in silence for a minute before my dad softened slightly.

'I'm glad to hear you're not dead, son, but I'm not getting involved with you and the Stoddarts.'

'Dad...'

'What?'

And there were a million things that I wanted to say, from blaming him for me being in this state, to begging him to come and take me home, but I couldn't trust myself to speak without crying, so I hung up the phone.

Sunday

Despite my tiredness I can't sleep. I'm going over and over in my head the events of the past few days. The painkillers Dr Evelyn gave me are wearing off and my face is hurting. I can't lie with my scar against the pillow because it hurts too much, but when I turn on the other side the cold air on it feels even worse.

Swinging my legs over the side of the bed I reach over and put the lamp on. Catching sight of my reflection in the dressing table mirror, I sit on the edge of the bed and take a good look at myself. I'm too thin. Too thin and too pale, apart from the bright red scar on my left cheek. My hair looks like it hasn't been washed for weeks, and I don't know if I'm imagining it but it looks like there's twice as much grey as there was a week ago.

I can't settle, so I get dressed and slip out of the houses as quietly as possible, trying not to wake Father Paul.

Once I'm outside I don't know where to go. I take a turn past the church and walk up to the Foot o' the Walk, the distance that Mrs Stoddart is supposed to have staggered while bleeding to death. Every step that I take confirms to me that it's just not possible that she could make it that far on her own. I sit on the bench for a minute and stare up at the statue of Queen Victoria. In this light she bears more than a fleeting resemblance to Isa Stoddart. Neither of them were ever amused.

My feet lead me on, and I wander up Leith Walk as far as McDonald Road. I cross the road then turn off along Brunswick Road past the Royal Mail sorting office and onto Easter Road. It's a beautiful morning and there's nobody about. I remember that it's Sunday, so that's not surprising. It's just as well it is so quiet – I'm not a pretty looking sight. I'd scare the living daylights out of anyone I bumped into. Well, almost anyone.

The road goes up a hill until I reach the Palace of Holyrood House. When we were little Grandad Joe used to bring Colin and me here on the days that the Queen was staying in town, in the hope that he would catch sight of her. The waiting around was pretty boring and on the rare occasions that we did see Her Majesty it was all a bit of an anticlimax; as far as we were concerned it was a lot of fuss over a middle-aged woman. Florrie never came with us so maybe she felt the same.

I wander further up the High Street, then turn along St Mary's Street onto the Cowgate; this is the heart of Edinburgh's Old Town now. A couple of minutes later I realise that I'm standing outside the building that used to be *Raiders* bar. It isn't called that now, in fact it's not even a pub these days. It's a pity *Raiders* closed down; it was a good place to work, and Rob was a fine boss. I wonder if he stuck with the pub trade. I hope Guthrie didn't break his legs.

Shortly after I deserted Rob for a life on the high seas I read a story in the papers about one of the neighbouring pubs. The pub had played a very minor part in the Cold War by assisting in the defection of a Romanian rugby player. The entire Romanian and Scottish teams had returned from Murrayfield to the pub, accompanied by the Communist team minders. The sympathetic bar owner, an ex-Rugby internationalist himself, helped the laddie to escape through the network of tunnels under the bar. The boy, all 6'6" of him, popped up several hundred metres away, and announced to a very surprised policeman that he was seeking political asylum.

Asylum. If only.

1999

Paula was an optimist, a 'the glass is half full' girl, a 'the world's not going to hell in a handbasket' sort of person. I'd stake my life that whatever situation she ended up in she'd make the best of it. I tried to take a leaf out of her book, I really did, and I wanted to make the best of things, but I just lacked some of her energy. I'd lost my wife and family, I was homeless and dependent on the whims of a psychopath for any kind of income.

I knew I should be out there looking for work, or trying to mend some fences with Dad and Florrie, but I just couldn't rouse myself. I'd always been one to go with the flow, relying on someone else to make things happen. I realised that in my whole life I'd only ever made two decisions: one to move to Edinburgh, and the other one to run away from it.

And unlike Paula, my glass was never half full. Mine was either full or empty. After a couple of months at Lachie's I really started drinking in earnest. Up until that point I could kid myself that I was a social drinker, that everybody had a drink too many when they're at sea, that everyone consoled themselves when their marriage breaks up. But you can only wake up on so many pavements, or strange flats, or Polis cells before you realise you have a problem. And realising you have a problem isn't the same as having the will to do anything about it.

Lachie, for all that he was an essential cog at the centre of the Stoddart business, didn't seem to have an awful lot more to do with his day than I did. We both appeared to have fairly vague job descriptions which involved keeping out of Mrs Stoddart's hair. There was no girlfriend or anything on the scene, so it usually fell to me to keep Lachie entertained.

Lachie had strong opinions on taking drugs. Heroin was for junkie losers, obviously, and cocaine was for yuppy bastards. Ecstasy, speed and blow were all acceptable. But Lachie's drug of choice was ketamine, which in its day job is a horse tranquiliser. Seeing as Lachie had the constitution of a horse, it was an appropriate choice. Lachie took K for its strong hallucinogenic properties, although Christ knows what he saw when he was tripping. It probably gave him delusions that he was a gangster.

The side effects weren't pleasant, particularly for me. Lachie's long-term use of the stuff gave him panic attacks. More than once we ended up in a taxi heading for the Royal Infirmary with him thinking he was having a heart attack, and me hoping that he was. It made him depressed, on top of the depression that he suffered from anyway, on account of being a fat, useless bastard. And my personal favourite: when he was lying there in a K-induced stupor he often pissed himself. If Isa Stoddart had had any idea how often I had to haul her deadweight son to the bathroom and wipe his backside for him, she wouldn't have complained about my wages.

The only positive thing about Lachie's regular drug consumption was the fact that 6 nights out of 7 he was off his trolley by 9 pm, and lying insensible in his chair. This allowed me the opportunity to get out of the house and drink myself stupid without Lachie peering over my shoulder. Knowing that at night I could escape from Lachie's madhouse for a few hours was the only thing that kept me sane. If sane is the right word.

I tried a few pubs before settling on a regular haunt. I knew what I was looking for in a pub, and I knew what I didn't want, which was: conversation, titillation, juke boxes or hot food. I just wanted somewhere I could sit at the bar on my own, and down pint after pint without anybody bothering me. When I walked into Shugs I knew I'd found what I was looking for.

The only thing wrong with Shugs was this mouthy git by the name of Murphy. The man had an opinion on everything, and he was happy to share it with the entire pub, whether we wanted it or not. He'd got a view on current affairs, economics, politics, philosophy, and history, with a particular focus on the economic and social history of the working classes. Not that I wanted to make anything of it, like I said, I just wanted peace.

One night, after a particularly hard day of humouring Lachie I decided I couldn't take Murphy's witterings about class war any longer.

'Hey – you!'

Murphy stopped open-mouthed. 'Are you talking to me, son?'

I nodded. 'Aye – going to knock it on the head will you?'

A hush fell over the pub, not that it was exactly noisy at the best of times.

He stood staring at me with his head on one side, as if he was examining me. 'Knock it on the head?'

I nodded again, not quite as confidently as before. 'Aye.'

He tilted his head over to the other side. 'Are you saying you don't want to hear what Ramsey MacDonald did in 1931?'

'That's exactly what I'm saying.' I was trying to be assertive but I wished everybody wasn't looking at me. It was like being out with Lachie when he started a fight.

The Murphy character got off his bar stool and hobbled toward me.

'Are you saying that you don't want to know about the incident that started the slow decline of the party of the working classes? Are you saying that you don't want an explanation of how a fine working man such as yourself came to be sitting at that bar stool, on your own, drowning your sorrows?'

The barman and the regulars were all trying not to laugh. I wasn't quite sure how to stop the onslaught of questions, and in spite of myself I was suddenly quite interested in what he'd got to say. If he could explain how I came to be here I was all ears. I took the bait.

'An explanation?'

'Oh aye, son.' He leapt on to the bar stool next to mine, with a great deal more ease than he made it across the floor. 'Buy me a pint and I'll tell you how you ended up here, sitting on that stool with your face tripping you.'

Without me saying yea or nay the barman poured us two pints of lager, and I could feel the tension leave the room. I think the regulars were glad that Murphy was preoccupied with me and leaving them to their pints.

Murphy downed half his pint, belched, and stuck out his hand. 'Michael Murphy, although most people call me Wheezy on account of my unfortunate asthmatical condition.'

I shook his hand with some trepidation. 'Joseph Staines.'

'Pleased to meet you, Stainsie. Now where was I?'

'You were about to tell me how Ramsay MacDonald was to blame for all my ills.'

He gave a gracious nod of his head. 'He is.'

'So it's Ramsay MacDonald's fault that I'm homeless?'

'Oh aye,' he said through a mouthful of lager.

'And it's his fault I haven't got a job?'

He wiped his mouth with the back of his hand. 'Undoubtedly.'

'And it's down to him that my wife is off shagging another man?'

He gave a broad grin. 'Old RM might as well have been porking her himself, he's so much at fault.' He downed the rest of his pint and ordered another one for himself, though I noted he didn't feel compelled to get me one.

'Picture the scene, Stainsie. It's 1931. Ramsay MacDonald is leading the Labour Party, who are only remaining in power because they've got the support of Lloyd George's Liberals. Are you with me so far?'

'Aye.' Just about.

'Britain is feeling the chill blowing across the Atlantic from America.'

I must have been looking a bit blank because he said crossly, 'The Great Depression – 1929 – Wall Street and all that.'

I gave an embarrassed nod. 'Oh aye – that.'

'And the Cabinet can't decide how to respond to the Depression. Half of them want to spend their way out of it, and the other half, including MacDonald, want to cut unemployment benefit and balance the budget.'

'Uh-huh.'

'There's a schism. MacDonald for the life of him can't get his Cabinet to unite, so you know what he does?'

I was in danger of getting interested in this. 'What?'

'He submits his resignation as leader of the Labour Party, and sets up a National Government with the Conservatives and Liberals.' He leant back on his barstool, and I sensed I was supposed to look outraged at this point. I did my best, and waited for him to go on. He didn't.

'Sorry, Wheezy, I'm not quite sure how this relates to me.'

He pokes me in the chest. 'Ramsay MacDonald gave into The Fear.'

'The fear? The fear of what?'

He slid off the bar stool and stood too close to me for my liking. Very softly he said, 'The Fear that us working class folk can't sort things out by ourselves. The Fear that had Ramsay MacDonald hanging on the coat-tails of his betters, The Fear that had Wilson running to the IMF, The Fear that had Callaghan running for shelter in Europe. Ramsay MacDonald gave into The Fear and it's echoed down the years, until it's come to rest on you, my friend.'

I'd got no idea what he was on about. 'I'm suffering from The Fear?'

He nods vigorously. 'Oh aye, pal. A classic case of

working class angst. You are sitting there, crippled with
the indecision that you have inherited from generations
past. Your situation isn't your fault, son. It's Ramsay
MacDonald's.'

Not my fault? I didn't think much of his reasoning, but
I did like his conclusions. I caught the barman's eye.

'Two more pints over here, pal.'

Sunday

When I return to the Priest's House I fall asleep in one of the armchairs in the living room. I'm woken up by someone hammering on the front door. I have a discreet look out of the window, but it's only Wheezy.

'Jesus Christ! That's one hell of a love bite!'

I pull him inside so I can get the door shut as quickly as possible. 'It's not funny, Wheezy. I nearly got killed last night.'

He holds up his hands by way of apology. 'Meikle?'

'Aye, he walked in on us at his office. Your Marianne is no great shakes as a lookout.'

He looks annoyed. 'She shouldn't have been there in the first place.'

I'm outraged. 'Neither should I! So don't come up with any more ideas that could get me battered.'

He looks as if he's about to argue further, then changes the subject. 'Did Meikle know who you were?'

I shake my head. 'No, I don't think so. He thought I was just some junkie looking for loose cash.'

'That's something at least.'

I nod. 'You want a cup of tea, Wheeze?'

'Aye.'

We sit at the kitchen table and I try to eat my breakfast without chewing, because every time I chew my scar hurts.

'I've been thinking about all this.'

I drop the spoon into the bowl. 'Oh, that's good, Wheeze, 'cause the last time you did some thinking you came up with an idea that ended with me getting my face cut open.'

His eyes flicker toward my scar. 'Aye, well, we've been going about this wrong.'

'Oh aye?' I couldn't be less interested in Wheeze's theories.

He nods. 'Aye. What we need to do is work out what the catalyst for all this has been.'

'The catalyst?' I say, then wish I hadn't encouraged him.

'Yes, what was the very first thing that happened that set all the events in motion. If we know that, we can work out what Meikle's up to.'

He's staring at me and I realise I'm not going to get my breakfast in peace. I have a couple more painful chews of my Rice Krispies then say, 'Well, the first thing that happened was Mrs Stoddart getting done in.'

He shakes his head violently. 'No, it wasn't. Cause and effect, Stainsie-boy – Isa's death was a *result* of the catalyst.'

This is hard work. 'OK. How about, if before Isa's death Meikle came to town.'

'Because...?' He circles his hand around.

'Because Guthrie Stoddart took ill.' I'm getting into my stride here. 'And remember those bank statements that we saw of Mrs Stoddart's? About six months ago she stopped paying the £20,000 into that Spanish bank account every month.'

'Interesting.' Wheezy nods. 'So Guthrie takes ill, and

260

Isa seizes the opportunity to stop paying him his monthly share. However, his associate out there on the Costa del Crime gets pretty pissed off that the income has stopped.'

I wave my spoon. 'He comes over here, intent on killing Mrs Stoddart...'

'Or maybe even just to talk to her, but ends up killing her...'

'Either way, Mrs Stoddart's dead, but he can't get his hands on her money, 'cause she's got it all tied up in her company.'

Wheezy nods again. 'So he tries to get hold of the money legally, well kind-of legally, by taking control of the company.'

'So, as a director he would have say over what happened to the profits of the company?'

'Well, up to a point.' Wheezy takes a long drink of his tea. 'The shareholders are the people with the real clout – they can vote the directors off the Board.'

Just when I think I understand, it all get's confusing again. 'So, why's Meikle bothering becoming a director? Why isn't he trying to get control of the shares of the company?'

'He's probably doing both – taking control of the company as a director in the short-term, and pursuing the shareholders as a long-term way of staying in control.' Wheezy gives a bitter laugh. 'I wouldn't like to be a shareholder with that bastard after me.'

'Wheeze.' I've got a sudden bad feeling about all of this. 'If somebody left you their entire estate would that include any shares they'd inherited?'

'I suppose so, why do you ask? Oh.' He leans back in his seat. 'You mean Lachlan Stoddart.'

'I really need to get out of town, Wheeze.' I dig out the remains of Meikle's money. 'But I've got £3.50 to my name.'

Before Wheezy can respond, my mobile rings.

'Mr Staines?' A woman's voice that I can't quite place. Then I realise.

'Miss Spencely.' I sit down. I'm not in the mood to deal with any lawyer crap, and epecially a lawyer that has a bampot for a boyfriend.

'I'm at Mavisview, Mr Staines, and...'

I think I can hear her crying at the other end of the phone. I'm tempted to hang up. The last weeping woman I was nice to was Marianne, and I think everyone would agree that virtue in that case really was its own punishment. Still, I'd better know what was going on.

'Miss Spencely - what's the matter?'

There's a loud sniff on the line. 'Oh, Mr Staines – there's another body. A young woman.'

Oh God.

'Mr Staines' – she's really bawling now – 'I think it's a friend of yours.'

This is surprising. The nearest thing I have to a friend is currently sitting opposite me stuffing his face with Father Paul's chocolate biscuits. 'Who?'

'Marianne Murphy.'

I stand with the phone frozen to my face. My first thought is that she's making it up, but then I remember her boyfriend thinks I owe him a tallybook that I've not delivered on.

'Mr Staines? Are you still there?'

I try to keep my voice level. 'Yes.'

'Can you come over?'

262

Wheezy looks up. 'What was all that about?'

Wheezy has to be physically restrained from heading right over to Mavisview.

'See sense, Wheeze, it could be a trap. Remember who Miss Spencely's boyfriend is? That Bruce chappie – nasty bastard?'

He pushes me out of his way. 'I don't care, Staines, this is my niece we're talking about.'

I grab a handful of his donkey jacket. 'At least let me phone her mobile first.'

Liam answers.

'Is your mother there?'

'No.'

'Where is she?'

There's a long pause.

'She wasn't here when I got back from my granny's.'

'Where's she gone?' I realise I'm shouting which isn't helping matters. For all we know Liam's just been semi-orphaned. I try to calm down.

'It's important, son. Do you know where she went?'

There's another pause. 'She left me a note saying she'd be back in a couple of hours but she hasn't come back.'

I try to sound reassuring, which is difficult cause I'm starting to panic. 'Why don't you phone your granny, son, and get her to come round, and I'll call you back later?'

I look round for Wheeze but he's already out the door.

2008

By the end of 2007 my drinking was out of control. I would tell myself that I was just popping out for a couple of pints, but more and more often I didn't make it back to Lachie's. Sometimes I went back to Wheezy's after the pub and fell asleep there. Other times I'd wake and find I was sitting in a doorway or lying on a bench in the Links. Lachie didn't take it well if I wasn't in the house when he wakened. He was like a jealous lassie if he thought I was off having fun without him.

One particular morning, having spent the night lying on Wheeze's floor, I was walking home on tenterhooks wondering what kind of reception I was in for. I'd just turned into the street when I saw two Polismen come out of our stair, with Lachie in between them. I immediately sidetracked into another stair. I didn't know what Lachie'd been caught for but I could do without getting tangled up in it.

I gave them ten minutes then headed up to the flat to consider my options. If Lachie's dealings had caught up with him, I didn't really want to be around when he got back. I wouldn't put it past Ma Stoddart to set me up to take the blame for whatever it was he'd done. It would kill two birds with one stone from her point of view – her beloved son off the hook and his waster pal out of her hair.

I put the chain on the door then went into Lachie's

room. The room was a disgrace. Your average teenager would be ashamed to live like this: there were clothes all over the place, plates with rotting food on them, and condoms scattered across the floor, which were a mystery to me because I wasn't aware of him having a girlfriend in all the time that I'd been living there.

I knew what I was looking for, though I didn't really want to admit it to myself. After half an hour digging around in the stour under Lachie's bed I found it: a cardboard box off a bottle rocket that he'd had since he was at primary school. I opened it and as I suspected, it was full of notes. There must have been thousands. I could be out of there, and set up in a new life.

I picked up an empty plastic bag that was lying on Lachie's floor and grabbed a handful of the notes. I was about to drop them into the bag when something stopped me. The picture of the rocket was bringing back memories of us as kids and I didn't know if it was nostalgia or what, but I felt a bit crap doing a runner when Lachie was in trouble with the Polis.

I heard a key in the door, which caught on the chain.

'Stainsie you tool! Why's the chain on?'

I dropped the box and kicked it back under the bed, hoping that I hadn't disturbed the dust so much that Lachie would notice that I'd been in his room.

'Staines!' Lachie was kicking the door in frustration, and nearly took my hand off when I loosened the chain and he threw it open. 'What are you playing at?'

He marched past me into the kitchen and I didn't have to answer. He poured himself a large vodka, which was unusual because he wasn't much of a drinker, least of all in the morning.

'Are you in trouble with the Polis, Lachie?'

He ignored my question and pushed past me into the living room. He sat down on the sofa and buried his face in his hands. Within seconds his shoulders started heaving up and down.

'Lachie – are you crying? What's the matter?'

He didn't speak for a minute or two, then ran his nose along his sleeve and said, 'It's my ma.'

'What about her?' I hoped the old bat'd finally been arrested.

He looked up at me with a tear-stained face and said, 'She's dead.'

Four hours later I was sitting in the late Mrs Stoddart's house with a broken-hearted Lachie. He'd downed the rest of the vodka and had started on the whisky, with the occasional snort of cocaine on the side. I was trying to be as comforting as possible, but I was struggling to think what to say, not least because I was glad the old bag had finally got what was coming to her. Lachie was in a mood-and-a-half, which I supposed was fair enough what with his Ma being murdered and all.

'She was a handsome woman, Staines.'

News to me. 'Oh aye, Lachie, a handsome woman.'

He poured himself another glass of *Johnnie Walker*. 'But people round here didn't like her.'

I thought that was understating the case a little. 'Oh, well, I wouldn't say that.'

He glowered at me. 'You know the difference between you and me?'

I shrugged and waited for him to start.

'People like you. But they don't like me'

I wasn't sure if I would annoy him more by agreeing or disagreeing with him, so I shrugged again.

Lachie leant forward with his best approximation of a hard man snarl. 'But I don't like you. I've never liked you. I didn't like you in primary school and I don't like you now.'

Lachie stopped for another line of coke, and rejuvenated, continued with his theme. 'See you – you've drank away every chance you've ever had. Your wife left you. Your bairns don't know you. And I've seen you lying face down on the street in your own puke.'

He wasn't wrong, but it wasn't nice to have to listen to.

'You are a first class jakey. But people still like you.'

Lachie stood up, a little shaky on his pins, and disappeared out of the room. Two minutes later he was back with a book. 'What do you think this is?' he said, thrusting it at me.

I leafed through it. There was page after page of names and addresses, with amounts of money and ticks and crosses next to them. I took a wild guess. 'It's your ma's tallybook.'

'It's a list of suspects!' He waved his glass at me and a tiny splash of whisky flew over the side. 'One of they losers murdered my mammy and I want you down that scheme using your charm to find out which one, before she goes into her grave.' He paused and leant forward. 'I want a name.'

I kept leafing through the book but I knew it was inevitable. I was going be chasing round the scheme trying to come up with an answer that'd save me from a kicking from Lachie's lackeys.

'Lachie?'

'Aye?'

I pointed to the book. 'Why is there a dog listed here?'

'Pissed on my mammy's shoes after Mass one Sunday. The owner's paying it off at a pound a week.'

I left Mrs Stoddart's with my napper spinning from the drugs, drink and unhappy responsibilities that had been thrust on me. Lachie'd given me the book away with me, which I wasn't happy about at all. The information in that book could get a man (or woman) killed. Under the circumstances I felt the need for a couple of beers so I stopped in at the offy on the way home, only to be accosted by Wheezy.

He threw his arm round my shoulders. 'Stainsie, Stainsie, Stainsie, my son – where've you been? I'm drinking on my tod here!'

I shrugged his arm off. 'Not tonight, Wheeze – I'm off home for a sleep.'

He grabbed hold of my jacket. 'C'mon now – a couple of cans with an old pal won't hurt you.'

I was drowning in the Water of Leith, and every time my head came back above the water, Isa Stoddart was standing there and booted me back under. The dream was so vivid that when I woke up I could still feel the water lapping round my feet. Then I realised that my feet were in fact wet, because I was sitting at the number 16 bus stop on Commercial Street with a pile of empty beer cans at my feet.

The Book. Sweet Mother of God, I prayed. Let the book still be in my bag. But the Blessed Virgin wasn't looking

268

too kindly on my pleas because there was nothing in my bag except a couple more empty beercans.

It took me two hours to track Wheezy down to a café on Leith Walk.

I slumped into a chair, fighting to get my breath back, while he tucked into his double egg and chips. 'Wheeze – see last night, whatever I told you...'

He held up a hand to stop me. 'Not a word my son, your secret's safe with me. Soul of discretion and all that.'

'Thanks, pal.' The waitress came over to take my order but I told her I wasn't staying. The thought of the kicking I was going to get if that book was lost had robbed me of my appetite. 'Wheeze, I'm in trouble.'

Wheezy finished off his eggs and started eating his chips using his fingers. 'If this is about your tallybook, Father Paul has got it.'

I stared at him. 'Father Paul?' Relief that the book was safe gave way to confusion, which was booted out of the way by fear. 'What the fuck does he want with it?'

Wheeze wiped a paper napkin across his face and stood up. 'Long story. I'll tell you on the way there.' He opened the café door and gestured to me to follow him. 'Are you coming or what?'

The door to the Priest's House was opened by Wheeze's niece. She did some cleaning, or housework, or something for Father Paul. Her torn-faced laddie was there as well, playing on one of those hand-held computer games. The noise of electronic gunfire wasn't helping my nerves any.

'All right, Marianne – is Father Paul in?'

She nodded. 'Aye, come through.'

I was still none the wiser about what was going on. Despite his promise to fill me in, Wheeze hadn't said two words on the way over. Father Paul was sitting at the kitchen table, resting an elbow on the tallybook.

'You want a coffee, Stainsie?' Marianne asked.

'Aye, I wouldn't say no,' I said, without taking my eyes from the book. 'Any chance of having my property back, Father?'

He smiled. '*Your* property, Stainsie? Or do you mean Mrs Stoddart's property?'

We stared each other out until Marianne handed me my coffee. 'If you are going to get technical about it,' I said, 'it's Lachie's property.'

Father Paul pulled the book closer to him and folded his arms on top of it. 'Oh yes, Lachlan Stoddart. Your best pal. Is he planning to continue the Stoddart debt-collecting business?'

Somehow I couldn't see Lachie running any kind of business. 'It's not really uppermost in his mind. He's more concerned about finding out who did his mammy in, and he thinks one of those debtors probably did it.'

Marianne's laddie's computer game chose this moment to announce 'Game Over'.

'Liam – will you get out of here with that.' He ignored his mother, and turned round in his seat so his back was toward her. She grabbed his arm, pulled him to the door and pushed him through it. There was a shout of protest from the hall as she closed the door behind him.

Father Paul and Wheezy looked at each other, then Father Paul placed a shoe box on the table. 'We've got a proposition for you.' He slid the box toward me.

270

I flipped the lid off. The box was filled to the brim with used notes. 'What's this?'

'It's £1,700. Ten pounds each from every man, woman and dog listed in that book. And it's yours. All you need to do is take that book, get out of town and never come back.'

I stared at the money. Maybe the Virgin was listening after all because this was the answer to all my prayers, my ticket out of Edinburgh and far, far, away from Lachie Stoddart.

And yet. Lachie Stoddart, fat, useless, Lachlan Stoddart, my oldest friend. My only friend. Who was sitting alone in his late mother's house, crying into his beer about his poor, dead mammy. Lachie, who had no idea what was about to hit him, when the sharks that circled the Stoddart empire realised that he was in charge. I gave him six weeks before some one put a bullet through his head. So, what was I to do? Stay, and try to keep Lachie out of trouble, or save my own skin?

The three of them were staring at me. I picked up some of the money and looked at it. 'Why do you care so much about that book?'

Father Paul thumped the book. 'The Stoddarts have been bleeding my parishioners dry for years. This is a chance to end that.'

I nodded. 'Aye, well, I can see that but what about you?' I looked at Wheezy, who I've never seen put his neck on the line before. 'And you, why...' I looked at Marianne. She was a bloody good-looking woman. I'd always had a wee thing for her; the only thing that had stopped me making a move was that in a certain light there was a strong family resemblance to her uncle.

271

I couldn't understand why she'd got herself mixed up in Father Paul's business and a thought flitted across my mind, wondering what the relationship was between the two of them. Was it one of those things where she was giving him more than housekeeping services?

Then suddenly it hit me. I realised why Wheeze, the tightest man in Scotland was buying me drinks all last night. I understood why Father Paul was out with the begging bowl round his parishioners.

I got to my feet and pointed to Marianne. 'It was you. You done Mrs Stoddart in!'

Wheezy punched my shoulder. 'No, she didn't. Don't you go telling lies like that!'

Father Paul said 'Sit down, Stainsie, there's no need for that kind of nonsense.'

But Marianne just stared back at me, until tears started running down her cheeks.

'I never meant it to happen,' she said very quietly.

'Marianne!' Wheezy grabbed her by the arm, but she shook herself free.

'I owe her a fortune, and I thought I could maybe negotiate with her. I saw her at evening Mass and followed her out the church but... but the things she was saying to me about how I could pay off my debts. I never meant to hurt her but I just snapped and hit her and...'

I can't bear crying women. 'Calm down.'

She didn't. She looked back up at me and said, 'Stainsie, please...' but then choked up. I didn't need her to finish the sentence, I got the message. Her uncle put his arm round her shoulders, and I looked away.

'So...' Father Paul put the lid back on the box. 'What's it going to be, Staines? Are you going to take our money,

272

or are you going to send Lachlan Stoddart and his thugs straight round to this wee lassie's flat?'

I thought about Lachie. I thought about Marianne. I thought about the money.

I sighed and reached over for the book, and the box, and shoved them both back into my rucksack. 'How do you know that I won't just take your money and give Lachie back his book?'

There was silence, apart from Marianne sniffing. Then Father Paul spoke. 'We're trusting you, Staines.'

I nicked back to Lachie's flat, picked up my things, such as they were, and got myself onto the first train out of Edinburgh. I planned to head to London, but on a whim leapt off at Newcastle. Maybe I didn't really want to be too far away. In the hotel room, I unpacked the tallybook. I couldn't believe that Father Paul trusted me with all this information about people. I knew I shouldn't look at it 'cause there are some things it's just better not to know. I couldn't resist, though, and flipped the book open at a random page. I ran my fingers down the page and read the names out loud.

Michael Mouse
Minnie Mouse
D. Duck

I flipped back to the first page and saw that the original pages had been cut out, and that someone, no doubt a priest of my acquaintance, had taken the precaution of removing the real contents. I opened the minibar and drank a toast to suspicious clergy, and their lack of faith in man.

I headed out into town and looked for a busy bar. I

made eye contact with a woman standing at the bar. She looked away, and then looked back and held my gaze. She'll do, I thought.

I fought my way through the crowd to her, and put a wad of notes on the bar. 'What are we drinking?'

Sunday

I manage to get Wheezy to hold back for a minute or two when we get to Mavisview, so I can work out what's going on. There's only one car at the house – a red Golf that I assume belongs to Miss Spencely. I'm still convinced that we're walking straight into some sort of trap set up by Bruce.

'Wheeze – this doesn't feel right to me. I mean, why is Miss Spencely at Mavisview anyway? She can't be there for work reasons.'

Wheezy ignores me and pushes open the iron gate. I try again.

'Don't you think we should phone the Polis before we go in there? Tell them there's a body?'

He turns on me. 'And what if she isn't dead and we're just drawing her to the Polis' attention? You can do what you like – I'm going in.'

I'm not used to this side to Wheezy. He's striding toward the house, and I find myself following him.

The door isn't locked so we push it open and go in. It's the first time I've been inside the house. It's impressive. Facing us is a massive staircase which must have been magnificent in its day, but is now looking a bit the worse for wear. They left the curtains up when Agnes moved out, and on the landing there are these huge velvet affairs that reach from the ceiling to the floor.

275

'Miss Spencely?'

There's no answer and I get a really bad feeling about all this. I'm about to say as much to Wheezy when I hear the sound of a gun being cocked. Wheeze cluches my arm and we turn round with him still hanging on to me. Bruce is standing there. I'm pretty sure he isn't holding a water pistol.

'Up the stairs and turn to your left gentlemen. Quick as you like.'

Bruce gestures up the stairs with the gun, like he's Humphrey bloody Bogart, but we aren't really in a position to argue. I take the stairs two at a time cursing my own stupidity. Wheezy's struggling along behind me, pulling himself up by the banister.

As instructed we turn to the left and into a room with two occupants – Miss Spencely and Meikle.

Meikle looks at me and bursts out laughing.

'This is yer man? This is the Staines that I've been worrying about? The little bollox that I found sniffing round my office last night?' He looks over my shoulder at Bruce. 'I'll say this for you Bruce – your powers of description aren't up to much. He's not what I was expecting at all.'

'Where's Marianne?' Wheezy shouts.

'Calm down, old yin,' says Bruce, still waving the gun about like he's in a film.

'She's safe,' Miss Spencely says quietly. 'I'm so sorry.'

Wheezy turns on her. 'Where is she?'

Bruce laughs. 'Last time I saw her she was getting out of my car somewhere round about the English border. Long walk home with no money. Has she got a thing for you, Staines? All I had to say was you were in trouble and she was out that flat and in my car quick as you like.'

Wheezy pipes up. 'My Marianne'll have gone straight to the Polis.'

Bruce laughs. 'No, she won't. I can be very persuasive on that particular issue – isn't that right, Charlotte?' Miss Spencely throws Bruce a look of such contempt that I feel the leather in my shoes wilting. Unfortunately, it seems to have no effect at all on Bruce.

'And I don't think your Marianne will be going anywhere near the Police,' Meikle says. 'After the right hook she gave Isa Stoddart I thought she'd saved me a job.'

'So it *was* you that did Isa in?' Wheezy just can't help himself.

Meikle laughs. 'Did you really think that slip of a girl finished off Isa? If she was that damn fragile she'd have been done in years ago. Do you want to know why I did it, grandpa?'

Say it's none of our business, Wheeze, and we might just get out of here alive.

'Aye, I do want to know.'

Meikle smiles. 'I did it because she wouldn't listen. I didn't come over here to make trouble. And, you know, Isa was pleased to see me when she came round after the punch your daughter...'

'Niece.'

'Whatever, had given her. I was there like an angel out of the blue, helping her into my car, taking her for a drive to calm her nerves. She couldn't believe her luck at seeing a friendly face in her hour of need.'

Wheezy snorts.

Shut up, Wheeze, please.

277

'OK then, boys.' He looks as us both, as if we are on some kind of quiz show. 'What happened next? Come on, Mr Staines, you haven't had much to say for yourself. Take a guess.'

I really don't want to go down this route, but there doesn't appear to be a choice. 'Well, I'm guessing you suggested to her, in a calm and reasonable manner, that she might like to cut you in on some of her business deals, what with all the sterling work you were doing with Guthrie out in Spain.'

He gives me a mock round of applause. 'Calm and reasonable is exactly what I was, Mr Staines. Well done. And what do you think she said?'

Seeing as she's now pushing up daisies I'll take a wild guess that she didn't say, 'Smashing idea, Meikle'.

'She said no.'

Meikle smiles. 'She did indeed. Giving me all this shite about how the business was hers and Guthrie's and how I'd been lucky to be working for them all this time. And there's Guthrie lying in hospital not even able to wipe his own arse and I'm having to run everything.'

Wheezy chips in. 'Aye, and she isn't even sending you the twenty grand a month anymore.'

Fortunately, Meikle's getting himself too worked up to listen to what Wheezy's saying.

'She said she's doing all this for that idiot son of hers so that when she dies he's got a nice little property empire that even he can't mess up. And I say to her again, "cut me in, Mrs Stoddart, I can look after the business on Lachie's behalf," but she won't listen.'

Wheezy is unstoppable. 'So, you battered her head in?'

Meikle grabs Wheezy by the throat and I can't help

278

but feel that it serves the gobby bastard right. 'I wouldn't quite put it like that.'

Wheezy's still going on. The man's got a death wish.

'Is that any way to treat your own mother?'

'My mother?' Meikle lets go of Wheezy in surprise. 'My mother's very well looked after in a nursing home in Roscommon. What's she got to do with anything?'

'Can I go now?' Miss Spencely says abruptly.

Everybody turns to look at her; I think we'd forgotten she was still here.

Bruce laughs. 'Aye, sure, sweetheart – unless you want to stay and chat to these nice gentlemen?'

Miss Spencely leaves without a backward glance. I'm guessing that's one romance that isn't going anywhere.

Meikle looks at Bruce. 'Are you sure she isn't going to do anything daft, like call the Police?'

'It's fine – she's under control. She knows I know where her family live.' He looks irritated at the question and I think that maybe this isn't a perfect working arrangement. Bruce is kidding himself if he thinks they're partners. This is Meikle's show, and Bruce has never been anything other than sidekick material.

'Gentlemen,' says Meikle gesturing to a couple of wooden chairs. 'Please take a seat. There are a few questions we would like to ask you.' He reaches into his bag and pulls out a length of rope. Good to see that he's come prepared. He must have been a boy scout. 'It could take a while so you might want to get comfortable.'

'I don't actually know anything about Staines' affairs, so I don't think I can really help you gents. Can I go?'

Now that Marianne's accounted for safe and well, normal service seems to have been resumed on the

Wheezy-front. Meikle isn't having any of it though, and he gestures him toward the chairs.

'Sit.'

We sit on the chairs and Bruce ties our hands behind our backs. I'm sweating and I can feel the scar on my face ache.

'Now, Mr Staines, do you realise that I flew in from Malaga as soon as Bruce told me you were in town?' Meikle perches on the side of the table. 'Thanks, Bruce. It was very inconvenient seeing as I had just got back there after completing a bit of business over here. But then as you lads seem to know everything, you probably already knew that.'

I close my eyes and wait for Wheezy to dig us in even deeper, but for once he keeps his mouth shut.

Meikle points at his sidekick. 'Clever laddie is our Bruce.'

I look at Bruce and he winks at me.

'Not only is he Isa's right-hand man, he's also got a great taste in women. Wouldn't you say so, lads?'

I'm not sure where this is going, but I grunt in what I hope is a positive manner.

Meikle carries on. 'That Charlotte – what a looker!' Bruce is smiling away to himself, as smug as the cat that got the cream. 'But not just a looker, brains as well. Not smart enough to realise that Bruce was after more than getting his end away, but knows her legal stuff.'

He looks at me like he's expecting me to comment. I do my best. 'Eh – is that right?'

'Oh aye.' Meikle nods vigorously. 'Very good at coming up with solutions to hypothetical legal problems, like say, somebody being overlooked in a will.'

280

I'm beginning to see where this is going.

'Now, gents,' Meikle rearranges his bum cheeks on the table. 'Have either of you brains every heard of something called a Deed of Variation?'

'Aye.' Wheezy pipes up. That man's urge to show off his knowledge can't be repressed even when he's worrying about getting killed. 'It's when the beneficiaries of a will agree to change who gets the money.'

Meikle looks surprised and bursts out laughing. 'Give the man a gold star. Exactly right. It's when a person renounces their legal right to benefit from an inheritance. Are you following me so far, Staines?'

Unfortunately, I am. 'Just about.'

'Good. I was worried I was using too many big words for you. Now Bruce here has young Charlotte draft him up a Deed of Variation, leaving out a few specifics to be filled in at a later date, like your name for example. Can you see where I'm going with this, Staines?'

I sigh. 'You want me to sign over all my rights to Lachie's inheritance and then get out of town, I'm guessing?'

'Well, you're right about the first part anyway.'

And it hits me that I'm not going anywhere. I'm going to sign his papers then Wheezy and I are going to end up part of the foundations of the Mavisview development. All in all, I wish Liam had shot me with a real gun and maybe at least then my bairns would have inherited the money.

We hear the sound of a Polis siren in the distance. Bruce looks out the window.

'That bitch.'

'I thought you said you had her under control?' Meikle moves toward me with the knife and for a minute I think

281

he's going to finish me off, but instead he leans forward and cuts the rope round my hands, then leans over and does the same to Wheezy. 'Let's get the two of them out of here before the Police come in.'

They haul us back down the stairs. We pass the door where we came in and I assume that we're heading for the basement but we stop at the next landing, and Meikle starts patting one of the bits of wood panelling. A section of it swings out like a door. A smuggler's hole.

'No nonsense out of you two,' Meikle waves the knife at us, and Bruce pulls the panel back to reveal a door.

'Right – in there.'

Wheezy backs away. 'Not me, son – I'm claustrophobic.'

'Tough.' Meikle shoves Wheezy head first into the darkness and pushes me in after him.

As the door closes behind us, the darkness is complete. The room is so narrow I can't straighten my arm in front of me.

'Jesus – this isn't doing me any good.' Wheezy clutches at my arm. 'I need my inhaler.'

'Calm down, Wheeze. Just keep taking deep breaths.' Even as I'm saying that I start worrying that the air in here might not be too fresh. 'They haven't taken my phone off me – if we can get a signal we can tell the Polis that we're in here.'

He elbows me in the ribs. 'Give it a go, then.'

I flip open my phone but I can see right away I can't get reception.

'It isn't working Wheeze.'

'Try sending one of they message things.'

'A text message? Who to? The Samaritans?'

He digs me in the ribs again. 'Text message 999.'

282

'Can you do that?' I'm suddenly hopeful.

There's a brief pause. 'I don't know, but you'd think so.'

'I've got a better idea.' I scroll through my address book to see if I've still got Danny Jamieson's number. 'I'll text Danny.'

I type as fast as I can.

'What are you saying to him?'

I read it out. 'Held prisoner in Mavisview. Need help. Not a joke.'

Wheezy snorts. 'That won't get him to shift his arse. Tell him you pumped his wife and he'll be here in record time.'

We sit in silence for a few minutes.

'Remember what that man said about suffocating in these places, Staines?'

'That won't happen to us.' I laugh bitterly. 'We'll survive our stay in here and Meikle will kill us later. And you know what, Wheezy? I think I'm prepared for it.'

He shifts around, trying to get comfortable. 'What do you mean prepared for it? You want to die?'

'No, of course I don't *want* to die, I'm just saying if it happens I'm prepared for it.'

He snorts. 'Bollocks.'

I'm getting annoyed that he doesn't believe me. 'No, I mean it. If we're going to die today then so be it. It isn't like anyone is going to miss me.'

There's a long silence before he says, 'That isn't true.'

'Who's going to miss me – the ex-wife who hates my guts? The bairns I haven't seen for years? The lads at Shugs? I've even pissed off my parish priest and they are supposed to care about everybody.'

283

Wheezy sighs. 'Much as it pains me to say it, I think my Marianne might miss you. Anyhow, you can sit here and wallow in self-pity but I'm getting out.' He leans past me and bangs on the inside of the door. 'Hoi, Polis! We're in here!'

'That won't work. The door's soundproofed.'

'You think of something then.' He sounds irritated. 'I'm not ready to die. I'm planning to rage against the dying of the light for some time yet.'

'Except there isn't any light in here.' As soon as I say it I notice something. 'Actually, Wheeze, I can see light in that corner there.'

'Where?'

I point, pointlessly given the darkness. 'Down at floor level – there's a wee bit of light coming under that wall. Move down the room, Wheeze – see if you come to an opening.'

I feel him tense up. 'Oh no – I'm not going any further into this place.'

'Well, move out of the way then – I'm going to have a look.'

Getting past Wheezy just about kills the pair of us. He has to squat on the floor while I climb over him. I'm right – there is light coming into the chamber. I edge my way forward and hit a wall. At least I think it's a wall, but there still seems to be air coming from the edges of it.

'Have you found anything?'

'I think it's a false wall, Wheeze.'

'Well get a move on – the Polis won't detain those two for ever.'

I run my hands along the edge of the wall and there's definitely a gap where the air is coming through.

'Is there a handle or anything?'

'Shut up, Wheezy.'

'I'm just saying – we've not got long.'

I start at the top of the wall and slowly move down. Nothing gives way. I crouch down and try to get my hand under the base of the wall. It crumbles slightly at my touch but my hand brushes against metal.

'I've found something!'

I pull at the lever but nothing happens.

'What's happening?'

'I don't know Wheeze – I think the mechanism's rusted.'

'Try it again.' He sounds excited.

I pull again and I feel it give, just slightly. I pull again with as much force as I can muster and the wall shakes slightly. I push my shoulder against it and it moves an inch.

'It's moving Wheeze!'

'Push harder!'

I put the whole of my weight against the wall and the wall swings round on a hinge, like a door.

'What can you see?'

The room seems slightly less dark but it takes me a minute to realise why. There is light shining through the floor.

'There's a trapdoor Wheeze.'

I feel around and find a latch. I pull back the trapdoor and I can see earth about three foot away.

'I think we can get out this way.'

'Right behind you.'

I crouch down and look at where the daylight is coming from. There's a wrought iron vent and through that I can see the garden. I give the vent a shove but it's solidly in place. I'm cursing. Meikle and Bruce will surely have got rid of the Polis by now and be on their way to find us. I take a deep breath and start feeling my way round the edges of the vent, and sure enough, as before there is a lever. It's stiff but it creaks into life. I give the vent a shove.

'What's going on?'

'It's a bit of a tight fit, Wheezy, but we're out.'

And after a bit of wriggling we're free.

'Let's get out of here.'

We creep round to the front of the house. The Polis cars have gone.

'Shall we run for it?'

'Aye. No – wait.' I've just seen Danny Jamieson's motor. He must have heard there was a 999 call relating to Mavisview and decided to check it out for himself. 'Danny's here.'

'Well, I'm sure he's got it under control. Come on now.' He tugs on my jacket but I don't move.

'He won't know that they're armed in there.'

'Aye, well, he'll have his radio on him for backup.' He yanks on my jacket again but for some reason my feet still aren't moving.

'What if he doesn't get a chance to use his radio? What if they're holding him up at gunpoint right now?'

'Stainsie – you've got a guilty conscience when it comes to Jamieson and rightly so, but he's a Polisman and he can look after himself.'

'No.' I can't believe I'm saying this. 'I need to know he's all right. Take my phone and you make a run for it. Dial 999 when you think you're safe.' I make a sprint for the front stairs before I can change my mind. I grab a big rock from the garden on the way – it's the nearest thing to a weapon I'm going to find round here. I'm halfway up the stairs when I hear Wheezy shout in a stage whisper.

'I'm not sure how to work a mobile.'

I keep going, hoping that the daft bastard manages to find a passer-by who knows how a mobile phone works.

Once I'm inside I'm not quite sure what to do. If Meikle and Bruce are handling the situation there might not have been any need for guns so far. They could be spinning him the same story that got rid of the uniformed Polis; I know from personal experience that Danny's a gullible bastard. Me rushing in there would just cause all kind of alarm.

On the other hand, if the guns are already drawn, me rushing in there isn't gonna do anything except give them two targets to aim at instead of one.

I creep up the stairs and position myself behind one of the full length curtains on the landing. It's a bit of a strain but I can hear what's going on. Just as well Danny's got a loud voice.

'Of course, you can understand why we have to follow up these calls. If we had realised that the lawyers had hired your security firm to protect Mavisview we would never have bothered you.'

'Oh yes, Detective Superintendent, I understand. I'm just sorry you've had your time wasted.'

It sounds like Meikle's pulled it off. I wonder where Bruce is; even Danny would be suspicious about Mrs Stoddart's right-hand thug suddenly being employed as security.

'Well, I think that's us…'

Danny's mobile beeps. That'll be my text message coming through now that I can get reception again.

'If you don't mind, I'll just…'

I wonder if Danny's any good at poker. There's a silence.

'While I'm here, I'll maybe just have a quick look round.'

Another silence.

'Whatever you like, Detective Sergeant.'

I feel the floorboards move as they walk past.

'I'll have a look upstairs first of all.'

'No problem.'

I give them time to get to the top of the stairs. Danny's got things under control so I reckon I can safely slip outside and check if Wheezy's still standing nearby trying to work out which way up my phone goes. I cautiously draw back the curtain and walk straight into Bruce.

'What the…?'

I hit him as hard as I can with the rock. He loses his balance and falls head first down the stairs. I'm just savouring the moment when I hear voices up the stairs, and Danny and Meikle appear.

'What's going on?'

'Danny – he's got a gun!'

Danny – being remarkably quick on the uptake for once – tries to throw a punch at Meikle, but Meikle is too quick. There's a gunshot and Danny crumples to the floor.

Meikle doesn't say a word but starts down the stairs, all the time with his gun aimed at my head. For the second time in an hour we hear Polis sirens in the distance.

Meikle's head jerks round in the direction of the door. I use the opportunity to run into the nearest room; he fires after me but it bounces off the wall. I lock the door and hope to God that he decides he hasn't got time to chase after me. I hear his feet pelting down the stairs, so it looks like I'm right.

Oh God, Danny.

I give it a minute then poke my head out the door. I can hear Danny speaking.

'I'm in urgent need of assistance.'

I walk out on to the landing. 'I'm here, Danny.'

'I'm not talking to you, you tube. Get up here and hold my radio for me.'

He's been shot through the upper arm. There's blood everywhere, but he's trying to prop himself up on his good arm to get to his radio.

'Shouldn't you be lying down?' I say, getting his radio off his belt.

He ignores the question.

'What are you doing here anyway?'

I stare at the Polis radio. 'It's a long story.'

'I'm not going anywhere.'

I try to work out where to start. 'Remember Isa Stoddart's thug, Bruce?'

He nods. 'Aye – we had him in for questioning about her death.'

'Well, he's lying unconscious one floor down from here, by the way, but him and this other laddie Meikle, who's been working with Guthrie Stoddart in Spain...'

Danny groans and shifts his position. 'Stoddart's still alive then? I always thought Isa had done him in after that business with the young lassies.'

289

'That's what I said! Anyhow, Bruce and Meikle lured me and Wheezy Murphy here...'

He frowns. 'How?'

I sit down on the floor next to him. 'Never mind that for the minute.'

'*Why* did they lure you here?'

I continue avoiding his questions. 'We'll come back to that. Anyhow, they lured us here but somebody called the Polis, and they took fright when they heard the sirens...'

'Somebody?' There's a tone of sarcasm in his voice. I ignore it.

'Aye. Anyhow, they bundled us into a smuggler's hole on the downstairs landing, but we managed to get out, and we were making a run for it when I noticed your car out front, and I thought I better try and let you know he's got a gun.'

Danny winces. 'Which worked out really well for me.'

I pat his leg. 'Aye. Sorry.'

'So, why did you come back when you were in the clear?'

I sigh. 'Well, you know...'

'Guilty conscience?'

He knows. I always suspected that he did. I just hope to God that Danny isn't about to die 'cause I don't want his last conversation on earth to be about me and his missus.

'Well, I suppose so, but it was a long time ago and I think we have all moved on since then...'

'What was a long time ago? Your involvement in Isa Stoddart's death?'

'What?' *Where did he get that from?* 'I'd nothing to do with any murder!'

290

He tries to move and yelps in pain. Through gritted teeth he says, 'Then what are you talking about?'

I get to my feet. 'Nothing. Nothing at all. I'm just havering.'

Fortunately, the Polis arrive at this point, followed by a paramedic. Danny isn't letting me off the hook.

'Sergeant McKenzie – this man has a full statement that he wants to make about today's events.' He props himself up on his good arm again. 'And see that it is a FULL statement that you make.'

I stand up and look down at him. 'Aye, aye. Look after yourself, Danny.'

As the Sergeant escorts me to a Polis car I note that Danny's never said thank you to me for trying to save his life, but I suppose getting shot can make people a bit ungrateful.

Sunday

I give as full and frank a statement as I can without mentioning Marianne in any way. I'd have liked to have left Miss Spencely out of it as well if I could, but I'm not a quick enough liar to work out how. I suspect that's her career as a lawyer over; I hope Bruce was worth it.

As I haven't actually committed any crime (well – none that I've admitted to) the Polis can't hold me, though I can tell by the glint in Sergeant McKenzie's eye that he holds me personally responsible for Danny getting shot. He may be right. Anyhow he isn't in any hurry to let me go and leaves me sitting in an interview room on my own for over an hour.

This gives me plenty time to think over what's happened. There are still some things I don't understand, number one amongst them, why was Meikle going to such lengths to get hold of a company that Miss Spencely was trying to tell me wasn't worth anything? Was that something Miss Spencely has been told to say by Bruce, or didn't Bruce and Meikle realise that there are other creditors? And if old Senga O'Neill is to be believed, and Isa had a son or daughter, where are they?

And the most important question, what impact does all this have on my inheritance?

Eventually Sergeant McKenzie gives up waiting for me to crack and escorts me back. When I walk back through the Polis Station I'm surprised to see Wheezy sitting in Reception.

'What are you doing here?'

'I came to make sure you aren't suffering any Polis brutality.'

The Desk Sergeant rolls her eyes in a manner that makes me think she's been listening to Wheezy for a while now.

I give her an apologetic smile as we leave. No point antagonising her; I'm bound to be back here at some point.

Wheeze rubs his hands together. 'So, what now, Stainsie? Round to Shugs?'

We stare at each other. I'm almost touched that he's waited for me. I nod. 'Aye, but there's a couple of things I want to do first.'

'Have you found anything yet, Wheeze?'

Wheezy turns round from the gravestone that he's been pulling weeds off. 'Naw. Are you sure this isn't a wild goose chase?'

'Maybe. But let's give it another ten minutes.'

Wheeze looks up at the heavens. 'That's the rain on. *Five* more minutes then I'm off. I'll have a look at they stones over there.' He gestures in the direction of some modern gravestones with the bunch of flowers that I made him buy.

Suddenly the air erupts with the sound of cheering. Hibs must have scored - the Eastern Cemetery all but backs on to the Easter Road stadium. I sigh and go back to looking at the graves.

The rain is picking up and I'm about to shout to Wheeze to knock it on the head when I find what I'm looking for. The grave has obviously not been visited for a while. I pull back the worst of the weeds and read the name out loud. *Margaret Sylvia Jackman 1952 – 1990.*

I have a furtive look round. The cemetery is deserted apart from Wheezy, and he's out of earshot. If I'm going to say my piece, it's now or never. I start talking.

'Mrs Jackman, I was a friend of your Shirley's. Well, not much of a friend to be honest, as you'll hear. I knew her when she was seeing Lachlan Stoddart. I really let her down, Mrs Jackman. I found out that she was only fourteen and I never did anything about it. I mean I'm not sure what I should have done about it, but I knew she was going to get into trouble. You can't hang around with the likes of the Stoddarts and not get into trouble, but for a fourteen-year-old lassie...'

I'm starting to get a bit choked up.

'Guthrie Stoddart... Guthrie... he had a thing for young lassies. We all knew it but nobody sort of mentioned it out loud, you know, and then one day I walked in on the pair of them and... and I just ran.'

I'm weeping properly now. My scar stings as the tears run over it.

'I'm not sure what I saw, Mrs Jackman. I'm not sure if she was just a daft young lassie who thought it was funny to shag her boyfriend's dad, or if it was something worse. And I don't know what happened between her and Guthrie – Lachie said she stole some money off him, but I don't buy that. Whatever happened, I'm sure that it was Guthrie and his pals that murdered her.'

My scar is stinging.

'I can't help thinking if I'd stuck around and done something back then Shirley might still be alive, and so might you. So, that's all I want to say, Mrs Jackman. Sorry. Sorry for everything.'

I wipe my eyes on my jacket sleeve, and shout on Wheezy. He waves the flowers at me to show he's heard, and starts to limp in my direction. 'Where to now, Stainsie?'

I push open the door to the church. The smell of incense hits me, and I can see Father Paul standing at the altar. I spot Marianne and Liam a couple of rows from the back. I point them out to Wheezy and we walk down the aisle and stop beside them. Marianne jumps when she sees us, but moves silently along the pew to let us sit down. She takes my hand and I let the hymn wash over me.